THE NIGHT GARDEN
FAIRYTALES OF THE LOCHS BOOK I
NICOLE NORTHWOOD

Copyright © 2024 by Nicole Northwood
www.nicolenorthwoodbooks.com

All rights reserved.

No part of this book may be reproduced in any form or by any electronic or mechanical means, including information storage and retrieval systems, without written permission from the author, except for the use of brief quotations in a book review.

No AI Training: Without in any way limiting the author's exclusive rights under copyright, any use of this publication to "train" generative artificial intelligence (AI) technologies to generate text is expressly prohibited. The author reserves all rights to license uses of this work for generative AI training and development of machine learning language models.

This is a work of fiction. Names, characters, places, and incidents are a product of the author's imagination. Locales and public names are sometimes used for atmospheric purposes. Any resemblances to actual people, living or dead, or to businesses, companies, events, institutions, or locales is completely coincidental.

eBook and paperback cover by Rachel A. Rosen
Hardcover artwork and interior illustration by Natascia Mora

Editing by Heather Ellis

Content Warning

Content warnings include: fantasy drug use, explicit sexual encounters, drinking, references to parental death and cancer.

To restless hearts and reckless lovers.

Chapter One

ELLIE

I first tried Allure when I was fifteen and at a party hosted by Padraig, one of the boys from across the meadow. He's married now to a girl from the next loch over, and they have two children who I can sometimes hear playing over the moors and between our families' fields. Their high-pitched voices always seem to travel farther through the countryside than I recall mine and my sister's doing when we were young. But what's stranger still is to think of Padraig the Allure supplier as having a wife and kids at all, working for the records department at Blossom Preparatory Academy and sitting on their administrative board as a director-at-large.

Of course, Padraig is twenty-two now and very serious, whereas I'm sure he'd claim that I'm foolish for a nineteen-year-old. Though I wasn't too foolish to have an affair with him in the spring of last year shortly after I'd turned eighteen, fueled by nothing more than Allure and magic. He says it was merely something that was only meant to span one season during his transitional period from a young man to an adult. Despite what he claims, our *encounters* have certainly happened on more than a single occasion, I keep reminding myself that Padraig and I have never been meant for one another. We're diversions…

and the temporary effects of diversions can be alleviated in many ways, though I do have a favorite.

I'm in my bedroom snorting pink, powdery Allure off the back of a tortoiseshell hand mirror. It's all in preparation for a grand party I'm hosting since my mother's gone to the city to stay with my aunt Matilda. I'm supposed to be in charge of my youngest sister and brother, but eighteen-year-old Sophia always takes over the role of being the substitute mother since I don't have a single parental bone in my body. Maybe that's why Padraig didn't want to marry me—not that I wanted to marry him either. Or maybe that lack of motherly instinct is why I'm being shipped away to Blossom Preparatory Academy at the start of autumn.

My mother calls me insolent and reckless.

Sophia says I'm lucky to even be allowed to attend such a school—an academy for society's castoffs who don't fit into the mold of a proper young person ready for marriage. She reminds me of my "fortune" every so often. In fact, over the course of the last few moments, she's been reminding me of it incessantly, watching while I inhale Allure off the mirror, a line of powder covering part of the hand-painted floral decoration on the back. Sniffing in the dust loudly enough to obscure whatever Sophia is saying, I realize a second too late that I'm disturbing the black cat lying next to me, his legs tucked underneath him. His eyes are only partially opened, like he's trying to tune out mine and Sophia's passive-aggressive arguing.

"I said, you really should give that up before you go to Blossom. You'll get addicted, and then you'll never be allowed to marry Colonel Gallagher, since I'm certain that making your own *hallucinogens* isn't something fit for those in the upper levels of society." Sophia is reclined in the corner of my disastrous bedroom, a haggard red velveteen chair spewing stuffing out of one arm where the cats of Loch Gàrraidh have used it for a scratching post. "As it is, I'm certain if he knew about your… experiences that he wouldn't be interested in the least."

"You mean my thing with Padraig? That was last year."

Sophia flicks the crinkled corner of a condom wrapper toward me from the bedside table, shuffling her pastel blue dress around her knees so the packaging doesn't get caught on the fabric. "Either it's been more than that or you desperately need to clean your room."

I let out a little grunt, pushing my long, ginger hair away from my face. The room has always felt representative of me in some ways: messy enough to be considered on the verge of disastrous, combined with the depressing atmosphere of the dead flowers on the nightstand. I find my life both disastrous and depressing, and therefore, I'm not sure if I'm supposed to be offended by Sophia's comment. I choose to disregard it. "What you don't know won't kill you."

"No, but what I do know is that it'll hurt your chances."

"My chances of what? Being married off to a colonel who I have no feelings for whatsoever? I'd rather be Padraig's elusive mistress. Or a spinster." I tack on the last bit to make Sophia gasp because I think being a spinster is probably the worst thing that she could imagine. There's so much weight put on being married and having children and continuing on with the traditional values of society. Solitude isn't something that is valued—especially not the type of solitude that can make a woman like me happy.

Sophia does gasp, just a little and just enough for me to chuckle as I wait for the Allure to start working. "Your chances of anything, Ellie. You can't truly think you're going to get any of Dad's inheritance if you don't marry or at least don't stop doing… that. And you don't want to be turned into a cat."

I place the hand mirror back down on the bedside table before running my fingers through the dark fur of the large male cat nestled on the blankets. He's not named, like all cats of the Loch—a superstition more than anything else. If we name the cats, it's said to show affinity and compassion for their rule-breaking. Every fairytale book, but especially the Blossom fairytales, have proclaimed that cats are not to be named as they could be Bèists. It's one of the only rules I've ever thought to follow because maybe I am just a little bit superstitious.

Outside my window, I see dusk is starting to set in, and soon the big male cat will make his way outside to hunt and I won't see him, or any of the other feral cats who frequent Loch Gàrraidh, until morning.

"That's just a folktale, Sophia. You know that." The Blossom fairytales we were told as children always stated that cats are the spirits of those who high society was unable to tame after sending them to Blossom Prep for reformation. Every parent is given a copy of the fairytale book when each little one born in their home, hence the reason why we have six well-worn texts in the house between all of us—if you count Father's copy, which I do because I know where it's kept. I personally believe one hardcover with the wretched stories would be more than sufficient to meet the goal of altering young minds... maybe two if I was looking for something to burn in the middle of winter to prove I don't believe in that shit and that it's ridiculous Sophia still does.

"You can't tell me you honestly believe in kids' stories anymore."

My sister rolls her eyes and leans back in the chair once again. "Stories have a foundation in truth most of the time, I've found."

"Well, *I've* found that I need to get ready for this party. Maybe you can take the littles somewhere so they won't disrupt the festivities. You're always welcome to join in, you know, once they're asleep."

"I'll pass on that. I'd rather read a book than listen to you and a bunch of drugged-up degenerates make horrible innuendoes."

"Suit yourself. But a little snort every once in a while would really loosen you up."

Sophia opens her mouth, probably to say something sardonic, but seems to think better of it before rising from the velveteen chair and straightening the skirt of her dress.

Her pink lips purse together and she gives me a once over as I feel the Allure start to kick in. I can tell I've done just enough because there's an aura around my field of vision like I've been staring up at the sun.

"Goodnight, Ellie."

"Night, Soph. Give Huntley and Pippa a kiss for me."

"You could do it yourself if you weren't so fucked up," Sophia mutters under her breath before she opens my bedroom door, walks over the threshold, and then closes me back in—alone, except for the cat.

I look down at the animal lying in my mussed-up blankets and gently wiggle my fingers under his fluffy body to encourage him to rise. "You should go too. You're going to desperately want out once people start arriving. Can't very well have you walking around the house in the dark when you should really be outside."

The black cat meows, hopping down onto the floor with a *thunk* before he saunters toward the other side of the room. Rising from my spot on the bed and crossing the space, I slide the window open and watch as he daintily leaps onto the frame and then to a branch on the closest tree before disappearing into the impending dark, somewhere toward the glistening Loch.

Fresh midsummer air flows through the bedroom. I hope it carries out the sickly sugar scent of the Allure mixed with oversized dust bunnies to lessen Sophia's scolding about the state of the room. Sophia's probably right. I could clean up a little, but I don't anticipate needing it tonight anyway, so it can wait until later. The house and the estate are vast enough that a garden party shouldn't venture inside unless we get rain. With the clear skies and slight breeze, I'm certain that the candlelight and lanterns in the common, and the abundance of flat surfaces, will create enough of an atmosphere to entertain a collection of inebriated nineteen-year-olds and twenty-somethings who are hoping for a summer filled with last chances and final flings before they're sent away to Blossom.

Before the Allure sets in and I'm too intoxicated to clothe myself easily, I pull a shimmering black dress from my armoire, slipping the gown over my head. The neckline crosses over my small breasts, the mesh in the middle and thin lace on top making an illusion of size and shape. The fabric itself is light and airy, exposing my shoulders, perfect for Loch Gàrraidh's depths of summer as we're experiencing them now. I debate momentarily what to do with my hair before settling on a loose braid that runs over my shoulder and lands near my hip. I tie it off in a makeshift knot, the moonlight reflecting off the red hues that show in the hand mirror.

I don't bother putting on too much make-up because the Allure has put me into a haze. After I finally manage to stain my lips, voices begin to filter in through my bedroom window. Shifting from my spot in front of the mirror, I look out through the glass.

Sophia must have gone out and lit the candles and lanterns because the yard is illuminated beautifully, and I immediately spot two young men standing in avid conversation next to the rock wall. One of them is blond Padraig; the other I don't recognize—a man with dark hair and a deep voice. Padraig's attendance at the gathering is a bit questionable, considering his wife and children are probably in bed in their home just over the moors. Plus, his employment with Blossom inherently makes me question if he's here to enjoy himself or here to spy on the others for some future committee meeting. I don't rush to find out his intentions because I'm more interested in whoever his friend is.

I'm just about to leave my room to head to the garden when I force myself to reconsider Padraig's possible objectives: to sell Allure, to drink all the wine that's been set out from the cellar, or to find satisfaction against a warm body. On nights like this one, more often than not, that body is mine. I think a piece of me wonders if I sleep with Padraig enough, that he'll be able to use his connections to save me from a year at Blossom and a lifetime with a man I don't love.

I pull out two pouches from my bedside table. Inside the smaller, pink one is Allure dust. I wrap the pouches' strings around my wrist like a bracelet to take them with me. Inside the large silver sachet are several vials of sparkling liquid contraceptive, and I pull out one of the vessels before popping its cork to drink the contents. I have to plug my nose to get the remedy down because the smell is enough to put anyone off intercourse for life. However, if one can get past the scent, the taste of pears is tolerable. Padraig makes such a fuss about condoms that it's better for me to take care of things on my end.

I slip one other bottle inside my undergarments, just to be safe.

Corking the vial, I place it back inside the pouch and drop everything into the drawer before nudging it shut and leaving my bedroom.

My shoes *click-click-click* over the stone floor as I cross the hallway to the staircase, descending carefully to avoid tripping on my dress. The back door is prodded open, also probably done by Sophia, letting fresh summer air into the bottom level and providing some nighttime coolness to our home's interior. I smile at the thoughtfulness before heading through the kitchen and out to the garden.

Candlelight and moonglow cascade over the hedges, and a few more people mill about in the yard in small circles of conversation. I recognize Kit and Lucy, the neighbors on the opposite side of Padraig, along with Agnes and Grace, Landon and Gregoire, and a few of their invitees. I know them all to varying degrees, but the thing that connects us all is our affinity for Allure, intimate parties, and the types of events that occur when the two of them marry.

It takes half a second before Padraig notices me, and he smiles in my direction before nodding to the shadowy, dark-haired figure next to the trellis. I try to catch a glimpse of the other man's face, a peculiar feeling of recognition crawling up the back of my neck, but I can't quite place where I might know him from. He seems to know Padraig though, which likely makes him someone I've met in passing at another gathering. I've probably just forgotten that we've already met due to my frequent cloudiness at parties.

"Ellie. You look beautiful." Padraig makes a note of gazing at me up and down, pausing at my breasts, probably thinking about the last time he had his lips on them when we were intimate in his sweet-smelling barn.

I smile in return, partially to be polite. "Padraig. I wasn't expecting you."

"I wasn't expecting to be here either. Sometimes I think our *friendship* is easier if we don't see one another at all."

"Uncharacteristic of a friendship, don't you think?" The words fall from my mouth in a way that almost sounds like I'm flirting with him.

"Well, we are strange friends." Padraig offers me that crooked grin that first convinced me to sleep with him. Something about the lopsidedness of his smile is charming enough to remind me of a time back before things got so complicated with him... and in my life as well.

My ability to make good judgments is quickly being sapped away by the Allure. "What brings you here, then, *friend*?"

"It's a gathering, Ellie. Everyone from the surrounding lochs near marrying age will be here."

"And yet, you're here without your wife." I raise an eyebrow, and Padraig shuffles from one foot to the other.

He hesitates for a moment before responding. "Someone needs to stay with the children."

"You're here on official business, then?"

"You know that it's not. I'm not here to cause trouble for anyone."

I nod very slowly, as if it's taking me a minute to comprehend exactly what he's saying, but I know he's here hoping I'll either share my Allure or that he will be able to sell his own. There are probably no consequences for Padraig and his side business because it's not as if anyone from Blossom would believe that one of their favored committee members is actually doing something against the rules.

I keep a straight face—I don't need him to know he's so transparent with his intentions that I can practically see through him. "Well, I hope you enjoy yourself then. I suppose I should greet the rest of the guests and attend to my hostess duties."

Padraig nods, giving me my space, bowing a little before he steps away. We break apart from our discussion like two people who don't have a deep-rooted secret, but somehow, neither of us can avoid looking over our shoulders at one another as we attempt to find others to engage with. I'm still staring at Padraig as he joins a chat with Kit and Lucy, watching the glint of his hair under the candlelight when I run directly into someone.

"I'm so sorry—" I begin, steadying myself against the other partygoer, but lose my words when I look up to find myself face-to-face with the raven-haired man who I saw speaking with Padraig from my window.

Up close, he has familiar green eyes and the soft scent of a garden: fresh, growing plants and something else I can't place. Springtime, maybe, if one could give springtime in

Loch Gàrraidh a scent: wet and mossy moors that span into the distance, cloud-spotted skies alternating between a moody gray and a brilliant blue, damp hair from swimming in the lake. He's all those things in aroma alone, but in essence, he feels like so much more. More in the way that the gaze he gives me under the candlelight is worldly, experienced, gentle, and doesn't show complete surprise.

"Do I know you from somewhere?" I ask, whispering the question like I don't want the world to overhear. Maybe it's because I'm embarrassed that I don't remember this handsome man.

He shakes his head. "I don't believe so. I'm Max O'Carroll."

"Ellie Blue Callaghan."

"My pleasure, Ellie."

We stand there for a moment longer before we both seemingly realize that we're connected at his lapel, Max's hand on my arm, though I no longer need his help to balance. Once I catch my breath, something I hadn't realized I lost, I quickly step away. Clearing my throat, I fiddle with my dress before bringing my gaze back up to meet Max's. He's watching me curiously, and it's then that it strikes me that I'm probably sallow and intoxicated-looking from the Allure I took.

"How do you know Padraig?" Max asks, and I wish that the earth would swallow me whole before I feel forced to answer the inquiry so as not to be rude

"We—we're friends," I manage to stammer out because what else am I supposed to say? *He deals hallucinogens to me and my so-called other friends in the Loch, and we've been sleeping together on and off for the last year in some kind of hopeless attempt to hang onto life before we are forced to follow the rules of society?* "It's complicated."

"I can imagine being a woman who is friends with a married man would be a little complex."

"Do you say that as a married man who is friends with a woman?"

Max chuckles, the deep sound resonating in my bones. "I say that as a single man who can very plainly see when someone is pining for someone else."

"I'm not pining for Padraig…"

Max tips his chin toward the rock wall where Padraig is now sitting with Kit and Lucy. "I didn't mean you."

I swivel on my heel in the grass; though the three are engaged in a vibrant conversation, Padraig is looking in my direction with an expression that can only be described as longing. I've seen that look on his face before, enough times that I can recognize it even at the distance that separates us. I know he's already thinking about disappearing between the hedgerows with me and removing my dress…

Turning back to Max, I do my best to explain. I'm not entirely clear why I should have to enlighten a stranger about my relationship with Padraig since I'm not the one acting out of bounds. So I pick the simplest excuse. "That'll be the drug."

"The drug?"

I hold up my wrist with the pouch of Allure attached. "Allure. Padraig's sort of... a supplier. Now my magic's strong enough to make my own."

Max raises an eyebrow, though he mostly seems unaffected by the realization. "Ah, so that's what everyone's on."

"Not everyone, I don't think. Just—" I look around at the groups of people disappearing into the gardens, snorting off flat surfaces, and generally acting inebriated. "Okay, well, maybe everyone."

"What about you, Ellie?"

Hallucinations caused by the Allure quickly come back into my peripheral vision; little speckles of brightness like I've been staring at the sun for too long. *Not now, not now.* This is the worst time for this to happen while talking to a charming stranger who clearly is unaware as to what kind of party this is supposed to be... "What *about* me?"

"Are you under the influence of Allure?"

I nod.

Max looks concerned. At least, I think he does based off his facial expression. "So, I'm the only sober person here?"

I bob my head, breathing in a sigh of his springtime smell again. Sophia once told me that scent can help fortify memories of people, places, and events, but I can't place this one outside of the water's edge in Loch Gàrraidh. It's going to drive me up the garden wall, and the Allure is telling me to suck in the aroma of this Max O'Carroll for the rest of the night.

"Why don't we take a walk and discuss something other than Padraig?" I suggest, opening my pouch to extract a miniscule metal scoop of pink powder. Max watches in silence as I level and then snort the dust off the spoon, the powder filling my nostrils with a temporary sugary fragrance that reminds me of honey confectionaries. I manage to only spill a little, or at least it seems like only a tiny bit in my state of intoxication.

I dispense another measure and blink at him. "More than enough for both of us."

Max pauses for a moment, as if considering the implication of the offer. "You made this?"

"I did."

He hums to himself for a second. "I can only presume that means you're going to get sent off to Blossom soon. Between magicking up hallucinogens and hosting unchaperoned parties, you're more or less—"

I cut him off, using the terminology I've long since learned is used for people who act like me. "A deviant, I'm aware. But you're here, and I see no wedding band on your finger. So that leads me to believe that you're headed off to Blossom soon as well. To try and cure you. Make you fit into society. It's either that or you've stashed the ring in a pocket to try and trick unsuspecting women into engaging with you."

"The former rather than the latter. Not married."

A stone weight lifts off my chest, and I'm not certain why. "So, what's your vice then? Gambling? Drinking? Sex?"

Max smirks, gently taking the spoon of Allure from my hand. His fingers brush against mine so delicately that it feels more like a breeze than a touch. "We've just met, Ellie. I'm not certain it's polite to ask about one's preferred depravity yet."

I can't help but let out a small laugh, during which Max snorts the scoop of pink powder so methodically it's as if he's been doing this for his entire adult life. "Now, come sit with me in the garden, Ellie. Before Padraig gets his hands all over you."

"You're worried about Padraig?" I ask. We begin to walk toward the vine-covered pergola.

"I can't help but be a bit worried tonight about every man's intentions with you." Max's shoulder bumps gently against my arm, and I'm not certain if it's on purpose or by accident.

"Why?"

"You're under the influence, and they look as if they'd like to take the opportunity to consume you."

A laugh escapes me. "If only you knew that half the men here have already had their lips on my neck."

"Well, I know now that you've told me." Max chuckles, and we pass beneath the arch to enter the hedge garden.

I suppose he does.

"What brings you to Loch Gàrraidh?" I quickly change the subject, attempting to hold some semblance of conversation as my heart pounds. I know he can't be from the area or I'd have seen him before—I'd surely remember him. That's one of the things about Allure. In between it making the user insatiable for certain things, it also makes them unbearably honest. At least I didn't tell him that I find him inconceivably handsome though...

"Visiting from Loch Lomond. Extended stay for the summer." Max breathes softly next to me as we ascend a small hill, craggy rocks jutting against the darkened wildflowers.

I nod. "I take it that means you've finished at Blossom and been cured of your own depravities. Probably all fit and proper to be married now. Destined for some woman back in Loch Lomond who fell in love with your eyes."

Fuck, Ellie. Too much Allure. That last scoop put me over the edge of being able to control my mouth, and now I'm on the border of having *it* control *me*.

"What's there to love about my eyes?" Max asks, a hitch in his step like he's going to stop right here in the middle of the hedgerow to wait for my answer. The smirk on his face is gentle, amused, and—*dare I say it?*—enticing. However, his eyes have the familiar glassed over look of an Allure haze.

I shake my head and keep on walking, holding back a laugh as we approach the shores of the loch.

Chapter Two

MAX

Ellie knows my name, but every story that Blossom tells to children insists that she's not supposed to use it. I feel as if I've cursed her by allowing it to unknowingly slip across her tongue and over her lips, but there's also a piece of me that loves the way she purrs my name like it's something decadent and desirable.

On top of having her violate a rule she doesn't know she's broken, I'm breaking about a hundred unwritten laws by being at this gathering. Every feral being in Loch Gàrraidh told me that getting dressed up tonight and coming to this garden party was a bad idea, but I've been staying away from Ellie for so long that it's now causing me physical pain. This pain has caused me to ignore every warning, every alarm that's been raised, and put on my suit. It's possible that I want to warn Ellie about the inescapable fate of poor choices. It's probable, too, that I want to save her from the inevitable destiny brought on by the choices that she's making tonight.

We're walking through the gardens in the back of her family's property toward the loch when Ellie asks me about my vices and what took me to Blossom. I think it's the Allure speaking more than her, though drugging is one of those things I'm somewhat familiar with. A hallucinogenic powder like Allure—particularly one that was created outside of a controlled environment—has a whole collection of issues that surround it, from moral to physical. Magic isn't something to trifle with, especially not strong and wild magic like I've seen that Ellie possesses. She's one of those rare people who has learned multiple types of enchantments on top of being born with an innate ability for water magic, which is highly unusual. Often, at least from what I've heard in books and from my time at Blossom, those with multiple natural "charms" are seen as dangerous and harder to control. In Scotland, unlike in other countries where magic isnt' meant to follow strict rules, we're supposed to have one specialty, one core elemental enchantment. But Ellie? Ellie's control over water is likely the weakest of her many skills.

And I know that Padraig, despite having just met him in my human form, isn't the type of person Ellie should be philandering with either. He's employed by Blossom, and therefore, I can't help but detest him immediately. I know from the things I've seen here in Loch Gàrraidh that he has horrible intentions with Ellie. She's not the only person he's mesmerizing with his enigmatic charms, all for his self-serving purposes.

My curse from Blossom Preparatory Academy is an enchantment too, but instead of being one that manipulates people, it is simply a magic curse that I once considered to be nothing more than a folktale. I now know it is something real.

"What brings you to Loch Gàrraidh?" Ellie whispers the words, and her voice breaks me out of my state of dwelling on my superstitions. I don't expect my body's reaction, my heart beating erratically in my chest as she speaks. After a moment, I realize it's being caused by the fact that I'm looking at her through a man's eyes for the first time.

I internally chastise myself. It's no wonder she's been taken advantage of—beautiful and wild and windswept, like the moors themselves.

I have to think about her question for a moment, in part due to the Allure that I snorted in her company, and because I haven't prepared a suitable lie to explain my presence in Loch Gàrraidh. It feels too soon to tell her I'm afflicted with the Blossom curse; that I'm one of the students who wasn't able to be tamed. Now, I'm paying the price for my own indiscretions by living the worst kind of enchanted life, which features the inability to exist as a human man except after sundown.

I'm a Bèist—a cursed and feral beast of the loch. I'm one of the damned, the tormented, the afflicted. A man with an unspeakable name, the lifeline of a cat, and a faded memory of home.

The Callaghans have been attending to the animals of Loch Gàrraidh as part of their volunteerism to high society for as long as anyone can remember, and it was suggested to me that their care has been what's drawn me to Ellie. What the other Bèists don't know and what I've never spoken about is that I've been with Ellie as she's snorted herself into a drugged oblivion, as she's fucked men who wanted nothing more than temporary satisfaction, as she's cried, and as she's read books in the springtime, sunshine flickering through her dark curtains and shining in warm patches on the floor. It's not about the watchfulness she and her family have over me. It's about the way I inexplicably want to keep her from losing her future.

The realization burns like a branding iron to the soul, and I realize then that I've been silent for too long.

"Visiting from Loch Lomond. Extended stay for the summer." I breathe softly next to Ellie as we ascend a knoll that juts against the shrubs and signals the end of the gardens and the start of the shoreline. It's the best answer I can think of.

Ellie nods, glimmers of silver reflecting on her hair in the moonlight as we walk toward the loch at the far edge of the gardens. The shade is like nothing I've ever seen before, and I wonder for a split second if I've ever looked at a woman with my human eyes the way I'm looking at Ellie now. There's something about the combination of her passion and force and recklessness that has me completely intrigued.

I can't help but continue to wonder what's going on in her beautiful mind as we stand there next to the glistening shards of moonlight on the water, my vision affected by the Allure that I was once so familiar with. Of course, I don't tell Ellie that I used to use my magic much like Padraig did—to make hallucinogens and other drugs to sell at gatherings like this one. I feel like it would make her think less of me, and I want her to think more. I want her to believe that I've changed from that sort of person—not just in corporeal form but in my mind as well, where I no longer try to get immensely fucked before parties.

Ellie turns away from me, unraveling the pouch of Allure from her wrist and placing it down on a craggy rock. Then she poses a question. "Would you save me if I fell in?"

I presume she means if she fell into the loch, and doubly presume that means she's never learned to swim, a peculiar characteristic for someone who lives so close to the water.

"You don't swim?" I ask.

"Of course I do." Ellie laughs, the sound echoing in the vastness of the gardens. I'm not entirely sure what she's getting at by acting the way she is, but I do suspect she's testing me because she's used to being treated a certain way by men.

"Then I'd take your rescue under consideration."

"Under consideration? What kind of gentleman are you, Max?"

To my surprise, Ellie slips the straps of her gown down farther over her arms, exposing her shoulders to the glow of the night. The ribbons on the back of her dress loosen a little, criss-crossed over her spine. I'm looking but am respectfully trying not to because it's indecent. Though I've seen her undress before, this somehow seems... different. I don't know what she's thinking, starting to strip herself bare here by the loch. *How much Allure did she do before she came downstairs?*

"I'm the sort of gentleman who is going to ask you what you're doing. Someone will see. Someone will presume something unsavory." The tone of my voice lowers, but the pitch feels as if it's raising on its own. I don't need to have to explain my entire history the first evening I spend with her as a man.

"Nobody will see; I'll cast magic over the loch so nobody will know we're here." Ellie meets her gaze with my own, shuffling the dress down to her waist, exposing her chest, daring me to break eye contact. There's no way that Ellie's magic is strong enough to be able to hide an entire garden despite what the Allure is telling her she's capable of. "You're also the sort who isn't quite averting his eyes. I feel as if that's saying something all on its own. Maybe you're more like Padraig than you care to admit. Maybe you have particular urges that you're looking to satiate."

I shudder at the name, though the reaction is at first unconscious . "I think that feeling is coming from you, Ellie. I'll look away, but if you don't know how to swim and I have to rescue you, that's going to be a whole other ordeal to try and explain. Also, that magic spell you're allegedly casting doesn't exist except in fairytales."

"Nobody will know either way, even if someone does come down. I'll tell them they were having a hallucination from the Allure." But still, she does pause, standing there in front of me, half dressed in her silk underwear, dress barely held up over her stomach.

"I'm starting to think this whole night might be a delusion."

"Close your eyes, Max. I'll just hop in for a quick swim. The water feels miraculous while on Allure. Every sense tingles."

"I'm fine," I murmur before closing my eyes.

There *should* be the sound of fabric puddling, the ripple of water, the noise of a woman entering the loch. However, after a few seconds pass, all I hear is Ellie's loud sigh. "You need to relax a little, Max O'Carroll."

Opening my eyes, I'm not sure she understands that I can't imagine feeling much better than I do right now under the cover of darkness and the illumined light of shooting stars. The very second that I look at her, she drops the dress the rest of the way, which gives me a whole other sensation—my heart in my throat.

"Ellie!" Her name comes out as a harsh whisper. There's a part of me that isn't certain what to do. Certainly, I had women before I was changed, but those women were nothing like Ellie. Almost all of them were quiet, private, and their deviancy revolved around things like drinking too much or flirting with multiple men at the same time. Ellie's different. She knows what she wants and she goes for it.

She's going to fail out of Blossom almost on sight, and maybe she knows that. It would explain the forward behavior—assessing her life for the limited time she has left to enjoy it before she's changed too. I'm also certain it doesn't help that she's been involved with Padraig; his reasons for being entangled with her are definitely barely more than surface-level.

"Come in with me." Delicately, Ellie tiptoes along the edge of the loch. Tiny waves lap at her feet, and I try my damndest not to look at her legs, her thighs, her long hair brushing the curve of her back in the moonlight. It's difficult because the silk of her undergarments is the same pale white as the stars, and my fingers itch to feel her.

But no.

"I can't."

She steps farther out, water covering her knees. "And why's that? You can't swim either?"

"I can swim just fine, thanks. I just—" I hesitate because the only reason I'm not getting in is because she's on a hell of a lot of Allure, I'm on a single scoopful, and because it would look awfully suspicious if someone were to come down here and see both of us half naked in the lake. I'm less worried about the partygoers, the people within her circle of influence—I'm worried about the others like me and their disapproval. I've already broken the rules of the curse by giving her my name... and allowing her to speak it without warning her of the consequences of being cursed to live life as a Bèist.

"Then you have ten seconds to get in here before I drag you in, fancy suit and all."

Ellie sinks into the water then, up to her shoulders, ripples of water playing off her pale skin and reflecting the distant candlelight from the upper garden.

I can't help but smirk. "You think you can drag me into the loch all by yourself?"

"Absolutely, I can."

"I'd love to see the attempt, especially with the amount of Allure I can assume you've taken."

"The pouch is still almost completely full. You can check. I didn't bring the good stuff because I figured I could sneak some from Padraig. He's usually pretty quick to dole out scoopfuls once he's inebriated and feeling carnal." She paddles her way toward where I'm standing at the edge of the loch, a little closer, still staying with everything below her neck under the surface. "But if you want to be dragged, I can do the dragging. I didn't take you for a submissive man, Max."

In a swish of water and one fell movement, Ellie rises from the water like a goddess, exposing her entire body. Her undergarments are translucent, and I can pick out her every detail in the glimmer of the night, moonbeams radiating off her collarbone and her drenched hair dripping into the loch. I could swear her pale eyes are glinting with the stars, playful yet intentional about the way she knows she's making me feel.

There's a twitch inside of my slacks, in between my hips, and for a second, I see nothing else but Ellie. Ellie, there in the water, showing herself off to me, all breasts and hips and laughter.

Fuck.

Before I even realize what I'm doing (and thanks to the little bit of Allure that I've had, ruining my usual inhibitions), I find myself shimmying out of my coat. Then, unbuttoning my shirt, I expose my chest against the heat of the season. The barely-there breeze feels significantly cooler without layers of clothing to block any airflow. My gaze is affixed to hers, even as she slowly sinks back down in the water, satisfied that she's found a way to get me to do what she wants. I hesitate before slipping out of my slacks, worried that she'll comment on the obvious way I'm feeling, aching between my legs for her.

I can't have her.

But I can have this *moment* with her. The disappointment will only come in the morning, again, if she remembers my existence. That's the part that will hurt—when she remembers me only as some unnamed pet who does nothing but shred her velveteen chair and sneak food from Huntley and Pippa.

Ellie blinks, and I blink back slowly, as if I'm trying to communicate a message to her without saying anything. I sort of am, but it's not in a language she can understand. It's barely in a language that I understand, despite my year spent living as a feral animal.

"Don't make me get up again." She chuckles, tossing her hair over her shoulder like a horse would with their mane. "Bottoms off."

"Ellie, I—"

"I already know you're of a... particular affliction, Max. We'll blame it on the Allure."

I nod, taking her word for it, sliding out of my slacks, and though I catch her peering down at my hardness, she makes no further comment. Even still, my face is hot, my cheeks probably a shade of bright red in the dark, and I immediately try to cool down by immersing myself in the loch at a healthy distance from Ellie.

She's right, the water of Loch Gàrraidh does have a particular sensation to it when one is on Allure. The undulations tickle like dusting feathers being run over my naked skin, a shiver cascading up my spine and settling itself as tingles in the back of my neck and in my fingertips. I traipse farther into the water, Ellie's presence calling me like a siren's song, until I'm paddling toward the empty spot in the water next to her in the blue-black night.

"Are you satisfied?" I ask, blinking against the light of the moon, the garden and pergola and the rocks of the loch somewhere behind her head.

"Very."

My heart is beating as fast as a galloping horse's hooves thundering against the packed dirt on the road to Loch Lomond. Ellie, meanwhile, seems perfectly at peace, twirling her finger around in the water where little white sparks come from her fingertips.

Her water magic is stronger than I thought. Much stronger than the elemental magic that I had before Blossom stripped it away following my dismissal from the academy. I have nothing left now that defines me as a sorcerer, other than the enchantment that turns me, day after day after day, into a roaming black cat.

"What're you doing?" I question, transfixed at her ability to charm the world around her out of thin air. It's strange to watch someone use magic now since it's no longer a part of my daily existence.

"Watch."

Ellie continues to swirl the water around, her body hidden underneath the surface. After a few moments of quiet, the space between us turns into a shimmering, milky white liquid, complete with rainbow-scaled fish that swim around in lazy circles. The fish aren't real, of course; they're an illusion—a trickery—but it's beautiful nonetheless, particularly with the blue whirls of the lake coming up from underneath the magic.

After a few seconds slip by, she takes her finger from the water, and it all disappears with a flurry of sparks and an otherworldly popping noise that rapidly dissolves into the atmosphere.

"Where'd you learn to do that?" I ask.

"A party trick from a romance novel I read once."

"Ah, so it's a Whimsey. It's lovely. How'd you do it?" I haven't seen a Whimsey in a long time. They're a unique optical illusion that seem quite simple on the surface of their magic, but allegedly require a lot of concentration to produce. The latter is intriguing, considering Ellie is high and yet still has managed to make one that is vibrant and well-defined, clearer than any I've ever seen.

"So many questions for a simple fantasy." Ellie stands—presumably on her tiptoes again—and pulls a little bottle from somewhere inside her bralette, the corked glass glinting. "But if you must know—liquid contraceptive. A few drops on my fingertip, and mixed with the water of the loch, it makes illusions. Every loch is different, according to the anthologies. Some say you can see what you most desire, though I don't think what I most desire is fish. I just find it somewhat amusing that the enchantment works. I haven't quite studied it in depth. I keep getting the fish here though, over and over and over. Maybe this loch has something to say about marine life."

"I haven't seen one of those since—" I cut myself off before I give away anything about my true nature, collecting my thoughts as quickly as possible "—for a long time. My grandmother used to show us Whimseys when we were children. She was attuned to fire more than any of the other elements. She'd send imaginary wolves from the fireplace when we wouldn't behave."

"Did they work? Make you behave, I mean?"

"When we were young, sure. But all the Blossom fairytales work when you're young. It's keeping the belief alive when one gets older that's a bit more of a challenge."

Ellie nods, lowering herself back into the water. With the moon behind her, she has a nearly ethereal glow. "Sophia—my sister—is the same. Just at the age where she shouldn't believe in the stories anymore since she's old enough to entertain the idea of marriage. But she believes them as strongly as she did when she was a child. I don't know how to break it to her that just because I like to do things my own way doesn't mean I'm going to get turned into a feral animal. Nor does it mean I'll fail out of Blossom."

I think the Allure is loosening Ellie's tongue.

I don't say anything for a second, but it's a second too long because she seems to take my silence as me agreeing with Sophia.

"Don't tell me you believe in that duty to society shit too. Is that why you finished at Blossom? Because you changed? Compromised yourself?"

"People do change, Ellie. I'm not sure I would call it a compromise."

"So if it's not a compromise, what is it?" There's agitation in her voice that wasn't there earlier, and I don't think it's due to the Allure.

"It's just… it's growing up. Getting older. Wanting more."

"More than what? This?" Ellie waves her hand up toward the night sky, water flying, her words a harsh whisper. I know what she's referring to: the parties, the casual sex, the drugs, the deviancy. "Because it seems a little bit like you don't want more than this. Unless we're talking about—"

She holds up the contraceptive bottle and stares at me, her gaze hard. "If this is what you want, we can just get it over with. I thought you were different, Max O'Carroll. I thought that maybe you weren't..."

"I wasn't what?" There are prickles of light in the corners of my eyes now, telling me that my single snort of Allure is wearing thin. It never lasts long enough, and this is one hell of a time for it to start to dissipate. I wipe at my face where beads of water have landed.

This time, I'm the one who doesn't want to wait for an answer, so I repeat my question.

"I wasn't what, Ellie?"

Letting out a small sigh, she stuffs the glass vial back into her bralette, the thin fabric cups barely coming up over the surface of the glistening water. "I thought that maybe you weren't a friend of Padraig's. But Padraig's friends come here for only a few things. And I can't for the life of me figure out what you came here for or why I so desperately feel the need to give you whatever it is."

"I didn't come here because of him."

The voice in my head wants me to tell her that I'm there because she is, that I want to protect her, that I want her to know that she needs to change in order to save herself and her magic. But she won't believe me if I tell her right now. Or maybe she'll forget in the morning after all the Allure and drinking from one or more of the bottles of wine that I saw on one of the garden tables have worn off. Then all my efforts would have been in vain.

"Who are you here because of?"

Her name is on the tip of my tongue, and if I open my mouth, it's going to fall out and metaphorically splash into the lake. So I force myself to swallow it down along with the remnants of my intoxication and visualize it as something sinking down to my toes, toes that aren't even visible in the water I'm treading. "Nobody, Ellie. Loch Lomond wasn't intriguing to me this summer, and I thought seeing some new scenery would be worthwhile."

"Summer is courting season in Loch Lomond," she notes, pushing her braided hair back from the spot where it has floated in front of her shoulder.

"It'll be courting season next summer too."

"No rush to marry, then? I thought after graduating from Blossom, that was everyone's primary objective. Why not for you?"

I look up at the stars then, wondering why she's asking me all these difficult questions. A glimmer of a shooting star streaks across the night sky, cascading into the nothingness that's beyond our world. The sound of faint laughter trickles down from the upper gardens, but not enough to be a distraction from the conversation at hand and the discussion I'm trying desperately to avoid. "Didn't I infer earlier that some questions are better asked the second time you meet someone?"

Ellie laughs, the sound as elegant as the falling of autumn leaves. I've heard it before, many times, along with other sounds that I'd rather be the cause of. But now, as a man, the noise of a simple laugh is doing complex things to me.

"I understand that commitment is difficult for some. I suspect it will be difficult for me, too, when the time comes for me to marry Colonel Gallagher. Mother says I'll grow to love him and that he's a good choice for me. I just... don't feel ready."

The notion of her marrying Colonel Gallagher isn't news to me, but the reminder of her thinking about growing to love him hurts. In the lochs, young women often don't get to pick the men they marry unless they are very fortunate, and it causes an ache in my heart to recall that she's headed to Blossom to prepare her for a life of being married to him. I try to tell myself that at least he's not Padraig.

"Maybe you'll be ready in a year when you're done at Blossom?" The words come out as a question, and Ellie shakes her head, little globes of water hitting the top of the lake with her movement.

"Maybe *you'll* be ready in a year when you go back to Loch Lomond." She lifts her hand and flicks a spray directly at my face with her thumb and forefinger before dashing underwater and beginning to swim back toward shore.

Chapter Three

SOPHIA

Ellie's using her enchantments again.

As I look out toward the candlelit yard from my bedroom window, I can see her water magic sparkling on the surface of the loch. I imagine she's down there with Padraig, trying to procure either Allure or sex, either option good enough for her when she's high as a kite. It's wrong—the things she does with Padraig—especially when she's promised to Colonel Gallagher. I suppose she wants to get those things out of her system, like Mother says she does, but I still find it hard to believe that this is a healthy way for Ellie to spend her dwindling days here in Loch Gàrraidh.

What kind of hostess leaves her guests to go off philandering with some man?

I heave in a deep sigh, my guilt and sense of courtesy nagging at me. I'm going to have to go down there, to that *party*, and fetch Ellie. She can't just decide to host a gathering and then leave everyone in our yard, snorting drugs off the rock walls like they're pigs, drinking the red wine that was supposed to be saved for the winter holidays. Plus, the people below my window are loud. *So* loud. I'm surprised I was even able to get Huntley and Pippa to bed, despite them being on the opposite side of the corridor.

Running a hand over my face in exasperation at a particularly noisy burst of laughter, I finally rise from my spot at the window and make haste down the staircase and out the back door.

God, these people—don't any of them have any sense? Can't they just go home, or at least be disgusting somewhere that isn't here? What am I even going to say to them? Get out of our yard? Ellie invited them here, so I can't exactly just send them away. I see them on a regular basis and I don't want to offend anyone by telling them to leave...

Thankfully, when I stomp out into the upper yard, it's none other than Padraig and some of the other usuals—Kit and Agnes, who are the first two I recognize. They're pushing around stones in some kind of makeshift game and chuckling to themselves. Ellie is nowhere to be seen, but Padraig is still here, which doesn't make much sense since I thought he was with her at the loch.

If Ellie isn't with Padraig, then who is she with?

"Sophia!" Padraig finally looks up from his game and greets me like an old friend and not like I'm the sister of the girl he likes to sleep with when he's bored. Despite Ellie's comments earlier in the evening, she can't fool me into thinking it's something that only happened last year. "Did you finally decide to come and join a party?"

I shake my head in annoyance, red curls bobbing around my cheeks. I'm certain after all this time, Padraig knows I don't feel any kind of fondness toward him or his presence, and I'm not about to try to hide my true feelings even though others are around. "I came to ask you as nicely as possible to shut up. The children are trying to sleep."

Kit lets out the loudest guffaw imaginable while Padraig raises an eyebrow at me like I'm a petulant child who needs some straightening out. "Are you aware that this is a social gathering?"

"I'm also aware that you're—" I almost tell everyone at the party that he's married and screwing around on his wife. The words are there on the very edge of my lips, but I keep them in because I know that if I said something and any of these troublemakers remembered, I could find myself next in line to head to Blossom. Padraig has a foolish amount of power at the school, something I've never quite understood "—you're all on Allure. Allure doesn't make you noisy; it makes you a degenerate. If you want to be loud, go be loud in the gardens *away* from the house. Or, better yet, why don't you go to *your* own houses?"

That's about the moment my bravery wears off, and so instead of allowing them the satisfaction of responding, I take off in the grass toward the pergola and the loch, stomping through wildflowers and dodging rocks with my bare feet. I should have put some shoes on, but I was too angry and frustrated when I left the house to have given footwear a second thought. A small benefit of not having worn anything on my feet is the energy of the earth that flows through my toes, and I absorb little bits of magic here and there. I don't have the same level of ability that Ellie does, but I can still feel the moments when my enchantments are stronger and more connected with the elements around me.

I don't use magic for much though, unlike my sister. I don't feel like I have any reason to. I have no substances to make, no man to impress, no real use for the fact that I can connect with the energy of the earth and seemingly store magic inside of me indefinitely. Though I am admittedly a little jealous of Ellie's talents with charms and sorcery, I know it's gotten her into more trouble than anything else. I don't want to be in trouble. I don't want Ellie to be in trouble either, but the fact that she's using her magic might be proof that she's about to find herself in a mess.

As I walk, I think about all the things I want to tell my sister. All the things that I've already told her tonight that clearly have fallen out of her ears. But one thought in particular sticks out: she's never going to get to marry a decent man with behavior like this. Even though she jokes about becoming a spinster and ruining our family name, I'm much more concerned about her becoming a cat and roaming around Loch Gàrraidh for the length of an average human life.

I probably shouldn't believe in those stories anymore, but something about the feeling I get from the fairytales of our childhood sits uncomfortably in the soft spot on the back of my neck, right where my skull joins my spine.

Breaking me from my thoughts, the sound of water splashing comes over the moors. Under the moonlight and between hedgerows, I spot my sister diving underneath the surface of the loch in her silken underthings, the ivory fabric of her brassiere glinting in the moon's glow. She doesn't notice me, and neither does the man she's with, his bare shoulders peeking over the edge of the lake, darkened hair blending into the evening like blotted ink. He's too busy looking at her, and she's too busy underwater, everything calm and quiet as I spot Ellie moving toward the shoreline that's nearest me.

Ellie has this way about her with men, and I'm not sure if it's a glorious thing to behold or a frightening one.

When she climbs out of the water, the man has finally broken from his trance and isn't far behind, rising from the loch and grabbing for his slacks that are puddled on a mound of rocks and flowers. I do my best not to stare at him because it's not appropriate to look at an unclothed man unless he's your betrothed. However, it's difficult to tear my eyes away from the gentle curve of his thighs, the creases in his abdomen, or the—

Focus, Sophia.

There's something strangely familiar about him, and it has me furrowing my brow and ducking back behind the prickly branches to try to place him. Heat rises in my cheeks as I glance at him once again before making a conscious effort to examine the remaining summer flowers on the branches. They're a blushing pink and crimson in the luminosity of the evening, and I can only imagine that my face must be a similar color once again.

Somewhere in my peripheral vision, I see my sister pull her dress over herself quickly, her movements graceful. I'm mortified that she thought showing this man her silk lingerie was a good idea, let alone wearing it in the lake. At least it's seemingly undamaged as she slips her arms through the sleeves of her dress. Mother would have a fit if she knew Ellie was practically skinny dipping in the Loch with some stranger. Though, then again, maybe she would be relieved that the poor societal behavior is at least happening outside of the house where Huntley and Pippa can't overhear or see.

"Can you dry us off with your magic?" the man asks, stepping a dripping leg into his pants. I swap my gaze to stare up at the stars for a moment and do my hardest not to ogle his bare legs, naked in front of me and my sister—along with the rest of him. "Might be a bit less suspicious than if we both show back up to the party soaking wet."

"Oh, yes. I should have done something earlier to repel the water, but I obviously was a little under the influence."

When I look back down at Ellie and the stranger, she's flicking her fingers toward where the dark-haired man is standing. He has one leg in his slacks and one leg out while carefully covering his manhood, and sorcery quickly flows from Ellie's fingers. Her magic winds a curl of ivory around his body for barely a moment before the tornado-like spiral sucks up all the water from his body and his hair and then disappears like fog into the night. When the charm fades, the man is as dry as a bone, probably looking almost exactly as he did when they came down here to the loch however long ago, minus the guilty look on his face.

"Thank you," he replies in a low voice, cladding himself the rest of the way in his slacks and shirt as I watch on like a curious child who is seeing something interesting for the first time. Once he has his pants on, I don't *quite* look away.

Though, to be honest, I've never truly seen a man without his clothes. And seeing this one, here, under the moonlight, is a bit of a shock to my entire body and mind. I think I'm frozen to the spot, trying to sort out a good time to let my sister know that I'm here without making it come across as if I've been spying. Because I'm not spying, not really. I'm just... trying to protect Ellie from herself.

Ellie smiles at the stranger before turning the spell on herself, the magic probably requiring double the effort to dry out her long hair. I can't help but watch, fascinated at the ease with which she performs her charm since enchantments are always so effortless for Ellie. There's a tinge of jealousy in there as well—deep inside where I've pushed the feeling into the recesses of my heart. I sometimes wish I didn't care about being proper and good and appropriate, the way that Ellie doesn't seem to worry about those things. But there's also this desperate need for acceptance, for protection, for all kinds of other things that places like Blossom teach us are important to our society's existence and our own. Maybe it's because Father's gone now and I worry that at some point his money will run out and we won't be able to keep our home in Loch Gàrraidh. After that, we'd be forced to sell our remaining horses, market the land, and hope for the best.

I feel a tickle in my nose—a sneeze threatening to escape due to the scent coming from the aromatic flowers covering the moors and the gardens. Almost as if she can sense it in some way—it's either that, or she knows of my presence—Ellie speaks.

"Come out, Sophia."

A knot forms in my throat as quickly as Ellie says the words. I could just not respond, make her think I'm not actually here in the lower gardens, watching and worrying. Unfortunately, my feet instinctively disobey my orders, and I find myself standing next to a gap in the wild rose hedge, sighing, half at myself and half at my sister. The man, meanwhile, raises his eyebrows, flicking his gaze between Ellie and me. He doesn't look surprised, exactly. It's an expression I can't quite place, that familiarity in his eyes sinking deep into my existence. Maybe Ellie feels it too, and maybe that's why she's gotten so... acquainted with him tonight.

"How long have you been standing there?" Ellie asks, picking up her little sachet of Allure from one of the rocks. She asks the question in a way that should make it sound like she is annoyed, but I can tell she is more amused than anything else. Meanwhile, the man—whom I haven't yet been introduced to—runs a hand through his luxurious hair and awkwardly shifts his weight from one leg to the other.

"Long enough," I retort, my throat dry. Does she know that I saw the two of them getting out of the water, practically nude? "Long enough to see the two of you doing what you shouldn't be."

The man seems indifferent, but I'm worried about my sister and not him. Ellie snorts, a sound that's rather unbecoming, in my opinion. "You shouldn't be peeking around in the dark."

"And you shouldn't be abandoning your guests at the house." I might as well tell her exactly what's on my mind now that she knows I've been here for a while. "They're going to wake Huntley and Pippa and then everything is going to be a disaster."

"You are aware this is a social gathering, Sophia?" Ellie's words are nearly an exact repetition of what was said to me earlier in the evening.

Words slip out before I have the ability to control my mention of the name that I suspect Ellie might not want to hear when she's with another man. "That's what Padraig told me. I told him to shut up."

Ellie freezes at the mention of Padraig, just as I should have expected she would, and it feels as if the air around us changes. A slight breeze blows over the water, and it brings a chill with it. I'm not certain if it's an aftereffect of Ellie's magic or just a coincidence, but the stranger must feel it too because he bites at his lip before speaking, a shiver clearly running up his spine and causing him to clench his jaw.

"I'm—I should be getting back to the gathering."

I have no control over water enchantments like Ellie does, but I still can give a deep, frozen glare when necessary. It's an attribute I think I got from our mother, and I'm using it in her stead since she's away. "That would probably be best."

"Max, don't go," Ellie whispers, though she's loud enough for me to hear. I wonder if she thinks she's being quieter than she actually is, or if it's the Allure affecting her. Is she even on Allure right now? She doesn't seem as fucked up as she did when she was snorting pink powder off her hand mirror. All I do know is that there's a pleading tone that isn't the same as when she talks to Padraig or any of the other men who I've seen her in *precarious situations* with.

This Max character looks between Ellie and me, seemingly trying to decide who to listen to. As is usual for a man in her company, it's a struggle for him to leave Ellie behind.

I sigh. "Fine, Max. You can stay. But you must dare to tell me your intentions with my sister."

Max suddenly breaks into a chuckle, picking up his coat from somewhere in the darkness. "I think that question should be directed at Ellie instead of me. It seems as if she may be the one with particular intentions."

Her jaw drops, and she flicks her braid over her shoulder defiantly. "You're the one who got *hard* at the sight of my—"

"Ellie!" I squeal before clapping my hand over my mouth. "Don't!"

Max appears unaffected by the blush that I know is creeping up my face, as if he's already grown accustomed to my sister's foul language and my crushing embarrassment. "It was little more than a surprise."

"Little more than a surprise?" Ellie huffs. "Would you like to see it again? I'm doubly certain it would have the same result if I gave you a warning."

She reaches up to the sleeve of her dress like she's going to pull it down over her shoulder to expose her skin and her chest but pauses with a smirk on her lips as her fingers twitch against the fabric. That's enough of a show for me, and I rush across the garden, nearly snagging myself on the rose thorns, grabbing my sister's hand away from her gown. The sachet of Allure sways against her thin wrist where the strings are wrapped around it.

"Okay, I think it's time for us all to return to the upper gardens and for you two to wean yourselves off whatever amount of Allure or drink you've taken this evening." I start to drag Ellie away from Max, and though my sister is nearly a full head taller than me, she's lithe and fine-boned like a little bird. All that to say that I nearly bowl her over into the hedges as I yank her from the edge of the loch.

Ellie whines under her breath. "I wasn't really going—"

"Come *on*!" I'm not having any of her behavior, and now I'm starting to worry that I've left Huntley and Pippa in the house alone for too long. Perhaps they've awoken and found out I'm not there? Perhaps something even more shocking could have happened, like Mother arriving home early, or some other uninvited guest like... "What if Colonel Gallagher shows up at this stupid party of yours and sees you down here with another man? Let's go. At least with Padraig, I know what to expect from you."

The name flies out of my mouth, and Ellie and Max both stiffen, as if there's something that I don't know. I feel as if I know so many things about Padraig—so many more things than what I want to be aware of—that there can't be something I've missed other than the intimate details that Ellie's shared with me. But Colonel Gallagher is more of a mystery, maybe because I haven't met him yet. However, I hear that he's a proper gentleman for a proper lady, though he could be putting on a show as much as Ellie is.

"You really think I care what Colonel Gallagher thinks of me?" Ellie's question comes out as a hiss under her breath. "He'll need to fall in love with me at some point as much as I'll be required to fall for him. But until then, Sophia, let me live."

Max shuffles into his coat and buttons the front. "Maybe she's right, Ellie. Let's go back up. We're dry, we're chaperoned now, and nobody in the yard is likely any less inebriated than we are. Nothing happened, and I wouldn't want to be the reason your future after Blossom is affected."

"But..."

"Come, let me guide you both back up to the pergola." Max's voice is stronger now, an edge of authority in it that wasn't there when I was hidden in the rose brambles. I don't think he's putting on a show—no, that can't be it. I think that, for some strange reason, he's trying to do what's best for Ellie instead of whatever gets him the single thing I'm expecting he wants.

It's an interesting quality that I'm not used to seeing in the men that Ellie associates with. Maybe I've grown too accustomed to men like Padraig who just want drugs and sex—an obsession with pleasurable sensations driving their every move and every motive. But Max? I don't know. It's only been minutes, but I can already tell that he's not as intoxicated as anyone up in the main yard. And, judging by my sister's conversational abilities, she isn't either, which is peculiar all on its own.

But where do I know this Max from? I must recognize him subconsciously from somewhere, because something about him still feels so familiar. And it doesn't escape me that he brushes his fingers against Ellie's arm as he passes us through the gap in the hedgerow, both a silent confession and a gentle admission of some sort that I don't understand. Maybe I would if I had gotten here sooner. Maybe if I had saved her from herself earlier...

"Sophia, come on. You're the one who wanted to go back to the house." Ellie's practically dragging me now, pulling me through the shrubberies and rocks and flowers so abruptly that I'm in danger of smashing my toes.

I mentally drop back down to the loch, furrowing my brow as I try to pay attention to where I'm stepping. The candlelit party slowly comes back into view.

"How do you know Max?" I finally ask her, my voice quiet enough that I hope he can't hear from where he's leading us up the lawn. "He seems... accustomed to parties like this one while not being a complete degenerate asshole."

The corner of Ellie's lips twitch up in a smile as I glance over in her direction. "Wouldn't you like to know?"

"I would, hence my asking. He's not your usual *Padraig*."

"Not every man is like Padraig, Sophia."

"More are than aren't, I seem to find."

We ascend the knoll in the moonbeams, grass tickling my feet and ankles as we step back underneath the pergola and leave the wildflowers and the sparkling loch behind. The laughter from the gathering gets rapidly louder, conversations dragging through the summer air and cascading over us as I notice that the party has made its way to the upper section of the garden instead of the lawn directly below my bedroom window. At least Padraig had enough sense to listen to something I said about keeping away from the house. Or maybe it was Kit. Either way, I just hope the children are still asleep.

Chapter Four

ELLIE

The entire time we walk back up to the party, I stare so hard at the curvature of Max's ass that I nearly trip over a tangle of wildflowers. I do my best to cover up the blunder by scolding Sophia for taking too long, even though she doesn't deserve it. I'm not actually annoyed that she saw Max and me in the loch together, soaking wet with the mystical water I was able to magic away from our clothes. However, I am slightly concerned that Sophia might tattle to our mother when she comes home.

We rise over the hill and exit the depths of the gardens, leaving the enchantment of the lake behind us—only by minutes, but still in the past. It only matters a little that Max is clothed now because the picture of him undressed is branded into my soul, along with the feeling I got when the Allure waned and my stomach started doing somersaults. As I walk underneath the pergola with Sophia, the noise from the party gets louder, Padraig and the others on the lowest part of the yard away from the house. Probably where Sophia told them to go to continue their noise; I'm a bit surprised they actually listened. Allure isn't exactly the kind of drug that makes you… obedient.

In fact, the moment I saw Max fully nude and fully *everything else*, the Allure didn't matter anymore. As much as I teased him, I wanted him too—I wanted him to want me in the ways that Padraig has had me but with a depth that is gentler, like mist over the moors on a late spring afternoon.

Max finally turns from leading us back to the gathering, his mouth set in a firm line, but his green eyes blazing with some kind of torment I can't put my finger on. "I'll fetch us some wine, if you'd like?"

The gentlemanly attitude is still there, despite the disappointment I assume he shares with me.

"That would be lovely, thank you." I put on my best manners so my sister doesn't get any ideas, though it's probably a bit late for that.

"I don't know if you need wine combined with however much Allure..." Sophia begins, but I gently cut off her thought.

"There's not been that much. We're sober. A glass of wine won't cause any harm."

"*More* harm," Sophia corrects, playing her motherly duties well as she stares at Max, hard, before directing a question at him. "You do know that you're playing with fire?"

I grumble, trying to ensure that only my sister hears me. It's the vocal equivalent of kicking her leg beneath a dining table. "Sophia..."

"Someone has to look out for you, and it clearly won't be yourself," she hisses under her breath as the three of us stand there amid the fading evening and the raucous sounds of laughter and merriment. Just then, Sophia and I are distracted by a movement near the back door—a tiny, pajama-clad person walking down the yard toward where my sister is still standing with Max and me.

"Ah, shit. The children are up." The curse falls out of my mouth more easily than it should, especially considering I should be practicing being proper for Colonel Gallagher. However, I'm more worried about Huntley being exposed to the inebriation of the partygoers than anything else. As much as I don't have any maternal instincts, I do have some sense.

"Stay here. Stay in the group. No more fucking around. Don't think about him; don't do anything that I wouldn't do." Sophia turns a stern glare to me, then another to Max. "That applies to you as well. Don't touch my sister."

With that, Sophia takes off with her skirts in her hands, rushing up the incline toward the spot where Huntley has spotted us. There's silence between Max and me for a few moments after she leaves, but no silence in the gardens can be found with the likes of the others playing games and finishing off Padraig's Allure stash. Instead, we walk—together, but apart—toward one of the tables where there's some uncorked wine, and Max pours me a glass underneath the vanishing light of the candles. He hands it over without touching me, honoring Sophia's direction.

Leaning against the edge of the table, I look out into the dusky night as I slowly consume my wine and as Max pours himself a drink of his own. Padraig is standing along the edge of the garden wall, throwing me pointed looks every few minutes. I think he's subliminally trying to get me to run off into the bushes with him too, pain in his eyes like I've fucked Max already and am satiated for the party's remaining duration.

It was nothing like that, even though I am more than willing to admit that I tried. I tested. I attempted to play all the appropriate games that a man would want: the teasing, the flirting, the banter. But Max? Immune—at least, mostly.

Time goes on, but the tranquility that comes from being with Max next to the table and under the increasingly hazy sky offers me respite. Respite primarily from the idea that in the morning, I'm going to face Sophia's wrath for waking up Huntley and probably Pippa too, and wrath for taking off in the dark with someone from Loch Lomond she most certainly doesn't know. Someone well within marrying age who isn't married, who isn't spending the summer courting, who isn't... a lot of things, as far as I can tell. Another degenerate, to her. Another notch in my bedpost, another man to add to my countless list of lovers, another person to potentially ruin my proper future after Blossom and with Colonel Gallagher.

She will disapprove and see everything about tonight as scandalous.

But there's something about Max that tells me he won't destroy me. He's not like Allure, or Padraig, or any other artificial sensation I'm familiar with. Perhaps that thought is much more frightening than the thought of being ruined—the thought of being made into something more than I ever expected.

The night persists, draws on, and dies.

The din of the gardens slowly quiets, Kit and Agnes and the others finally disappearing into the night as they walk around the front of the house and make their way back home. Padraig reluctantly leaves me in the candle glow with Max, waving a defeated-looking goodbye, shoulders slumped, as he treks over the field back to his wife and children in an Allure-induced fog. I probably wouldn't have noticed at all if I'd have taken another snort of Allure within the last hour. But I haven't. Just sips of cherry wine and the intoxication of breathing the same air as Max, whose hand dangles close to mine as we find a seat on the rock wall together while the guests pair off and leave.

Max tells me stories of Loch Lomond, and soon, it's just us left in the yard. True silence consumes us, along with the death of the black candles that line the lawn and hang from the pergola. Amid the tranquility, I dangle my legs off the edge of the wall, my shoes discarded on the grass and my toes peeking out from underneath the fabric of my black gown. When I peek over at Max, he's twirling an empty glass in between his thumb and forefinger, staring off into where the sunbeams are just beginning to waterfall over the moors.

Has the entire evening really passed by? How many bottles did we consume? How long were we at the loch before Sophia came?

"I should make my way back. Let you get some sleep." Max offers me a smile, a knowing one, one that begs for me to kiss him and seal whatever tonight was with another intimate moment.

He sets the glass down on the gray stone, along with his hand.

"You know," I say in a whisper, brushing my fingertip along his skin. "Sophia only said you couldn't touch me. She didn't say anything about me touching you."

He chuckles, looking down. "I think that was a given."

"Maybe she should have been more specific."

Max groans gently before saying my name, clearly caught somewhere between desire and obedience. "Ellie..."

Frowning, I drag my hand away, feeling like I'm pulling away every essence of my being. *What is it about him that's making my heart and my body feel so strange?*

He must feel it too—or feel something, at least—because he twitches the corner of his lips up in a grin. "You'll see me again. I promise you that. You're not going to be able to be rid of me that quickly."

"Who says I was trying to be rid of you?" My heart is pounding so hard in my chest that I swear my ribs are going to break from the pressure and the need. It's a different sort of need than what I felt in the past with other men, including Padraig, this one is deeper, darker, and more dominant. It's enough to jump into a loch almost naked with Max and enough to feel like I want to skip out on

Blossom Academy entirely and move to Loch Lomond just so I have a chance of being properly courted by him next summer.

There's a strangled laugh then, a noise caught in Max's throat, as he slides himself carefully from the wall. He gazes back up at me, the morning sunshine glinting off his dark hair and reflecting in his bright green eyes. "Goodnight, Ellie."

I'm breathless as I respond, screaming in my head for him to close this gap that's been created between us... and for me to suddenly have the ability to control not only water but time itself.

My wish doesn't come true, and instead, I'm forced to say the words I've been dreading since I created a Whimsey in Loch Gàrraidh. "Goodnight, Max."

Max gives me a little courtesy nod before he turns and walks off across the lawn, only looking back over his shoulder once as he's about to turn the corner by the front of the house. The fact that he peeks back at me as I'm sitting on the wall, disheveled, hair falling out of my braid, has my heart skipping a beat. Something in his eyes tells me he doesn't want to leave, but something in his gait tells me he must. I can't pinpoint what the reason could be—nothing he said hinted at anything untoward. He was even honest, though hesitant, about his history at brothels in the surrounding lochs. I don't suspect a man would admit to something like that if it wasn't true.

And, therefore, I'm intrigued. Unfortunately, I'm also exhausted.

I pick up my sachet of Allure before slipping into the house through the back door, leaving the relics of the party behind. Unexpectedly, Sophia's sitting at the kitchen table, eating a bowl of porridge that has steam rising from it, which tells me she's not been up all that long. Huntley and Pippa must still be asleep.

"You're up early," I murmur, tiredness falling over me like a warm blanket.

"Or late," she replies, not even looking up from her breakfast. Her tone of voice is annoyed, edgy. "Depending on your perspective, that is."

"It's been a while since I've stayed up all night."

Sophia doesn't say anything for a moment or two. Her silence persists long enough that I assume she has nothing further to say to me, and I take a step out of the dining area before she calls me back. "Ellie."

"Yes?"

"You never did answer my question about knowing Max from somewhere."

I furrow my brow, pushing my hair away from my face where tendrils have fallen from the braid. "I don't remember you asking that."

"I'm asking now." She finally breaks her stare from her porridge and swings around in her chair to look at me, nightdress gathered and bunched around her legs.

"I don't know him from anywhere, Sophia." I shift my weight on the cool floor.

"So, getting him to take his clothes off and swim in the lake with you was *what*?"

"A mistake, probably."

Sophia runs a hand along her jaw, presumably exasperated with me and my carelessness. I know she's concerned about repercussions that could hurt our family, and I know she wishes I'd share in some of the responsibilities while Mother is away instead of throwing parties and making Allure. But I don't think Sophia understands that my time to do these things is so limited that I need to take the opportunity to do them before I'm forced into a life that I never wanted to live in the first place.

"I have a feeling you don't think it was actually a mistake," Sophia notes. "Unfortunately for you, I do think it's a mistake, and I'm certain our mother will think it was as well. If you ever wondered why you're going to Blossom, this is part of it, I'm sure. You probably don't even remember that Colonel Gallagher is calling on you tomorrow, and you'd better not be sickly. You can't just toy with men the way you do, showing off with your magic."

I did forget about Colonel Gallagher's visit, but she doesn't have to know that.

"And why is that, Sophia? Is it because you can't and you're jealous?" The questions fall from my mouth before I have a chance to bite them back, which is exactly what happens to me when I feel as if I'm being backed into the corner during an argument. I'm not good at arguments, and the hurt expression on my sister's face tells me that I've taken this one a step too far.

She smashes her spoon down on the wooden table. "Oh, fuck off, Ellie. The last thing I am is jealous of you and your *mischief*."

"That's not the language of a proper lady," I remind her, venom lacing my voice. I'm past the point of controlling what I'm saying. "Better be careful. If Huntley and Pippa start repeating it, you might find yourself being shipped away too."

"I'm not going to get sent to Blossom—" Sophia starts, but before she has a chance to finish her sentence, I'm already halfway up the stairs.

Once I make it to my room and close the door, I deflate. I hate arguing with Sophia, and even though she's a year younger than me, she's right more often than not. However, her worldview is so contrary to mine that she makes it easy to get into spats like the one we've just had, be it about Blossom or Colonel Gallagher or my preferred uses for magic.

I consider flopping down in bed with my dress still on, but the same black cat from last night is entwining his paws in my blankets right next to my pillow, eyes closed.

"You look comfortable," I say to the cat as I place the sachets of Allure and contraceptives back in the drawer next to my bed. The cat, of course, says nothing back. In fact, he doesn't even bother to open his eyes as I slip out of my dress and release my long hair from the now loose braid, strands cascading over my back as I stand in the middle of my room in my underwear. Sunlight streams through the small opening in my heavy curtains, the summer day outside already brightening but with an undertone of fog that seems to be persistent here in Loch Gàrraidh. The scent of freshly picked wildflowers and the cherry wine waft around the enclosed space as I reach forward and give the curtain a tug to encase the bedroom in almost complete darkness.

It isn't until I've woven my way underneath the blankets and around the big male cat that I think about what Sophia said regarding Colonel Gallagher's visit tomorrow morning. It's a thought that's in short consideration as I lie on the mattress because Colonel Gallagher isn't on my mind—the way Max made me feel over the course of the evening is what pushes all other thoughts aside. I don't recognize the feeling, and certainly don't recognize it from any of my other interactions. It's confusing because it's not like anything truly happened between Max and me, at least not physically. But emotionally, I'd swear as if something's happened.

Petting the cat on the head, the animal purring from somewhere deep inside its body, I stare up at the stippled ceiling. I'm intimately familiar with the bumps and swirls, having stared at them night after night, waiting. Waiting for something about my situation to change, waiting for a lover to finish, or just waiting for the latest snort of Allure to knock me out. Today, though, I imagine that Max and I are looking up at our own respective ceilings, thinking about last night and the loch, and the way it felt when his hand brushed my arm before we went back to the party.

Like lightning touching skin.

In the times before when I've met Colonel Gallagher, I've never once felt like that. Never felt the zap of inclement weather on my skin, the prickle of a desired sensation, or had the heat of lust flush to my cheeks. Of course, my exposure to him has been limited and very nearly always chaperoned, though we managed to sneak away once for a brief conversation when Mother knew he was going to ask me to marry him after I completed my studies at Blossom. I think Mother likes to believe that particular interaction was the only one where I was alone with a man, her willful blindness helping her maintain some semblance of control over me until I'm sent away.

Time goes by, a blink of a moment with each purr of the cat.

What if Max and I had kissed? What would his lips feel like against mine? Would they be gentle and soft or insistent and burning? Would he taste like the cherry wine we consumed mixed with the sweet scent of Allure, or something else entirely? Mint and charcoal, licorice root and tangerines, herbal tea and clove cigarettes?

I find myself staring up into the darkness, considering these questions over and over again until my eyes close and I fall into a restful slumber.

Chapter Five

MAX

The stippled ceiling is familiar, considering the number of days and nights I've spent here in Ellie's room. It almost always tends to be the quietest space in the house, Huntley and Pippa—the younger children—not used to having cats around as companions rather than playthings and therefore frequently making loud noises when we're around in that form. They'll learn in their own time, though it's not that I don't like children. I'm just certain they still believe in the bedtime stories and the fairytales about cats and are taught to be wary of us. Since Sophia still believes the stories and she minds the children much of the time, I'm certain the little ones haven't been told any different.

But Ellie? She doesn't. If she did, she wouldn't have taken me down to the loch and stripped half-naked into her lingerie. She would be terrified of Blossom, but she's reckless—much in the way that I was reckless, too. It's a somewhat wistful feeling to see her that way, carefree and wild. I don't have that luxury anymore.

The moment she starts to sigh in her sleep, I know it's my cue to leave. I'm exhausted from my own lack of rest and the filter I had to put on much of our conversation, as is true with any of the other people I interact with when I'm in my human form. Though I initially was energized by the evening air and, admittedly, Ellie's magic, there's nothing here for me at the moment.

I hop off the bed onto my paws, stretching out my back from the spot where I was curled and resting. Then I cross the room, batting at the curtains to make a tiny gap so I can spring onto the ledge. The ground is only a few stories below, and my whiskers rustle in the light summer wind, the scent of wine and wildflowers and cooking breakfasts on the breeze. Leaping gracefully onto one of the larger branches next to the house, I shimmy my way down the large, gnarled tree until all four of my feet hit the soft grass. Before I venture off into the flowers on the moors, I flick my ears back and forth to listen for something encouraging me to stay with Ellie. But all I hear is the distant sound of families talking, the cry of a sea bird, and the hollow ringing of a church bell.

The latter has an eerie echo, the church long since abandoned and taken over by the cats as their—*our*—shelter in the winter months, and a gathering spot in the summers when we aren't busy hunting.

I decide to head that way, following my nose toward the distant sea and my ears to the *clang-clang-clang* of the windswept bell's clapper.

The morning is borderline gray, and I find myself leaning toward being disappointed. Maybe it's because I know there's no possibility that someone like Ellie would have feelings for someone like me, or perhaps it's something to do with the fact that my affections toward her are stronger than anything I've ever felt in my life, human- or cat-wise. It makes me wonder what my world might have been like if I'd have met her before going to Blossom—if I would have stopped my reckless ways. Because that's what I want to do now. I want to take it all back and paint the night sky with pretty words and show her the way she makes me feel.

But it doesn't matter right now, I think as I cross over the moors in little more than a casual run. *She's promised to Colonel Gallagher, and she's convinced that she'll fall in love with him if she tries hard enough. I was nothing more than a one-night diversion.*

I know I need to accept this truth, but it's difficult medicine to swallow.

Breathing in the warm summer air as I sprint between hedges and windflowers, I try to empty my mind into a state of meditation, try to focus on my senses. There are things I can feel, hear, see, taste, and smell, and they stem from all directions: north, south, east, and west. The sea in the distance, the scent of roses, the softness of the blades of emerald grass under my paws, the taste of wine as it exists in a cat's mouth. It's a strange and beautiful thing.

The intrusive thoughts fall in line with the positive ones. As I dash across an open field, a forest far to my right, I find myself thinking about the curse and how it has afflicted me over the last year or more. One would think I would be counting the days, but I have nothing to count on, no reason to number my existence into human years spent as an animal. From what the others have told me, I'll be like this until my natural date of death as a person, just in the body of an animal that is meant to only live for a portion of that time.

I find myself pondering the memory of Allure and the other magical substances I used to consume, the clove cigarettes I'd smoke, the people I used to fuck. Ellie was never one of them—of course not, or I'd hope we'd at minimum remember each other—but she was never the type I had my eye on. I ventured through brothels and bawdy houses in Loch Lomond and beyond, finding warmth in the beds of those who found my peculiar eyes enchanting. Now, though—now things are so different, it seems like those days in Loch Lomond occurred during an entirely different lifetime.

Maybe because, in many ways, it was.

I make it to the old church after some time, having picked it as my destination out of habit rather than anything else. When I meander through the crack in the large wooden door, the atrium is empty, the others likely in various hiding spots or gone out to hunt the mice in the fields and flowers. Possibly, some of them had late nights enjoying the moon and the sea through the eyes of a human, lounging on the rocky shorelines, making fires and laughing and trying to enjoy some semblance of being normal. I don't expect any of them to be around this morning, and so I find a spot on one of the least broken pews and stretch my body out in the shattered reflections of the cracked stained-glass windows.

Sleep cascades over me easily, and when I dream—because cats *do* dream—I dream of Ellie in the moonlit water of Loch Gàrraidh, like a beautiful and ghostly pale shadow of a woman. A woman who is more than certain that I can't stop myself from needing her. The memory of the shadows in the Callaghan family's floral gardens haunts my very existence.

Hours later, I wake to a rumble of thunder across the moors. The sound flows effortlessly across the fields and forest and is lapped up by the waves of the tumultuous sea. There's a storm slowly rolling in that I can feel in my bones, and soon the other cats will congregate near the old altar. They'll all have questions for me—where I was last night since I wasn't at the regularly scheduled bonfire—and I'm certain at least a few of them will question whether my soft spot for Ellie's family has expanded to include an affinity for Ellie herself.

It's written all over my face and paws and fur, stained like the cherry wine on my breath and her touch on my skin.

I decide it's better to leave and find another place to wait out the storm than to get involved in a conversation I'd rather not have. Leaping from the pew into the quickly fading sunlight, I squeeze out around the gap in the frame of the northern window just when the first fat raindrops start to fall. Shaking them out of my fur, I break into a quick trot. As I rush along toward the breakwater, the humidity in the air heavy and thick with the storm surge, I notice there's a familiar silhouette sitting on the edge of the rocks. Sea spray flickers up into the air, and the old ginger cat speaks first once I approach.

"Ah, Maximilian. Another late night?"

"As if I have many late nights to begin with," I joke, padding my way across the rocks toward Alastair. If anyone was to notice my absence, it would be him. "I don't spend much time wandering as a human, despite what many may think."

"You spend much of your time wandering in general. You're very restless."

His observation isn't incorrect.

"You never used to find yourself restless?" I take a seat on the boulder nearby, listening to another rumble of thunder as it combines with the crash of a wave on the rocks. The moment I ask the question, I peer over at Alastair. His orange fur has seen better days, matted in some places, disheveled in others.

"Of course," he replies, attempting to hide a smirk playing at his mouth by licking the salt water off one of his big paws. "It was often my state of being when I was younger and found myself with a distraction on my hands."

"I've no distractions." It sounds like a lie because it *is* a lie, though Alastair doesn't have to be made aware of that.

"Maximilian, I may be old..."

I let out a little puff of air that almost sounds as if it's a sigh, but there's something distinctly cat-like about it. "What are you thinking then?"

He blinks at me slowly, larger droplets of rain starting to fall around us. "I'm thinking you should be careful."

"I'm restless, not reckless, Alastair."

"Maybe not as a cat. But when we turn back into humans after sunset, sometimes we don't always think about what might make us come completely undone."

He's seen enough in his time as a feral animal to know that maybe, at some point, we all have human desires inside of our hearts. We aren't supposed to. At least, we aren't supposed to give into them because of the shame and humiliation we could bring upon those who follow society's conventions and customs if they were to be found with a Bèist in any way.

"You think that I—"

Alastair lifts a paw toward me, showing his marred pink paw pads, a signal to pause and listen to what he's about to say. "You smell as if you've been swimming in Loch Gàrraidh. The air around you tastes like expensive cherry wine. On top of that, your avoidance of the rest of the *Clodder* marks the evidence that you were absorbed in something you don't want to discuss."

He knows.

"I'm not avoiding it. I just needed some space."

"You're outside and a storm's coming."

I could remind Alastair that he's outside as well, the winds and particles of salt water battering his ginger fur, but he's so old that I don't think he cares much for any arguing. Instead, I don't say anything in response as I consider washing myself away into the sea. I could become one with the waves, broken bones pounding on the gray-clad breakwater as I crash over and over and over.

"What's her name?" Alastair asks after a pause, the wind rustling his whiskers.

I try to remain mysterious despite the stupidity of even bothering. "Whose name?"

"The woman who's gotten you occupied with the act of falling in love."

I nearly choke as I suck in a deep breath of sea air at the old cat's use of the word "love." "It's not love. It's a fleeting infatuation. I'm lonely and she's nothing more than an… irresponsible diversion. Plus, she's promised to someone else."

"Does she love him?"

"She thinks she can."

Alastair hums to himself, nostrils flaring as he sniffs at the air of the growing storm. "Maximilian, I know that you know how the curse works. Yours won't break unless she loves you back."

I shift my weight on the rocks. "I know. And if she loves me back, she'll be turned into one of us by the Academy. It's the worst kind of paradox."

"If you're both found, my boy."

"What do you mean, if we're found?"

Alastair doesn't get to respond because there's another crash of thunder close by, the sky immediately lighting up in a flash of bright white electricity. Then the rain crescendos into a downpour. It's not a usual rain, a light sprinkle that slowly grows into a deluge and later fades into a drizzle. This is as if a bucket of water has been dumped on Alastair and me, a torrent of heavy showers that cascade over our fur and soak us to the bone in mere seconds.

"Come!" Alastair hollers before leaping across the rocks deftly as he heads back toward the church—the last place I want to go. There will be questions. And those questions are why I came out here in the first place. But I can't disobey Alastair. As one of the elders of the *Clodder*, I know he'll keep the whispers to a minimum. At least, the whispers that I can overhear.

I break into a run and catch up with him quickly, making it back to the building before the worst of the weather hits. Alastair ushers me down the curved staircase onto the lower floor where we shake ourselves as dry as possible, licking the storm's residue from our fur.

The cellar is quiet and well-appointed with carefully crafted, antique furniture that's probably been here at least as long as Alastair. When I arrived here after being changed into a Bèist—a beast—I was told of a legend of a man from the loch coming to the church in an attempt to turn it into a proper oceanside getaway. I'll admit that the location is ideal, with the ability to listen to the waves from nearly any of the dilapidated rooms. However, it seems this man only reconditioned the basement before abandoning the project, and depending on who is telling the story, he either simply disappeared into the ether with all his worldly possessions left in the cellar or he fell in love and turned into a Bèist himself.

At least, that's what the legends say, and they feel very much like the Blossom fairytales.

I just know that he never made it to replacing the windows on the old church, as there's a dampness to the basement as the rain patters against the window, the thickness in the air resting on me like a blanket. My favorite part of being down here isn't that there's a soft mattress, or dark rugs, or coverlets of stitched-together rabbit fur. It's that there are all sizes of chemist jars that line one wall in multiple colors, and they shine with the dayglow in rainbows along the furniture when there isn't a storm raging outside. The cellar window is small, but it lets in enough light that the underground apothecary possesses a mystical appeal. Even in the grayness of the weather, I can feel the warmth of the amber and jade glass vials as they seem to stare at Alastair and me.

"You never did tell me her name." Alastair's voice breaks through the pitter-patter of the storm against the window.

"Does it matter?"

He blinks at me slowly. "Does *she* matter?"

The question isn't meant to have an answer, because we both already know what I would have said. Instead of giving an unnecessary response, I pace the room as Alastair takes a tentative leap onto the black velveteen chair in the corner. I try my hardest to not look like I'm watching him, but I am—he's staring at the flashes of light against the bottles. The quiet isn't uncomfortable but is the sort of silence that could last forever without self-consciousness.

Her name sits on the tip of my tongue until approximately the fifteenth time I lap the room when I finally allow it out.

"Her name is Ellie."

Alastair doesn't flinch.

"Ah, one of the Callaghan girls. I should have guessed." He chuckles, curling his still-damp tail around his paws as he lies down on the seat. "The family's always been kind. But she's promised to someone else?"

"Once she's finished and reformed from Blossom, it seems."

"Blossom? Sounds like she's one who has a mind of her own if they're sending her away to reform school."

I can't help the smile that breaks across my face as I think about Ellie slipping off her dress and coercing me, naked, into Loch Gàrraidh with her. I'd say she *absolutely* has a mind of her own. I'd also say that some parts of me seem to have recovered their own convictions, in particular everything below my waist.

But it's more than that.

It's more with her than just my dick flinching like at the bawdy houses in Loch Lomond, and it's more than just the need to take Ellie to bed. There's a deep longing in my heart to feel her flame-red hair running through my fingers as we embrace, to taste a droplet of cherry wine off her lips, to watch her undress again under the light of the moon and just for me instead of with the intention of... whatever her intention was last night.

I don't want Ellie to be thinking about annoying Padraig when we walk through the gardens in the lower yard. I don't want her to be thinking about the stars or the moon or the way the flowers scent the air around Loch Gàrraidh as I lay her down in the grass and kiss her. I don't want her to think about anything other than the way the world feels when we're together, the way it feels when I show her what it means to—

"Are you still with me, Maximilian?" Alastair's real-world existence breaks through my daydream. I immediately drop back down to earth and realize I'm standing in the middle of the cellar in a puddle of pale light.

Has the storm passed already?

"Yes, Alastair. I'm still here."

I watch him carefully. The elderly cat sighs, resting his head on his outstretched front legs. He looks pained. "It must be getting late."

"Hard to tell with the stormy weather."

"My bones tell me what time of day it is. They're saying it's getting late. Almost time to change again."

"Your bones are probably tired of being in this damp basement all the time. You should go up with the *Clodder* in the warmth. Not much down here but old bottles and things that are meant for humans."

Alastair chuckles, eyes closed. "I like it here. Nobody disturbs me. Except for you."

"You brought me down here."

"You were going to whinge about everyone asking you where you went yesterday," he reminds me. "Now you can run off again to your fancy parties and avoid the group for another night. You should be offering me your gratitude for distracting you. Now go and enjoy yourself. While you still have the time. We don't always have the time, you know."

I look up at the window to check the sky, droplets of rain slowly sliding down the glass and indicating the storm has almost passed. As I step away toward the spiral staircase that leads from the cellar up to the main rectory and the wedged-open front door, there's a familiar tingling in my veins that tells me it's almost time to change again, just like Alastair said.

Or Alastair's bones, depending on what one believes.

Chapter Six

SOPHIA

A thunderstorm rolling in keeps Huntley and Pippa up later than they should be, and I do my best to soothe their worries and get them to sleep. As the predictable fog cascades over the moors and the loch, the two of them finally doze off, allowing me to escape their bedroom and retreat to my own. I shuffle down the hall with a lantern in my hand but pause when I notice that Ellie's door is slightly open. She's sitting in her worn-out chair reading from a leatherbound book. I should say I'm sorry for the way I treated her earlier. My comments about Colonel Gallagher weren't necessary, and my thoughts around her betrothal to him haven't been all that considerate of Ellie's personal preferences for her life.

A second after I knock lightly on the wooden panel, Ellie looks up from her story and I see her shoulders heave in a sigh. "What, Sophia?"

Her tone suggests that she's still unhappy with me, but I'm certain my apology will make her feel better.

"Can I come in?" My voice is so quiet I'm not completely sure if Ellie's even been able to hear me.

However, she does respond. "Fine."

She doesn't sound all that interested in having a discussion, but I'll take whatever opportunity I can get. Pushing open the door, I let myself into my sister's room. I'm immediately smacked in the face with the scent of lavender, dying roses, and wet grass.

Ellie wastes no time in letting her mood show through her tone: sharp and to the point. "Well, what else do you have to criticize me about?"

I should have expected that she was going to be annoyed, so I cut right to the main point I want to make. "I just wanted to apologize for what I said earlier when you came inside from the party. I should have been more understanding."

She stares at me for a second before looking down again at the pages of her book. I can't tell what she's reading based on the dark leather jacket but it must be interesting given that it's taking her attention away from the apology I'm trying to give. "I appreciate that."

More silence, punctuated by the crackle of the flame in my handheld lamp and the flicker of candles next to Ellie's bedside. I can't tell if she's ignoring me now, waiting for me to leave, or if she's trying to memorize her place on the page so we can continue this conversation with at least a little bit of grace.

"Do you forgive me?" I finally ask, shifting my weight from one foot to the other. I'm doing my best to make this as painless as possible while Ellie seems to be trying to achieve the opposite.

"Forgive you? You've been implying that I'm not worth Colonel Gallagher's time since before he proposed."

A sigh escapes my lips before I can stop it. "It's obvious you don't love him."

"Am I supposed to?"

"I think that's how marriage typically works, yes." I take a half a step forward into the bedroom but then stop myself because it's clear I'm not welcome.

Ellie flips another page, scanning it for a second before going back to the original one she was looking at. "Maybe for everyone else. Everyone else who wants to be married, that is."

"You don't want to be?"

She scoffs, finally snapping her book closed. "It's complicated, Sophia. You wouldn't understand."

"I can't understand what you don't explain."

My sister groans, swinging her arm to gesture toward the bed. "Ugh. Sit down."

Padding across her dark bedroom, the moonlight is completely blocked by Ellie's thick curtains. She waits for me to clear a spot for the lantern on the bedside table.

"Have you ever loved someone?" The interrogation comes point-blank and without hesitation. I'm still trying to get comfortable on the edge of the mattress, and I nearly fall off at her bluntness, tripping on the hem of my dress as I curl my feet up underneath the skirt to keep them warm.

"I—I don't know," I stutter. "I can't even begin to imagine how to answer that."

"Okay, let me try again. Have you had sex with someone yet?"

I nearly choke. I'm certain she already knows the answer—she's slept with plenty of men and I haven't even kissed one. Not a real kiss, anyway, unless you count one summer when Ellie and I were younger. I was twelve and she was thirteen, and we were playing outside in the gardens with the neighbor kids who no longer live nearby.

I never did tell my sister that George kissed me next to the heather bush and underneath the old pergola that fell down in one of the larger winter storms. That kiss didn't mean anything because it didn't feel anywhere near what I expected from all the descriptions in my storybooks.

"I hear sex and love aren't always intertwined," I say after a few moments pass.

Ellie cringes a little, her face crumpling, and it strikes me that she probably thinks I'm referring to her affair with Padraig.

"I just mean that... Mother said she didn't love Father when she first met him. She's always told us grew to love him as they got older and as he was kinder and more affectionate to her. Don't you believe that sort of thing can happen? I swear I wasn't talking about you and..."

"Don't say it," she emphasizes. "I don't want to hear his name."

I run a hand along my cheek, feeling the warmth from the lantern's flame on my skin, combined with a sudden flush of embarrassed heat. Clearly, there's some piece of Ellie's story from the party yesterday evening that I'm missing. "I didn't say it. But now I'm worried."

Ellie leans back in her chair and stares up at the uneven ceiling. "Nothing should be troubling you about my situation. I'm just realizing that *he's* an ass."

"We both already knew that. I refuse to believe that you weren't aware of it before now."

She sighs again. "Awareness and acknowledgement are two separate things."

"Like sex and love?"

A smile twitches at my sister's lips, and that's the moment I know she's going to forgive me for being so rude to her about Colonel Gallagher. "If you're referring to knowing about *him*, then yes, I suppose I've been aware for a long time. If you're trying to ask me in a roundabout way if I've ever been in love... the answer to that is no. So, I suppose that means you're right on all accounts. Sex and love don't always have to be interconnected. I don't even know if it makes a difference if they are."

"I feel like it has to. I mean, in every story—"

"That's all they are, Sophia. They're stories to make us behave until we're so controlled by society that we don't even know how to think for ourselves anymore." Ellie sets her book down on the corner of the bedside table before pulling the top drawer open, exposing her usual collection of vials, bottles, and pouches. "If I'm going to have to be a disciplined military wife in the near future, I'm going to use my current freedom to do as I please."

"Like swim nude in the loch with a handsome stranger?" I raise my eyebrow, amused.

My sister's face flushes, just barely, but enough that I notice. "Ah, I knew you were looking. To be fair, there was quite a lot to look at."

"Ellie!" I hiss her name from between my teeth, looking toward the ajar door, hoping Huntley and Pippa haven't wandered from bed and overheard the crude comment. It's not that they would understand the underlying joke anyway—they're much too young for that—but I sometimes wonder if I'm even old enough to find such remarks to be appropriate.

Ellie dips her hand in the drawer and pulls out a pouch that I know has Allure inside. "Oh, calm down. You're fine. Between Max's presence last night at the party and Colonel Gallagher visiting every so often, there's been a lot to look at."

My face burns with heat that I'm certain is unrelated to the lantern or the overwhelming number of candles that my sister has lit around the bedroom. "You find both of them attractive, then?"

She pulls the strings of the Allure pouch and extracts a tiny spoon that already holds a pinch of pink on the end. "Of course. It's not like I'm not allowed to think that way."

"But you don't want to marry Colonel Gallagher?"

My sister snorts the minuscule mound of her enchanted drug before she answers me. "I'm not sure how many times I have to say no. But it doesn't matter. Do you really think anyone cares? He's handsome, smart, and wealthy. Mother is pleased with his proposal, and Father would be too, if he was still alive."

I nod slowly, wiggling my toes anxiously under the skirt of my dress at the mention of our father. His passing was a year ago, but it sometimes feels like it was yesterday. "But you'll be wealthy, too, with Father's inheritance."

"Once I *marry*. And a one-time inheritance isn't quite the same as Colonel Gallagher's annual salary." Ellie tucks the pouch back into the drawer next to a handful of small glass vials that clink against one another.

"Is it about the money? The reason why you agreed to marry him, I mean?"

She barely stifles her laughter. "I'd opt to run off to the seaside first rather than marry someone for money, Sophia. And I know you're not that naïve. You know just as well as I do that there's nothing for a young woman to do here in the lochs other than raise a family and continue the tradition of persuading children to believe in fairytales. All I know is that some people leave the lochs and we never hear from them again. I know leaving can be part of growing up, but at least if I marry Colonel Gallagher and we have little ones, then…" Ellie pauses, her explanation dragging off as her eyes grow increasingly glassy. The Allure is taking effect, and soon she'll fade off to some other world that I don't ever plan on being part of.

"Then what?"

She brushes a lock of hair away from her cheek. "It's nothing. Just reminded me of something Mother told me once."

I tilt my head a little to the side, waiting for her to elaborate, but all Ellie does is sigh and lean back in her chair. She stares up at the ceiling again, unblinking, and for a moment, I think that maybe she's completely lost it.

"Ellie?"

She doesn't look at me but continues glaring at the ceiling. "I'm thinking."

I adjust my position, starting to get the pins and needles feeling in my foot from sitting so awkwardly at the edge of the mattress. "What about?"

"Dying alone."

"Dying alone?" I can't help but let out a chuckle. "You're nineteen. I don't think you need to worry about dying alone right now."

Ellie finally rises from her chair, and she stalks across the bedroom to fling open the heavy curtains. Moonlight floods through the window and puddles on the floor, the foggy night feeling thick with tension.

"*You* might not need to worry about it yet, Sophia. But if I turn down Colonel Gallagher, who else will want to marry me? He's doing our family a service by marrying me." She stares out the window, her silhouette accenting the background of the Scottish moors as I listen to her. "I'm everything Mother says I am: insolent and reckless. At some point, I thought Padraig—that he would want to. That he'd be my last chance when we were nearly too old to still consider courting. Then he had to go and fucking get married to someone else and now I'm left with the option of graduating from Blossom, marrying Colonel Gallagher, and having a family, or failing out of Blossom. Then who knows what happens? There's no third option. There's no option where I run away and go live at the seaside and fall in love for real with a man who doesn't want to have to lie to their own children."

"You don't have to lie."

"About curses and enchantments and an academy that's formed the backbone of our society for hundreds of years? Which part of that am I not supposed to lie about? What about the part where I tell Colonel Gallagher that I'm petrified at the idea of having children? Or the part where he could literally be anyone in private, away from the eyes of you and Mother? He and I have met a handful of times, Sophia. We've only shared a dance, but soon we'll be expected to share a bed."

A sudden and overwhelming feeling of sorrow for Ellie hits me like a thorny branch. I always thought she was just being contrary when she said she didn't want to marry Colonel Gallagher. I agreed with Mother about condemning Ellie's preference for decadent and immoral behavior. But it sounds like it's not about Ellie being rebellious for the sake of it. It's about her being *afraid*.

"Do you think he feels this way, too?" I ask, my voice quiet again.

"I don't know." Ellie slowly turns away from the window. As the moonlight hits her face, I spot tears glistening on her cheeks. They make her skin look as glazed over as her expression. "Sorry, Sophia. I just... I want to be alone. Can we forget this conversation ever happened?"

My heart sinks, half because of her question and half because I know it's entirely possible that she won't remember this conversation when the Allure wears off. It's not worth fighting her on it or trying to pry for more information. It's getting late, she's getting high, and there's been too much to think about already. "Sure, Ellie. My lips are sealed."

She walks back to her chair and sinks into the velour seat as I rise and pick up the lantern. I give my sister a half-smile before I start to head toward the door, but I barely make it ten steps before Ellie calls to me.

"Sophia?"

"Yes?" I turn around.

Ellie's already dug out her pouch of Allure from the bedside table again. "I forgive you, by the way."

I nearly forgot that was the reason I ended up in Ellie's room. "I'm glad."

"Aren't you going to remind me to be quiet or something before you leave?"

Shrugging, I offer her a gentle smile instead of my usual criticism. "I think you have enough to worry about. Just… remember that Colonel Gallagher will be here early tomorrow. Mother will have both of our heads if we make fools of her."

"I'll be here, either buried under a pile of romance novels or a heap of blankets. Perhaps both."

"Goodnight, Ellie." I step out of my sister's space and close the door, listening for the quiet click of the latch before I walk down the corridor and into my own bedroom. It's only partially dark inside, the moon shining through my sheer curtains and onto the furniture, while the lantern in my hand radiates a warm, orange glow against the cool tones of the night. I hang the lamp near the door before casting out the flame with a flick of my hand, and quickly change into my nightdress amid the silence of the house.

I consider reading one of my books for a short while, but I find myself in bed moments later, curled underneath a light summer blanket while staring out the window at the starlit sky. Normally, every ambient whistle of the summer breeze and rustle of the leaves would lull me into a deep sleep. Tonight, though, I can't help but keep thinking about the way Ellie's face looked when she turned away from the windows and essentially told me her fears are coming true.

It's at that moment that I realize something important.

Last evening at the party, Ellie was happier than I've seen her since her betrothal was announced. Happy enough to spend the evening with a strange man where I could sneak a look every so often to make sure they were at least making an *attempt* at keeping their hands off one another.

When Ellie meets a handsome man who intrigues her, it very nearly always turns into an intimate affair. Therefore, it's peculiar that she strayed from her party for the evening with Max and didn't bring him to bed. Instead, I only overheard whispers and the gentle clink of their wine glasses as they sat on the rock wall of the upper yard. I was so tired that I didn't even think to ask her about the stranger again, and now it's late and Colonel Gallagher is coming in the morning for a visit.

Though... everything Ellie said encourages me to think about what I want my future to look like. I know I promised my sister that I would forget that tonight's conversation ever happened. However, as I watch the flicker of the stars and the occasional leaf scatter past my window, it becomes clear that I don't know if I only want children and marriage because it's what's expected, or if I want them for *me*. Ellie's fears have me doubting the life that I was certain I needed in order to be considered a proper member of society. But what does it mean to be proper? Does being proper equal happiness?

Suddenly, I'm unsure of what my own heart desires.

Trying to find comfort outside of my own head, I wrap myself up underneath a second blanket that was previously crumpled at the foot of my bed. I think I want love, but I know that I've never experienced it. What if I don't like the way it makes me feel? If Ellie is scared of not ever falling in love with someone as attractive and wealthy and kind as Colonel Gallagher, what chance do I have at the kind of storybook relationship that I was taught exists?

The night—and my worries—draw on, until I finally find myself drifting off to a restless sleep filled with strange dreams.

Chapter Seven

ELLIE

I don't know how much Allure it would take to kill someone, but I do know that the powder I make myself is stronger than what you'd find in the restricted section of any underground apothecary. I suspect this is problematic in a lot of ways, but particularly because my magic isn't supposed to be as effective as it is without any formal training. Plus, with Allure being the potent drug that it is, I have to admit that it's conceivable there's danger in creating—and possibly supplying others with—something so strong.

In fact, the only Allure I've come across that's been more powerful than mine has been Padraig's. I can only assume that's because he graduated from Blossom and learned how to tame his magic enough so remnants of his powers don't get lost in the creation process. My enchantments are usually so out-of-control that sometimes it's a miracle I manage to make anything at all, whereas he's always had a calm and steady hand that's only been further refined through his education.

It's strange, though, because I recall stories and experiences about those who have gone to Blossom and what happened to them and their magic. Other than Padraig, they all appeared to be completely reformed by the academy. I don't know if a piece of their soul gets broken while they're there, or if they learn more about the ways of society and decide they truly want to be part of it, but I've always found it such a strange contradiction. I suppose I'll find out once I get there because my future education is intended to teach me to control my own deviancy, magic, and impulses. Fortunately, I don't have to worry about any of those things tonight. Except the part about where I told Sophia… that I don't want to die alone. That part doesn't leave me. In fact, the more Allure I take in order to try to make every coherent thought go away, the more I think about my father and how I found him dead a year ago.

Cringing, I shove the tainted memories away while snorting more powder from the miniature spoon. The room is already spinning, but that's fine. If nothing else, I'll eventually pass out, and when I wake up in the morning, it'll be time to play pretend with Colonel Gallagher. Pretend that everything is okay. Pretend that I want this. Pretend that I'm madly in love with him.

Love.

As if that would be possible.

For all intents and purposes, it should be. It should be like Sophia said, and like all the fairytales from our childhood. Colonel Gallagher should be saving me from myself, and I should want him to. But as I tuck my Allure pouch back into the bedside table—for what, the third time tonight?—I know that I don't want to be saved. I want to be as wild as all the cats that roam through the countryside and in the grasses that lead to the seaside. As untamed as the roses that we planted in the lower gardens by the loch after Father's untimely death.

With a sigh, I rise from the ruined chair before pushing the heavy curtain aside. The branches of the tree directly outside of my window are brushing softly against the glass, and it seems as if every leaf has a pink aura around it. The haze is a telltale sign the Allure is taking effect, and I feel the sensation of insatiableness spread throughout my body. Maybe consuming this much without an outlet was a mistake.

There's a faint flicker of lanterns from over the hills.

I could walk to Padraig's. It's not that far to his home, and I'm certain I could make it back to take the straw from my hair and change my dress well before Colonel Gallagher's arrival. Padraig's always been an awful sleeper no matter the time of day or night, and a voice in the back of my head is saying that maybe his sweet-smelling barn would be a little sweeter tonight once I've been satisfied. I'm nearly certain he'd accept my proposal as he most always does, though that might be the Allure-induced fog that I'm falling into.

I pause just as I'm about to drop the curtain.

The only problem is I've acknowledged that Padraig's an asshole. But I'm positive that selfish sex with a complete bastard is better than staring out my window as I chew the inside of my lip into oblivion. I'm also positive that I'm on a limited timeline to do whatever the fuck I want, so I release the curtain and cross the room to the armoire. I flick through a few dresses that are carefully placed inside until my fingers brush a bundle of bright green ribbon.

A jolt in my stomach suddenly wrenches me back to memories of the party, and it's as if I'm staring into Max's eyes. The sparkle of the fabric in the glow of the candles is reminiscent of the twinkle in his gaze as he tried not to watch me undress and swim into the loch. It also reminds me of the way the moon glowed over his skin as he slipped off his slacks, exposing the entirety of himself—an entirety that I couldn't help but glimpse at from the corner of my eye.

Recalling the finer details of the encounter feels like it is forbidden to think about the night before I'm supposed to meet with Colonel Gallagher, and, as quickly as possible, I slam the drawer shut. Maybe the next time I open it, the ribbon will be gone. Or not green. Or any other possibility that would have me not recollecting the Allure Max and I shared, the starlight against the garden's flowers, or the way I certainly felt—

I peek into the drawer again.

The ribbon is still there.

Wrapping my fingers around it, I pull the length free from inside the armoire, trying to regulate my breathing. The more I unravel, the more I remember about those green eyes, like I'm pulling every detail of that night from the inside of the cupboard and reliving it. The wine, the Whimsey, the way our hands brushed after Sophia told us to keep them to ourselves.

Max O'Carroll. I shouldn't even remember his name.

But I do.

A memory that cannot be controlled is a terrible thing. It provides a sense of nostalgia that eats away at your being and doesn't let go of the gnawing, gaping hole that it has left inside your heart. I recognize the sensation immediately, and it offers a glance into my true feelings and the opportunity to lie to myself. Typically, I'm an excellent liar. But tonight, alone in my bedroom, I'm awful.

I liked Max.

I liked him more than I like Colonel Gallagher.

I liked him more than I like Padraig.

Those three facts combined make for a feeling that sits dangerously in my heart and makes me want to do something reckless: hitch a ride to Loch Lomond and try to find either him or someone who might know where he's staying in Loch Gàrraidh.

Ellie, you're high, says a tiny voice in the back of my head. *You wouldn't know Loch Lomond from a hole in the ground right now.*

Maybe not, I respond to my own consciousness. But—

But what? But am I seriously considering how to get to Loch Lomond to seek out a man I've met once, or am I simply thinking about running away? Would either choice make a difference? Could I go live in the seaside and find happiness?

Running the ribbon in between my fingers, I make a loose knot and set the length down on my bedside table. The color feels as if it's staring into my soul, and I can't help but stare back, the haze of Allure changing from a pink speckled fog to a bright green streak that cascades over my vision. Whatever cologne or spray Max was wearing last night—the combined scent of springtime and roses—falls over me just as there's a peppering of something hard against my window.

I suspect one of the cats is trying to find a way into the warm bedroom, fur probably wet from this evening's thunderstorm. I push open the window. However, there's no animal to be found, no claw marks on the sill, no annoyed meow chastising me for taking too long. Instead, a low voice rumbles my name.

"Ellie?"

My heart pounds, skipping at least one beat as I instantly realize who is waiting in the yard only by their tone. When I look down, I spot a tall man with green eyes that practically glow in the moonlight—eyes that ignore the color-draining fog crawling along the moors like it doesn't exist.

"Max?" His name comes out breathy, soft, and surprised. "I didn't think I'd see you again."

He hesitates for barely a second, as if he might be rethinking showing up at my bedroom window unannounced. "Did I get the wrong impression of what happened last night?"

I shake my head, a smile creeping across my face. "You think I take off my clothes like that for just any man?"

Max lets out an audible sigh, his pose relaxing as he repositions himself near the garden gate. "I don't know what to think. All I know is there's something... consuming about you."

"Are you sure that wasn't the Allure eating away at your delicate sensibilities?"

"A spoonful of Allure? Ellie, I've done enough drugs in my lifetime to know when my attraction to a woman is a side effect or something real." He laughs, the sound trickling over me like a gentle river.

"What am I then?"

He runs a hand over his jaw, lowering his voice. "You're a menace."

"I don't think that was one of the options."

I can just barely see Max rolling his eyes at me in the dark, but the expression is more amused than annoyed. "You know, I didn't come here to debate technicalities. I wanted to take you for a proper walk in the garden."

I swear that the smile on my face is going to be permanent if he continues to speak like he is now. "What does a proper walk entail?"

"I'll show you when you get down here."

"That sounds awfully ominous."

"Good, then maybe you'll hurry before your sister finds out I'm doing a terrible job of keeping my hands away from you." Max smirks.

"You haven't touched me," I remind him, delaying the gratification of his close company. I'm not sure why I do it because I want to be near him, and I want to see him unclothed in the loch for a second time. But I'm not certain I can convince him to jump in the water with me again, despite it being dark. He seems like he might have other plans based on the words he's chosen.

My suspicions are confirmed when he utters a single word. "Yet."

I immediately drop the curtain, and there's a satisfied feeling in my stomach, like I'm on a galloping horse in the middle of the moors and all that's in front of us is a grand expanse of nothingness and fields of yellowed grass. I don't know what to call it, but it makes me think I'm doing something wrong and also something right at exactly the same time.

As quickly as I can manage, I pull on a proper dress—black with a light summer feel—and run my fingers through my hair. The amount of Allure that I've taken makes the task a bit more difficult than usual, and I use the wall and the armoire to balance myself as the initial prickles of pink in my vision completely fade. By the time I make it to the back kitchen door, I'm mysteriously sobered from the drugs and intoxicated by Max instead. I don't know how he manages to make me feel this way, but it's so peculiar and enjoyable that I hope it never goes away.

"Max," I say, nodding politely to him as he steps forward from the nighttime shadows. I keep my voice quiet just in case Sophia has her windows open. I don't want her to overhear that Max is here, and I absolutely wouldn't want her to know that I'm sneaking out with him.

"Ellie." We gaze at each other for a moment, two moments, then three, before Max finally speaks again. "I wasn't sure I could convince you to come out in the middle of the night."

"I took Allure for courage." I don't know why I say this, but it falls out of my mouth before I have a chance to even think of stopping the words.

"Ah." Max sounds a little disappointed, but he still gestures toward the gardens. "Shall we walk some of it off then?"

"It's not that bad," I assert, forcefully willing everything in my body to try to process the drug faster so I can enjoy this secret midnight affair with Max. "I'm mostly coherent. The rest will wear off soon. It never lasts long enough, no matter how strong I make it."

"Blossom will teach you how to control that." Max's words cut, even though I know that's not what he meant for them to do. However, he seems to immediately recognize the blunder, possibly based on the fact that my entire body stiffens. "I just mean that—"

"I know. It's okay. Let's just get away from the house before Sophia wakes up."

He nods, and slowly, we make our way back to the pergola in the upper yard, ambling along until we get to the spot where I quite literally ran into him the night before. It doesn't feel like this all occurred so recently. I can't put my finger on it, but there's something about Max that makes it feel as if I've known him for months. But then, there's something else about him that feels brand new—like I'm opening up a new side of him that I hadn't experienced before.

We descend quietly into the hedgerows and flowers, the moonlight glowing above us on a dark blue canvas of night. My fingers graze the greenery, the overwhelming aroma of plants mixing with Max's scent, while his clothed arm brushes against my bare one every so often. It's a song and dance game that we're playing, I think. And while I usually don't like doing the song and dance game with men—I'd rather get things over with—I'm oddly enjoying his flirtatiousness. And that, maybe, I'm returning.

"Why did you come back?" I finally ask, curiosity eating away at my insides.

Max continues to walk at my side. "I told you already."

"Tell me again. I like hearing you talk."

"You do? I've often been told I don't talk enough." His arm touches mine again, but neither of us moves away. "I sometimes feel I have so much to say but the words won't come out. Like they don't exist in our language. I used to use magic to express myself instead."

"Used to?"

Max hesitates, and when I look over from under the twinkling stars, I can see him clenching his jaw like he believes he's made a formidable error by sharing that. "Well—Blossom, you know. I feel like it sapped all the expression right out of me."

"I've heard as much from others who have attended. I'm not looking forward to going."

"It's for the best, I'm sure. Your marriage and everything else—"

I grit my teeth, stopping my forward momentum and pausing along the garden's crushed rock path. "And what do you know about marriage, Max? You told me you were going to summer here before returning to Loch Lomond. You didn't sound enthused about your potential upcoming marriage rites. From what I've heard, men like you usually find themselves in brothels and bawdy houses instead of the bed of a wife."

"Men like me?" Max has stopped walking as well, the light breeze blowing a strand of hair across his forehead like a black scar on his skin.

That wasn't what I meant.

"I just... men either want to fuck or they want to be married. Our conversation from the party led me to believe it's possible that you strangely don't want either."

He doesn't cringe at my curse word, which is something I'm used to other men doing. Instead, Max tilts his head slightly to the side, appearing curious. There's a little glint of amusement in his eyes. "And what made you think this?"

"The fact that you didn't try to… be intimate with me last night."

"And you're disappointed that I treated you with respect instead of trying to fuck your dress off?"

The way Max swears sends a surge of lightning into my heart. The word is low and growled from somewhere deep in his throat, and it takes everything inside of me not to push him into the bushes and steal a kiss. Ten kisses. Enough to last until morning.

"Maybe."

"I could have." He grins, taking a step forward before waiting for me to follow, which I do.

I furrow my brow, plucking out a tall and gangly weed from a spot where it doesn't belong. "Could have what?"

"Fucked your dress off."

"And how do you know that?"

"Because I think it's possible that you see something in me, too. Something that doesn't have to do with my family's title or their money."

"Is that how most people see you?"

Max nods as we turn a corner in the garden toward a section of perennials, and when I get a glimpse of his face again, there's sadness lingering in his eyes. "I grew up with the expectation that I would get married, carry on the O'Carroll name and have lots of children to inherit my family's wealth and estates. I was the first born—like you. I had to set an example for my siblings. Unfortunately for my parents, I didn't want to set an acceptable example. I never knew for sure that a woman wasn't looking at me because of my name or money instead of me as a person. I guess that means you're right, in some ways. I am the type of man who is found in brothels and bawdy houses instead of the bed of a wife."

"Then your parents sent you to Blossom?"

"They did."

"And you became one of the people that society tamed."

Max looks up at the moon, sighing. "Not... not exactly."

I wait for a moment, the late-night crickets chirping in the grass in the distance as I hope there will be further explanation. However, Max leaves the longest pause as we approach the loch, and I can't tell if he's avoiding the topic and waiting for me to change it, or wishing that I would forget the conversation due to the influence of Allure.

"This got serious so fast," he notes after several moments pass, but I won't let him get away with the comment so easily. I'm not on enough Allure to ignore what he might be implying.

Max plucks a rose from the hedgerow behind him and then gingerly hands it to me before taking a seat at the lakeside. Our hands brush when we sit, blistering heat pouring over my skin, and I twirl the deep crimson flower around and around in between my fingers. The scent of the velvet petals drifts into my nose as I sit next to Max and wrap my dress around my legs. The water laps gently near our feet, and I think about casting out a Whimsey just to see him smile again.

Max and I sit there for a while, inching closer and closer to one another until our knees are touching and I can practically rest my head on his shoulder.

"Remember how you asked why I came back?"

"Of course. It's because I'm a menace." A smile plays at my lips, and he tips his body and presses it against mine. Neither of us moves away, and I hold my breath, thinking that Max might pull away before I do, breaking the spell of being close to one another. But he doesn't retreat from the touch, instead slipping one arm delicately behind me to encourage my closeness.

And I allow myself to close the gap between us, leaning on Max's side, cautiously placing my hand on his knee. I haven't been cautious around a man since the first time I slept with Padraig and learned of his connection to Blossom.

"It's because I needed to tell you something."

"Don't say you love me already."

Max laughs, seemingly not at all put off by my attempt at humor. The sound resonates throughout my entire being. "You must give most men a run for their fortunes, Ellie."

"I'm not particularly worried about fortunes. I'm worried about—I don't know. I mean, I do know. It just feels kind of silly to say out loud." Thoughts roll around in my head about my own anxiety concerning marriage. But it comes from more than anxiety about my lack of love for Colonel Gallagher. It's a deep-seated concern that I won't be as good at being a wife and a mother as I'm supposed to be. That I won't be able to control myself the way I'm told I need to. That everything society says a good woman will be is something I can't fulfill.

Max seems to understand the silence that follows, waiting a few moments before replying. "You can say it all out loud to me. I won't even respond if you don't want me to. You can just declare your fears into the universe, and only the moon and the darkness and I will hear. I'll tuck your secrets into my pocket and carry them with me so you can let them go."

His words are so beautiful and poetic that I can't help but wonder what he might say about everything else. "What if I want to know what you think of my worries?"

"Then you can tell me when you feel it's safe."

I nod, looking at the spot where my hand has met the leg of Max's slacks. I run my finger along the fabric and feel the strange softness—where I expected a starchier material of typical men's pants, Max's are soft and seemingly freshly laundered. Maybe that's where the springtime scent is coming from: castile soap combined with crushed herb oils from the local apothecary.

"Okay," I cave. "But you can't laugh. And you can't look at me."

Max's right eyebrow twitches. "Can't look at you?"

"If you're looking at me, I'll be distracted by those eyes of yours."

He chuckles, averting his glance from mine and staring up at the blanket of stars coating the sky. "Fine then, I'm ready when you are."

Chapter Eight

MAX

I desperately need to tell Ellie that I'm one of the students Blossom couldn't tame. Alastair's words are echoing so loud in my head amid the silence that she can probably hear them—*we don't always have the time, you know.* However, when the subject changes to Ellie's anxieties around marriage, it seems as if she needs to get something off her chest more than I do. On top of that, her hand lying on my leg, fingers fidgeting against my slacks, is giving me that same fucking cock twitch I used to get in the bawdy houses of Loch Lomond.

Only it's somehow different, too.

I don't look at Ellie because she asked me not to, but I listen for her subtle sounds—gentle breathing and shifting weight and finally, an eventual sigh. "I was the one who found my father after he died."

Heavy silence encompasses us, and the words hang in the air like wet clothes on a line. I promised I wouldn't say anything, so I sit there next to the loch despite the fact that I want to envelop her in my arms and never let her go. And that's not my dick speaking; that's my heart, which is something I haven't let speak very often before now.

"Dad was kind of a strange man, near the end, in the sense that he would lock himself in his study for days on end. I do my best to remember him as he was when I was a child. You know those core moments when you know you're creating memories with a person? I try to remember those." Ellie sucks in a breath of night air, and I imagine the warmth filling up her lungs and giving her comfort. "Going to the seaside as a family every other summer. Teaching me to ride a horse when I was four after I begged and begged him for a pony of my very own. Sitting on his lap as he read thick books and hummed over the contents. I recall very specifically one time he found me in his office with a stack of novels tumbled around me, and he wasn't even mad at the mess. He plunked me onto his lap in his armchair and asked me what I thought of the stories."

The star I'm staring at twinkles; a wink in the sky that flickers as Ellie slightly changes the direction of the conversation.

"Either way, he only lasted a short time after he started acting odd. He would wake up in the night and we'd find him in the kitchen filling the cupboards with old papers, or standing on the garden wall reciting words that didn't make any sense. It was almost like he wasn't awake at the end. Until the night I found him. He had been awake then, because I'm certain he knew what he was doing."

I suspect Ellie brushes a tear from her cheek because she sniffles quietly before lifting her hand from my knee. When she sets it back down, a little higher on my leg than it was before, my breath hitches in my throat.

"That was around when I started to get scared. I don't want to get married and have children like is of me expected because I don't... I don't like the idea of leaving anyone behind, in case what happened to Dad happens to me. I've been scared for a year, Max. I'm exhausted and I don't know what to do anymore."

She stops speaking for a long time, her breathing ragged as she stifles her sobs.

"Can I look at you now?" I ask, trying to use my gentlest tone as I attempt to peek at Ellie from my peripheral vision. "I want to look at you when I tell you that everything is going to be alright."

"You just told me," Ellie says. "But yes."

I sigh, reaching over and running my fingers along the back of her hand. I can't resist touching her, despite being sure her sister would have my head if she knew that Ellie and I are out here by the loch, carefully pushing the boundaries of what would be considered proper. It doesn't matter, though; I don't give a single fuck because I like her. I want her to be happy, and I want her to be happy with me. I feel that need so desperately in my chest that I think it's going to burst out of me at any moment..

I never felt like this in Loch Lomond. I never felt like this in any of the brothels. I never felt like this in anyone else's bed, and I haven't been in Ellie's. We haven't even kissed. We've barely touched. And yet I know. I just *know*.

I don't want her to marry Colonel Gallagher. I want her to marry *me*.

But she can't. She wouldn't. Not if she knew the truth about what I am. And she probably doesn't even feel the same way, even though her hand is on my thigh and she's in tears after admitting something so personal.

"Max?" Ellie's voice breaks through my internal monologue. "Do you really think that everything is going to be okay?"

I blink once, resting my gaze on her beautiful face as my fingertips continue to brush downward. "You're not going to be like him. You're not going to come to an end like that. I swear on Loch Gàrraidh that I…"

Shit. What am I doing swearing on a whole loch?

"You'll what?"

"I mean—fuck, I don't know. I don't know, Ellie. I just have a feeling that nobody would let you suffer like that."

"Would you?"

Shaking my head, I turn her hand over so the underside of her wrist is exposed and slowly slide my thumb along her skin. Gooseflesh rises on my arms as Ellie inhales sharply, like I've done something more than what's actually happened. "I think you're suffering now, but I don't know how to make it stop," I say.

Ellie leans into me just a little more, and the warmth of her body offers heat to me as well. Her sniffles are beginning to subside the more she speaks. "You could tell me what you were going to mention earlier. Before I started giving you my entire family history."

Oh no. I can't. Not now. Not after that. I don't want her to think—to think something untoward. To think I'm using her for my personal entertainment. To think that I'm taking advantage of her while she's vulnerable.

"It's fine. We can talk about this. Or we can sit in silence and just enjoy one another's company," I say.

"Is whatever you have to say that bad?"

I bite my lip, hard, before responding. *Is telling her that I'm a broken member of society worse than her telling me about finding her father's dead body?* I try to act nonchalant, but I'm not sure it works. "Maybe."

Ellie scoffs, a little laugh escaping her. "Just tell me."

Maybe Alastair was right. Maybe I should just tell her and get things over with because it's better to be honest upfront than lie and be found out. But how do I tell her that I started falling for her when I was a cat, and that's why I took the risk of showing her my human form at the party? While I've been processing these feelings over time—days and weeks and months since I was expelled from Blossom and changed into my cursed form—Ellie moves so fast. She wants everything immediately, and now I'm finding I just want her.

"I'm not really sure how to tell you this." I lift my hand from hers, but she reaches out and takes it in her own, clasping her fingers around mine. Shocks run up my arm, and it takes a few moments to remember to breathe again. I should remember the way she feels right now, right at this instant, because everything is about to change.

"One word at a time," she responds.

I nod. "I went to Blossom, Ellie."

I can't tell her anything more than that. I can't, I can't, I can't. It's going to ruin everything. She's going to think I'm deceptive, that I'm ruined, that I'm an entire mess that's only been made bitter and difficult by my experiences.

"You said." She looks at me curiously, squeezing my hand just a little bit, which gives me an immediate sense of relief. "Did something happen there?"

"It did."

"Do you want to talk about it?"

"I... actually don't want to talk about it at all. But I feel like I should. I know I should because you deserve to know."

Ellie nods, peering down at our entwined fingers. "I can stare at the sky while you tell me if that would make you feel better?"

"I'm not sure anything could make me feel better about this."

The silence that follows gives me a few seconds to re-evaluate everything that's going to happen next. I'm going to tell her I'm cursed. She's going to get up and leave me here in the garden, and I'll never see her again. She'll never open another window for me. She'll go off to Blossom and she'll marry Colonel Gallagher and be miserable and scared for the rest of her life. There's nothing I'll be able to do about it.

But I can't lie to her. I can't let her think I'm holding this from her in an attempt to get what I want. The last thing I want is to be another selfish asshole who only thinks about himself and his own satisfaction.

"Did you get hurt there?" Ellie's tone is both quiet and intensely serious.

I shake my head. "Not exactly. It's that... I didn't quite graduate in the same way as someone like Padraig."

"What do you mean?"

I heave in a deep breath. It's really now or never, and while I'd prefer for it to be never, I know that it has to be now.

"I was cursed." The sentence drops from my mouth, and I swear that for a split second, the entire world stops turning.

Ellie blinks and her shoulders slump in what appears to be disappointment. "Those are just kids' stories told to scare us, Max. Don't start trying to frighten me with fairytales, too. We're much too old to believe in those."

"It's not something I'm making up. I'm a Bèist."

"Come on, Max. All the Allure has worn off, so it's not like I'm intoxicated enough to consider what you're saying is remotely true." She pulls her hand away from mine, and there's a warm emptiness that covers my bare palm.

I sigh.

"Ellie. I wouldn't make something like this up. It's true. The stories about Blossom and the enchantments and what happens to the ones who society couldn't tame are all true. Why would I create something like that? For attention? For pity? I don't need attention."

She shakes her head, shifting herself away from me like I've just declared I'm contagious. "No. You can't be. None of it can be true."

"Ellie, I *am*, and it is. I wake up every morning and there's nothing I can do about what I've become, and the best I can do is try to remember why I rebelled in the first place. Why I rejected the idea of 'doing my duty' by giving my family children to inherit the O'Carroll name. Because I didn't want to buy into the empty expectations of the lochs. And I know you don't either. I'd rather pay someone for the use of their body and bed and drink than do any of those things for duty."

I expect her to get up and walk away right then, but instead, Ellie picks up the plucked rose that's still resting beside her and delicately twirls it between her fingers. I don't say anything for some time, and neither does she, staring down at the flower like it holds all the secrets to the universe and the truth in the Blossom fairytales we were told as children. Thoughts flow like rivers and I wonder what Ellie could possibly be thinking. Is she angry or fearful or concerned?

Maybe I shouldn't have said anything.

Correction: I *definitely* shouldn't have said anything.

But, then again, there's some small chance that this might be something more than just a fleeting infatuation. That whatever's between Ellie and me, whatever is giving me these feelings, might be the reason my curse will eventually be broken.

The stories say the enchantment can be destroyed if a Bèist finds someone who falls in love with them. If someone can see the individual with value and compassion despite their past poor choices and tumultuous background that is implied by the affliction. Unfortunately, there's also a horrible side to the truth found in the fairytales—if one falls in love with a Bèist, they are to become one themselves. That person will be considered a scourge on fine society, and Blossom will find them. Blossom will turn them, and they will be changed for the rest of their life. But the person who was the Bèist that they fell for will be freed. An eye for an eye, a Bèist for a Bèist. If Ellie falls in love with me, I can be freed from the prison. But she will be captured in it instead.

But, as Alastair said, they would have to find us first.

Us?

Now I'm being presumptuous, writing my own fairytale in my head with an ending where Ellie and I live happily ever after. I don't even know if that's possible. It's not as if my family would ever accept me if my curse was broken—and they certainly wouldn't accept Ellie and her wild magic. Blossom Preparatory Academy promises parents with a Bèist in their family that nothing they could have done would have protected them from the misfortune of having a reckless child. That the unruliness and irresponsibility have nothing to do with parenting or lineage or customs but rather are engrained at birth and products of poor luck that only Blossom has a chance of correcting. I'm certain it's a way of persuading society to continue to follow the rules and remove those who show independence against them.

Ellie's still staring down at the rose when she finally speaks. "Can we fix this?"

I furrow my brow, a little surprised at her reaction. "I don't know. I don't even know if it matters. And your marriage—"

"Fuck the marriage."

"I don't want you to become like me."

Ellie shakes her head, reaching for my hand again and sending my heart soaring. "We can leave, Max. The curse will break, and we'll run off in search of something better and away from where we can be found. We'll do our duty by leaving society in the way we found it. But we can run and run and run until we're at the seaside and nobody will be able to find us. We can spend our lives together and never show our faces in Loch Gàrraidh or Loch Lomond again. Colonel Gallagher will find someone else. Mother will be glad to get rid of her insolent daughter. You'll be a man forever, and I'll be everything and nothing more than yours."

She doesn't do anything slowly, and for the first time, I realize I'm glad for it.

"Do you feel—?" I cut myself off because I don't know what words to put to my emotions. In any other situation, it would feel like it's all happening too instantly, but in this one, it feels as if it's not happening fast enough.

"I feel everything."

"Ellie..." My insides are a jumble of emotions, many of which are bigger and more complex than any I've experienced in the past.

"Don't," she says. "Don't try to take this back. I'm scared. But deep inside, I know that I've been waiting for you. I think that when I saw your eyes, something in the back of my mind told me you were the black cat on my bed all those mornings. You were the cat that would leave when I was getting changed or sleeping with men or being a deviant. You watched over me as I dosed myself full of Allure and cried over everything. I know now. I knew then, but I know now, too."

"I just wanted to save you," I respond, grazing my fingertips along Ellie's arm, up to her shoulder, daring them to dance along the curve of her collarbone.

She leans further into my touch, one hand finding the front of my shirt and pulling me into her. "You have."

The moment our lips brush, I find myself sinking into an ocean of her—every thought and emotion and fuck I've ever had disappears into the ether of a past I don't want to remember. Ellie wraps her small hand in the fabric of my shirt as she lets out a tiny sigh into my mouth, like she's been holding her breath for days while waiting for this moment. Naturally, the sound she releases makes my heart skip a beat, and I can't hold back any longer. I deepen the kiss, dragging one hand through her long hair, while Ellie draws me closer.

We are together like that for several minutes, the water of Loch Gàrraidh lapping at our feet and our mouths that are giving and taking from one another like we need the kiss to breathe.

After some time, I grasp Ellie's hair, gently releasing her and tugging her head back to expose her throat. Tracing a line down her neck, my mouth finds the softest parts of her skin, nipping at the smoothness just hard enough to leave small red marks, but not enough to bruise. I can't help myself. I want to devour her, and seeing the crimson blemishes drives me wild.

At the same time, the way I feel doesn't simply consist of hollow emotions and a flinching dick. It contains multitudes—a beating heart that might as well have been dead up until this point. She has brought it back to life. She's brought *me* back to life.

I draw a line with my tongue down Ellie's collarbone, her floral perfume and the scent of soap exhilarating me. My lips and teeth find the neckline of her dress, which is low enough that I could kiss the top of her breasts if I wanted to. I do want to, desperately. I want to put my mouth on every inch of her and listen to her whimper as I prove that not every man wants to use her for their own satisfaction. I want to give her satisfaction in return with my hands and my fingers and my mouth and my cock. I want to feel her tighten around me as she—

"Max."

Pulling myself away, I release her from my grasp and slip my hand from her neck back down to her shoulder, arm, and hand. "Are you okay?"

She nods, but there are tears in the corners of her ocean-colored eyes. I suck in a deep breath, trying to ascertain telepathically why she might be on the verge of crying. *Was I too rough? Does she think this was a mistake? Does she regret coming out to the garden after midnight again?*

"Ellie, did I hurt you?"

She shakes her head. "No, I'm not hurt. I'm surprised. Nobody's ever kissed me like that before. My heart is beating a mile a minute. I just need to breathe."

"What do you mean nobody's kissed you like that before?" I furrow my brow, lifting my hand to brush a single tear from her cheek.

"Max, you kiss me like I'm the only person who matters to you. Like we're alone in a moment that nobody can interrupt because the two of us are caught in a whole different world. I don't know what to do with that realization. I didn't know something so simple could be so intimate."

"There's nothing simple about a kiss."

"Prove it."

I smirk, reaching to tip Ellie's chin toward me before running my thumb over her jaw. "I thought I just did."

"Prove it again, then." She's breathless, and I kiss the words right out of her mouth as we crash into one another a second time. Slowly but surely, we lower our bodies to the grass, our lips telling wordless stories of how much we need one another.

I find myself atop Ellie at the edge of the garden, moonlight streaming onto her face as we separate again. Her dress is disheveled and up around her knees, and my shirt collar has been crumpled in her hands; grass stains probably present on both of our garments as we've tried our damndest to get as close to each other as possible while still being clothed. My fingers have combed through the longest strands of Ellie's hair, clenching them along with the grass, and her chest now heaves in a seemingly contented sigh.

Tonight's not about sex or the potential for it but about escape and truth and the unbridled need for something more than empty futures and societal expectations.

Ellie smiles at me from her spot underneath me, and then she gently pushes her hand against my shoulder until I roll into a patch of flowers. My back and shoulders thump against the soft earth, and I lie there and stare up at the stars for a second before she repositions herself and curls against my side. I can pick out a few fading constellations as we rest in the garden in near silence, but most of my attention is on Ellie and her quiet breathing.

After some time, the sky starts to turn a gentle pink, and I know it's almost time for me to return to the church and the seashore.

"You have to go, don't you?" Ellie asks.

"Soon."

"Will you come back again?"

I kiss the top of her head, lingering. Even her hair smells like flowers. "If you want me to."

"If I had things my way, you'd never leave."

"You'd get tired of me."

There's a tingle up my spine, and signaling that I'm going to change back into a Bèist soon.

Ellie props herself up on her elbow, staring down toward where I'm lying in the grass. The glow from the vanishing moon accents her hair like a gingery halo, the sun just starting to rise behind her. "I don't think I know how to be tired of you."

I should go. I should go now because otherwise I'm going to be with her when I shift. She shouldn't have to see that. Even after all this time, I don't always know how to process the things my body does to switch between cursed forms.

"Will you meet me in my bedroom once it's dark again and you're unenchanted?" Ellie asks.

"Your bedroom?"

"It's not like you've never been in there, Max."

She's right, but being in there as a feral cat and being in there as a man are two separate things. Going into her bedroom in the dark with the flowers on the nightstand and the curtains drawn and the summer breeze blowing through the windows makes me think that maybe…

"Are you sure?"

She grins, rising from her spot next to the loch. "It would at least be a little more private than standing in the middle of the garden and taking our clothes off."

My heart leaps into my throat at the exact same second I get another quiver along my back.

Chapter Nine

SOPHIA

I've been lying awake for what feels like forever when I hear someone approaching the house on horseback. Thankfully, I've been ready for Colonel Gallagher's arrival since the sun peeked over the edge of the hills, fog dissipating into nothingness as it always does late in the morning. I've selected my second-best dress to wear and tied my hair back at the nape of my neck in a valiant attempt to tame my curls. Mother always says it is important for me to look presentable \ when men come to visit because they have a tendency to speak to one another about the women of the lochs and beyond. If I was to look disheveled or disinterested, my options for betrothal could be limited.

To make matters more complicated, I'm also not permitted to take the attention away from Ellie, hence wearing my second-best dress with a simple hairdo.

The hooves slow from a canter to a walk, and then pause entirely as I imagine Colonel Gallagher dismounting and leading his horse to our empty stables. I rise from my reclined position and head out of my bedroom to attend to the arrival, pausing only momentarily to knock on Ellie's door. *I hope she's awake. Awake and sober, preferably.*

"He's here. You'd better be up and ready."

Silence.

"Ellie. Don't tell me you're still asleep."

Still nothing, so I gently prod open the door. It's mostly dark inside her bedroom. The curtain, haphazardly pushed to one side, lets in a single bright strip of sunlight along one wall. It takes a few moments for my eyes to adjust, but once they do, I realize my sister isn't in her room. She's not in bed—there are no lumps in the blankets to be found—and her ripped reading chair is empty.

I don't know why it surprises me that she isn't here. It's not the first time she's disappeared overnight to go for a walk or to do something untoward. But I did remind her of Colonel Gallagher's visit today, and you'd think she'd be back from Padraig's or wherever she went by now.

Where is she?

I back out of the room and look toward the stairs, wondering if maybe Ellie's already gone down to the main floor. I don't want to call for her as Huntley and Pippa are quietly amusing themselves in their bedroom, so I descend the steps first.

"Ellie?"

There's no response save for the ambient noise of our house in the late morning. She's not here. She's gone somewhere and hasn't come back. *What am I supposed to tell Colonel Gallagher? What am I supposed to tell our mother when she returns from visiting with Aunt Matilda? Will Ellie get in trouble and be sent to Blossom even sooner?*

My heart beats erratically as my palms begin to sweat. I wipe them on my dress, sucking in a deep breath in an attempt to calm down. It only partially works, and I feel a little bit of frustrated magic starting to rise inside of me, which is something it tends to do when I'm anxious. It's like it uses the opportunity to take advantage of me, which I don't like because it reminds me that reckless magic is a reason to be sent to Blossom. I could be sent to Blossom too, if I let it control me in the same ways it seems to control Ellie sometimes.

Blossom could teach me to control it if I was a deviant. However, I'm not out of hand like I'm told my sister is, and I'm also not usually this worried, so I guess the little sparks I feel aren't worth being concerned about.

I have something else to be concerned about, though, because I don't know what to do alone with a man coming to the door who is supposed to be staying here overnight from his long journey. Can I even allow him to without Ellie here?

As a thousand thoughts ramble through my mind, the back door to the kitchen crashes open, and there's my sister, her dress's skirt wrinkled and pieces of grass hanging in her hair.

"Hi," she says, breathless. "Is he here?"

I set my mouth in a firm line. "You know that he is. Where have you *been*?"

Ellie shrugs, picking a flower petal from the end of her long locks. "Just out."

"With who?"

"Max." She doesn't bother trying to lie to me.

My eyes could roll right out of my head and drop to the floor because I should have known that something more was happening between the two of them. I shouldn't have believed any comments stating otherwise. "The stranger from the party?"

She bobs her head, a flush creeping across her cheeks. "That's him."

"You can't do this, you know," I hiss. "It's not fair to anyone. You're going to marry Colonel Gallagher after you're done at Blossom. Mother and Father already made the arrangements for your inheritance and for the wedding."

Ellie's shoulders slump, but there's no denying that she's still glowing from her nighttime jaunt. "I can't marry him, Sophia. I know that you of all people believe in the existence of love. And while I might not love Max yet, I have a fondness for him that's infinitely stronger than how I feel about Colonel Gallagher."

"But does Max have that same fondness for you? You can't throw away your future for a couple of nights in the back garden." Our father's logic is starting to come out in me, and I can't help but ask her.

"He told me about his secret, Sophia."

"What secret?"

Ellie's eyes are serious, and she stares at me. "You have to promise you won't say anything to anyone. Not Mother, not your diary, not whoever else you speak with."

I haven't had a diary since I was twelve, which makes me wonder if Ellie and I are as close as I thought we were. "Who would I have to tell?"

"I don't know. Just promise."

"Fine. I promise."

The act of a verbal promise feels so juvenile that I wonder if Ellie's going to make me swear on my pinkie; however, Ellie smiles and says four words I didn't ever expect her to say.

"Max is a Bèist."

I suck in a sharp breath, like Ellie's just told me of someone's sudden death. "He failed out of Blossom—"

"—and they cursed him. But you know I can save him. He and I... we can save each other."

Ellie looks so full of hope and happiness that I don't know how to remind her that if she loves Max and his curse gets broken, that Blossom will find her and enchant her in return. They always keep track of those who have been turned—the stories have declared as much, though the books and lessons have never specified how Blossom manages to keep records. Maybe it's nothing more than a threat, but it's not something I think should be tested. *She has to remember this is a risk, right? She can't still think that everything about the fairytales from our childhood aren't true?*

I'm not fast enough to respond, and Ellie's voice breaks through the questions buzzing around in my head.

"You think I'm being ridiculous." My sister's demeanor deflates just enough that I can tell she was expecting a different response.

"Not ridiculous. Just short-sighted. You can't just—"

A series of knocks at the front door interrupts my response: one, two, and three. Ellie flinches, running her hands over her rumpled dress.

"Shit. Can you entertain Colonel Gallagher until I'm changed? Mother will have a fit if she knows I presented myself to him this way."

I think about saying that our mother will have a fit if she knew that Ellie was out having some kind of middle of the night date with a Bèist. I should just keep my mouth shut, so I nod despite my anxiety and magic making my fingers tingle. "I'll do my best. Just... would you hurry? I don't even know what to talk about with a man, let alone one I've never met before."

Ellie rushes toward the stairs, then pauses on the bottom step. "Whatever you want. I don't care. He's just another person, Sophia. Treat him like you treat Padraig—as an annoyance. That way, maybe he won't want to come back."

I snort out a laugh, which I know is unflattering, but I can't help it. Thankfully, half of the sound is stifled by another series of knocks, and Ellie runs the rest of the way up the stairs before I even make it to the front door. As I push through the threshold and walk to the entryway, her words echo in my mind: *He's just another person, Sophia. Treat him like you treat Padraig—as an annoyance. That way, maybe he won't want to come back.* That seems like a rather rude way to treat my sister's future husband, so I vow to be polite and offer him tea. How long can it take Ellie to get changed, anyway?

I was off visiting Aunt Matilda on holiday in Loch Tadhg when Colonel Gallagher came by the last time. I assumed I wasn't missing much. Probably a lot of Ellie being Ellie and another man doing his best to get under her dress. Yet, when I open the door to greet Colonel Gallagher, I find myself speechless. He's a tall man—at least a foot taller than me—with chestnut hair the same color as the hide of the horse Father owned when Ellie and I were young. His eyes have a gentleness to them and the shade matches his hair, both reminding me immediately of nights spent reading leatherbound books while drinking hot cocoa. There's a military bag slung over his shoulder that I can only guess contains his overnight things.

My heart flutters when he smiles, and guilt eats at my heart because I'm not supposed to find my sister's betrothed so... *attractive.*

I have no doubt this is an attraction. It doesn't feel empty, like when George kissed me. It feels like it's filling me up from my toes to the top of my head.

"You must be Sophia," Colonel Gallagher says. His voice is husky and deep, but still with the undertone of a young man who is trying his hardest to be formal and proper. "It's lovely to meet you. Your mother sent her regrets that she wouldn't be able to be here for this visit, but said that you'd be more than happy to preside over my company with Ellie."

Okay, Sophia, now's the time where you say something that isn't completely idiotic.

"How wonderful to meet you as well, Colonel Gallagher. Can I get anything for your horse?"

Good start.

He smiles. "Please, call me Iain. I drew some water and fetched hay from the loft, so I think she's more than well for now, thank you."

I nod, stepping away from the door to allow the man to enter. "Would you come in, then? Ellie will be down to greet you shortly. She's a bit... indisposed at the moment."

He doesn't question the pause or my choice of words, instead wiping his boots and entering the house. Closing the door behind us, I guide him to the formal front room. Iain—is it actually polite to use his first name as he requested?—takes the seat next to the piano that nobody's touched since Father passed, setting down his baggage at his feet.

"Can I get you something to drink or eat?" I do my very best impression of Mother when we have guests, though my heart is so far in my throat that everything I say comes out with a squeak. "Or I'd be happy to show you to your room if you'd like to rest. I know it's a long ride from Edinburgh."

Iain smiles at me again, and I feel like I'm about to turn into a metaphorical puddle here in the doorway. "I'll take tea if the water's already boiled. But don't go through any trouble."

"No trouble at all. I'll be back in a moment."

I practically run out of the room and into the kitchen, closing the door that adjoins the room with the corridor before balancing myself against the wooden countertop. Smothering a nervous laugh, I stare at the stove's flames. They lick at the kettle I placed there earlier in the morning, crimson and lemon-yellow flickers, the low burn against the iron teapot somehow reminiscent of my own emotions.

How could Ellie not want this man? If I was matched with him, how would I feel about it? Would I be as scared and upset as Ellie is to imagine waking up next to him? I could be matched to a man just like him in a year or so. I'm almost old enough. Once Ellie marries, it'll be my turn. I'll certainly feel this way about anyone Mother finds for me as a husband.

Hopefully, the fiery feeling comes again at that moment too.

Inhaling a deep breath of the aroma of the wood stove and remnants of the porridge that I made for breakfast,

I aim to fetch a serving tray and a teacup. Mother has special ones in a high-up cupboard that she uses when we have visitors, keeping them near the top of the pantry so Huntley and Pippa don't accidentally get into the more formal dishware.

I reach up into the open cabinet and try to select the cup that looks like something a military man might drink from. A blue paisley pattern on a white background comes closest to satisfying my parameters, and I slide my finger through the handle to remove it from the shelf. Unfortunately, the teacup was apparently set atop its matching saucer and I don't have a grasp on that, and the small plate comes tumbling down off the ledge. I scramble to catch the saucer but lose my grip on the cup as I do. The two dishes go flying to the floor and, consequently, smash into approximately a thousand and one pieces.

A curse word nearly slips out of my mouth, and I cringe at the little blue and white pieces that have been strewn across the kitchen. I'm carefully stepping across the stone floor toward the tallest cupboard to fetch a broom when a brown-haired head peeks through the kitchen door that leads to the hallway.

"Are you okay?" Iain inquires, glancing down at the broken dishes. "Did you hurt yourself?"

I shake my head, heat flushing to my cheeks in embarrassment. "I'm okay. Just dropped a cup. And a saucer. Not to worry, I'll get it all cleaned."

He flicks his gaze toward me. "Your hand is bleeding, Sophia."

Looking down, I see that he's right. There's a thin trickle of blood coming from my palm. I almost curse for a second time, but thankfully, I stifle the word just as Colonel Gallagher extends his own hand in my direction.

"May I see?" he asks, pulling a clean handkerchief from his pocket. "I know a thing or two about tending to wounds."

If any other man was to say something like that to me, I wouldn't believe him. I would think he was trying to get close to me under false pretenses. But with Iain, I offer up my hand straightaway. *A colonel would know a thing or two about minor cuts and scrapes, right?* Anything he would come across in battle would likely be worse than a tiny kitchen injury, but that doesn't mean he can't treat this as well.

Iain gracefully takes my hand in his and dabs at my palm with the square of fabric before looking at the split in my skin. But something peculiar happens. My fingers prickle with magic every time he blots away the blood, the sensation of him touching me causing shivers to flow from my arm and up and over the rest of my body. The feeling is intimate and warm; evocative of only minutes before when I welcomed him into our home and tried to understand my attraction to his handsome face and pleasant demeanor.

After a short period of time, the blood stops, but my heart continues to pound.

If Iain notices, he doesn't say anything. "I think we should wrap this, to be safe. I have some bandages in my bag. Come with me."

"What about the broken pieces? I should sweep them up just in case."

"I'll take care of it once we get you sorted. Don't worry. I'm more than capable of tidying up."

I nod, following Iain back out through the corridor and into the formal front room. I take a seat on the wooden piano bench as he rummages through his luggage on the floor. *If I get blood on Mother's ornate rug, she's going to be so upset.* Thankfully, Iain locates a strip of fabric quite quickly, and I hold out my hand for him to wrap it before the cut has a chance to start bleeding again. He kneels in front of me, bringing my hand into the proper position for him to doctor it. His fingers' nimble and yet meticulous movements entrance me as they coil the bandage with a perfect pressure and evenness before he fastens the end with pins.

"That should do." He grins, looking over his handiwork.

I'm breathless as I whisper a "thank you" because my magic feels as if it's going to explode out of my fingertips.

He could release my hand, but he doesn't.

I could pull away, but I don't.

Neither of us lets the other go—not even once Iain speaks.

"Because you're Ellie's sister, I hate to do this, but I need to ask something important, and I'd prefer it if you didn't tell her that I did."

I'm screaming curse words inside of my head in a vain attempt to keep my magic under control and distract myself from everything that I'm feeling. *I don't want to talk about Ellie. I want to understand why this man is making me feel like this. Like I'm the only person who exists in all of Scotland besides him.*

Gently, Iain drops his grasp on my hand and, because I'm only half paying attention, my arm flops to my side.

"Sorry, maybe I shouldn't ask anything."

I shake my head. "No, please ask. I promise I won't tell Ellie."

He nods, looking toward the door that leads to the kitchen, as if Ellie's going to appear through it at any second. "Does Ellie even want to marry me?"

It's a loaded question, and though I can't help but think about all the reasons why I should tell him the truth, I find myself nodding in affirmation to his inquiry. "Why wouldn't she want to marry you? You seem like a very nice man who would genuinely care for her."

Iain drops his gaze to my bandaged hand for just a split second. "I know it's silly, but she's never excited to see me, and now she isn't even here and... maybe I'm reading her wrong. Maybe I'm just scared to get married."

"It's okay to be scared. I'm sure she's scared too."

What I really want to say is that my sister has been taking so much Allure that I'm not sure she's coherent most of the time, and she's been out at night with a multitude of men trying to forget about her own duties to Loch Gàrraidh. But I don't think Iain needs to hear that right now. Not from me, anyway, because I'm sure he already knows the truth about Ellie somewhere in the back of his mind. There's no way that he couldn't—someone's told him, *right*?

"Do you think so?" he asks, his deep brown eyes looking for reassurance.

"Absolutely."

I hate lying, but in this case, I'm certain it's warranted because the truth isn't going to make anyone in this situation any happier.

Iain lets out a long exhale, and I watch his body relax. The stiffness that was previously in his shoulders dissolves into a position that appears much more comfortable, the strong, thick muscles in his arms suddenly eased of their tension. I can't help but quickly let my imagination wander, wondering what it would be like to be embraced by Colonel Gallagher—no, a man *like* Colonel Gallagher. Would I feel safe? Would I feel protected? Would I want to live in the intimate moment of his hold?

"I'm so relieved," Iain says with a smile.

I realize I've been ogling him since my mind started wandering. *Sophia, stop staring at the way Iain's biceps press against the fabric of his shirt. It's unbecoming.*

Quickly, I change the subject in hopes that he hasn't noticed my gawking.

"I should get the tea and sweep the floor before Ellie comes down to greet you. I wouldn't want her to get a cut."

"Let me help you. It'll be hard to use a broom with a bandage on your hand."

I give him a dismissive wave because I need to be alone. I need to be away from him, even just for a moment, to sort out my thoughts. "I can manage. Will you be alright alone for a moment?"

"I'll be fine. And... thank you for humoring me."

"Think nothing of the matter. It stays between us."

Before Iain has a chance to say anything more, I escape toward the kitchen for a second time, Ellie still nowhere to be found and only quiet giggles coming from Huntley and Pippa's bedroom, the noise cascading down the stairs.

Chapter Ten

ELLIE

The sound of dishes breaking downstairs interrupts my thoughts of Max and the way he kissed me in the garden, though only for a second. The sharp noise abruptly fades into the normal hum of the house, punctuated by Sophia's gentle voice and Colonel Gallagher's low tones. I imagine Sophia dropped something in the kitchen, and Colonel Gallagher—being the proper and polite man that he is—has offered to help her clean up the mess. Though I don't know him well, our meetings always supervised to some degree or another, the way he's acted in the past tells me that he has the same strong sense of duty as Sophia.

Maybe he should marry her instead. At least they'd have something in common.

I've been up in my bedroom long enough that I could have changed into a completely new dress and also fixed my hair, but instead I've been sitting in my reading chair with the curtain pushed away from the window. Staring off into the moors toward the direction of the seaside seems like a much better choice than picking grass from my tangled hair and pretending I'm happy about what's planned for my future. In fact, jumping out of this window and scaling down the tree trunk to the back lawn also seems preferable.

For a moment, I picture myself racing along the hedgerow toward the small buildings in the distance, climbing onto a boat with Max, and metaphorically disappearing into the morning sunshine. It would be a beautiful existence, living on our own amid the trees and the shoreline, maybe finding somewhere else in Scotland to call home. Not everywhere can be like Loch Gàrraidh, I wouldn't think. It can't be possible that every society functions the same as it does here. I've read enough of Father's books to know there have to be places where Max and I could go and be together without Blossom keeping an all-seeing eye over us.

The academy can't rule the whole world, can it?

A crow flies in front of my window and lands on one of the tree branches, breaking through my daydream. I can't keep Sophia down there alone with Colonel Gallagher much longer or I'll get a scolding from Mother when she returns home. She'll reprimand me for my poor manners and impolite behavior toward my future husband and will remind me that I'm being ungrateful for the promising future I don't deserve. I could do without another of her lectures for the rest of my life, so I quickly change into the first dress I pull from the armoire: lavender fabric with a touch of ivory lace on the short sleeves. It's not my favorite dress, but Colonel Gallagher isn't my favorite visitor, so I feel the outfit adequately represents how much I care about this visit.

I peek out the window again, secretly hoping I'll see Max standing underneath the tree branches, ready to take me away. Unfortunately, I have no such luck. There's no handsome, raven-haired man to be seen anywhere—not even a silhouette coming across the moors. The only other being in the vicinity is the cawing crow with dark eyes and a violet tinge to its feathers.

"Well, you're not much help, are you?" I say to the crow. The animal stares for a second before shifting on the branch. "It's not like you're going to be able to take me to the seaside and away from whatever my future with Colonel Gallagher holds."

The bird continues to look at me, tilting its head to the side like it might be listening through the glass.

"You know, if I was a crow like you, I wouldn't have to worry about the opinions of others or get married to a man I don't love. Do birds even have opinions? Do birds fall in love?"

Of course, it doesn't respond. I'm not sure why I'm even trying to hold a conversation with it because Sophia is definitely downstairs waiting for me to come and save her from what I can only assume is the most awkward encounter in the entire world.

I release the curtain and watch it fall, blocking out the crow and the sunlight—save for the strip that brightens the farthest wall. As I'm about to turn to make my way m to the door, I can't help but consider what might happen if I took some Allure. Just a little. Might it make this entire thing more bearable? Could I maybe pretend that Colonel Gallagher is Max, even just for a short time? Enough to be temporarily happy?

My mother would have my head if she knew I was taking these types of substances before meeting with my future husband, so I leave the room before I have any further opportunity to change my mind.

When I descend the stairs into the kitchen, Sophia's attempting to sweep teacup detritus off the floor, her hand wrapped in a bandage.

"What happened?" I ask, stepping down to the main level. "Are you okay?"

Sophia looks up at me for a second, flicking her gaze over my dress before resuming her cleaning. "Dropped some dishes. Iain's in the front room waiting for you."

"Iain?" I'm surprised to hear Sophia use Colonel Gallagher's first name instead of his title. She's never done that before—at least, not in my presence—so hearing it come from her mouth makes me curious.

Sophia freezes mid-sweep, her face turning red like I've just caught her doing something she shouldn't be doing. "He said for me to call him that. I didn't really think anything of it and just presumed he was being polite."

Doing something for the sake of being polite does certainly sound like something he would do, so I choose to drop my interrogation before it even starts. Does it really matter why Sophia's calling him Iain? "Sorry for taking so long. I had to find the right outfit."

"I see you opted for your least favorite dress." The flatness of Sophia's voice is not at all lost on me.

"It's not my *least* favorite."

She rolls her eyes, ignoring my quip as she reaches for the dustpan on the counter. "Will you bring him that cup of tea, please? He'll be happy if you take it out. I get the impression he's excited to see you after all this time."

"That makes one of us."

"He seems like a nice man, Ellie. I don't know what your problem is." The pieces of shattered dishware clink together as Sophia kneels to scoop them into the pan. Her posture and words are calm, but there's something in the tone of her voice that tells me I'm very close to treading on her last nerve.

"He's not Max."

The sigh Sophia lets out as she rises reminds me distinctly of our mother. "You're right. He's not. But if Max is a Bèist like you said, either you set him free and become one yourself, or you reform yourself at Blossom and marry *Colonel Gallagher* and live happily ever after. The end. I know which one I would choose."

"You're not me."

"No, I certainly am not. If I was, this entire situation wouldn't even be happening."

I can't help my reaction. Crossing the kitchen, I stomp toward the teacup and saucer that Sophia's placed on the opposite countertop. The cup is filled perfectly to the brim and spills a little when I grab it, tea dribbling over the edge.

Sophia would have been able to carry the cup to the front room without a drop landing on the saucer.

"It must be nice to be so perfect," I hiss, loud enough that I'm certain she's heard me. I regret the words the moment they come out of my mouth because, as always, I lament the times when I get into disagreements with my sister.

Instead of allowing the comment to dissolve into silence, which often requires an apology from me afterward, Sophia responds. "It must be nice not to give a shit about anyone else. And it must be nice to feel like you're being hard done by when you're the one causing every single problem for yourself. Instead of fucking around any longer, I would encourage you to get the hell out of this kitchen and go meet with your fiancé before I magically lose the ability to censor myself regarding the dubious *activities* you've been participating in when he hasn't been around."

"You wouldn't."

"Don't make me prove you wrong."

Usually, I would laugh at Sophia's threats because they're often so empty and meaningless, and I know she wouldn't actually take action on any of the things she's saying. However, I can't be completely sure this time, and this isn't the right moment for a challenge. I kick the bottom of the kitchen door and it flies open, allowing me to escape.

Colonel Gallagher—Iain—is standing next to Father's piano, running a fingertip along the wood. I want to tell him not to touch it, but I keep my mouth shut because Father isn't alive to play the piano anymore and he'd probably be happy that someone is paying attention to the instrument, even just temporarily.

"Ah, Ellie. You look beautiful," Iain says, nodding in my general direction. "It's been too long, hasn't it?"

I stare down at the teacup and then the saucer, where there's now an entire puddle of liquid instead of only a few drops. "A long time, indeed. I've brought you the tea Sophia made."

"Is she alright? I told her I'd tidy the kitchen for her, but she—"

"She's fine." I cut off whatever it was that Iain was going to say about Sophia. Probably something about how she's kind and polite. "How was your trip from Edinburgh?"

Iain runs a hand over his face as he finds a seat on the sofa that overlooks the windows. "Long. Happy to have a comfortable spot to rest until tomorrow. Please, don't stand in the doorway. Let's sit and have a proper conversation."

I cross the room and set the teacup down, trying my hardest not to stain the table with the trickles of hot tea. The last thing I want to do right now is have a "proper conversation." I want to run screaming out the door and never return. It's nothing to do with thinking that Iain might be a bad man, but everything to do with the reality that I don't love him, likely will never love him, and that I feel guilty about both of those things.

He should be with someone kind and gentle and who wants him. Not someone he's obligated to marry.

It doesn't matter though. Not here in the lochs. Maybe not in all of Scotland.

Taking a seat on the opposite side of the table, I smooth the skirt of my dress like I've seen Sophia do a million times. Iain watches me over the rim of the teacup, neither of us certain of what to say, or what makes up a proper conversation.

As he sips, I look him over. He's gotten more muscular since the last time I saw him six weeks ago. There's a light shadow of a beard growing along his jawline, his short hair coiffed by the wind, while his brown eyes remind me of the color of the chocolates Father used to bring home from town. They aren't the shade I adore, though. They aren't the green of desire and envy and so many other things that we've been told are dishonorable.

I don't think Iain is destined for some woman back in Loch Lomond who fell in love with his eyes. Or even me, here in Loch Gàrraidh. I'm not in love with his eyes because they don't belong to Max and because they don't remind me of small growing plants and floral arrangements. They are eyes meant for someone else—someone who appreciates the tranquil way that Iain looks around the formal front room and leans back on the sofa cushions instead of asking me to run into the garden in the middle of the night with him.

Iain isn't the type to skinny dip in the loch while high on Allure, or to kiss me amid the roses after midnight. In fact,

I'm not even sure Iain's been with a woman. He must have though, right? Most men who make their way to Loch Lomond visit the brothels and bawdy houses like Max did before he was cursed. Therefore, I can only presume that Iain's known women before.

Is that something I can ask? Does he know I've been with other men? Is it possible that none of that will matter once we're married—like all our indiscretions and reckless behaviors will be erased from society's memory because we'll have been "cured?"

"Ellie?"

I look up at the sound of my name and quickly realize Iain's been speaking the entire time I've been lost in thought. "Yes?"

"Is everything okay? You seem distracted."

I'm able to come up with a half-truth so seamlessly that I almost amaze myself with the cleverness of it all. "I—I wasn't able to sleep well last night so my mind feels a bit muddled. Had to take a walk to clear my head."

"What kept you up, if you don't mind my asking?"

I was kissing another man and the whole world around us disappeared.

"Blossom, the end of summer, the betrothal," I lie. "It's a lot to think about. How everything's going to change so soon. How we barely know each other and yet so much is going to be expected of us. How you're expected to save me."

"You strike me as the kind of person who would rather save herself." Iain's smile is infectious, and I find myself grinning back.

"Something like that."

"Maybe when we write our vows, we can pledge to salvage our individuality," Iain suggests, reaching for the half-empty teacup and taking another sip.

I almost laugh because I'm not certain Iain is aware that "salvaging my individuality" would likely mean I'd concoct daily enchantments to keep us from having children and spend my days running off from our shared home in Edinburgh every chance I could get. Thankfully, I manage to choke down any remnants of laughter and force myself to nod instead. "That would be a lovely sentiment."

It's at that moment I know that I don't actually dislike Iain. Rather, I dislike what's expected of us so much that I'd be willing to burn the whole country down to avoid it. Unfortunately, it seems as if engulfing my own world in flames would involve destroying his, too.

That might be a risk I'm willing to take, but there's a little voice in the back of my head that belongs to Sophia, and it eats away at me: *you can't throw away your future on a couple of nights in the garden.*

The conversation grows easier the longer I sit with Iain, but it doesn't change the way I feel about him—or about Max. Several times in our chat, I find myself drifting off into a daydream and replaying the memories of the party and of Max's lips against mine. However, Iain is courteous enough not to point out my distraction and fills the gaps in our discussions with careful mouthfuls of tea, which I can only presume must be cold by now.

Sophia doesn't show her face in the formal front room until the afternoon when she presents us with a tray of sandwiches, a teapot, and small cakes. My stomach is grumbling by that point, but I've almost not realized it because I've been swapping seamlessly between loosely paying attention to Iain's childhood stories and wondering if Max actually will show up after dark. However, the smell of strong tea reminds me I haven't bothered to drink anything today, and I'm parched from the room's warm air.

"There's hot tea in the kettle." Sophia sets a tray down on the table between Iain and me, and I note there's not a drop of anything spilled. "I just did something light for the sandwiches—roasted chicken and then fresh cucumbers that I picked from the garden topped with salt and pepper. You must be hungry after that long journey and all the conversation."

Sophia's not talking to me at all, directing her words only to Iain. It's clear she's still mad about what I said earlier, even though I did what she asked and got the hell out of her way.

"This is lovely, thank you," Iain responds. He selects a napkin from the tray and places it over one knee. "Will you be joining us?"

"Would you mind?" She finally turns toward me, and even though I want to kick her out of the room out of spite, I find myself nodding and gesturing to the empty spot next to me on the sofa. Before she sits, I grab a sandwich and start eating.

If Sophia stays, maybe she can talk to Iain instead of me, and I can focus on shoving chicken and cucumber sandwiches in my mouth.

Sophia smooths her dress before reaching for a small sandwich triangle. "It sounds as if you've both been having an agreeable afternoon?"

I can only assume this means she's been eavesdropping around the corner, though I'm not sure why I would have expected any less. I wouldn't be surprised if our mother told her to.

"I'd like to think so," Iain responds. He politely bites into his own sandwich, chewing a few times, and then dabbing his mouth to clear any crumbs before speaking again. "It's been lovely to have the opportunity to talk."

"Mother can be overbearing sometimes when we have guests, so I can see why it might be nice for you and Ellie to have time to yourselves."

"She seems to care about you all greatly," he notes. "Being overbearing as a mother might not always be a bad thing. Sometimes children need that extra supervision."

I nearly choke on a bit of cucumber, but neither of them seems to notice that I might be asphyxiating.

"Do you like children?" Sophia asks, the words likely sounding innocent to naïve ears. "You should meet the little ones, Huntley and Pippa, once you're fed and rested. They're upstairs playing."

"I do enjoy children. They look at the world in such a unique way. I'd love to meet Huntley and Pippa. Why don't you tell me about them?"

Where I would probably struggle to recite stories of either child, I know that Sophia has so many of them that they would take ages to detail. It's not that I don't like children and don't have an affinity toward their care, it's more that I've never felt any particularly strong attraction to the idea of having my own. That, and I'm terrified of everything surrounding the possibility of them. The potential things that I could fuck up are innumerable. I've already fucked up enough lives for one eternity. If I did have children, I can only imagine they would be as reckless and wild as I am, destined for a future that I now know isn't just something in fairytales.

Mother says unruliness runs in my blood. Then again, Mother says a lot of negative things about me. However, when I think about the things she's mentioned—about my personality, my deviancy, the stories in the books we read as children—I'm no longer sure any of them were lies.

As I tune back into the conversation, I realize that Sophia is still telling stories of Huntley and Pippa as if they were her own children, and I can't help myself when I again remove myself mentally from the discussion. It doesn't really feel like it's meant to include me, so I doubt Sophia nor Iain notice that my eyes have glazed over.

In my head, Max and I are back in the garden amid a downpour. The precipitation causes ripples on the loch's surface, and we are staring at our own reflections, fingers entwined. As the weather drenches us, he gives my hand a gentle squeeze, and I look up into his bright green eyes, the scent of cologne drifting into my nose. Rainfall beads off Max's hair, running down the side of his neck, and the trickle disappears underneath the collar of his soaked shirt. For a moment, I wish I was a droplet of water, caressing Max's bare skin as I find my way along the grooves of his chest.

"Ellie," he whispers my name. "I think we should run away together."

The imaginary version of me nods before smiling. "I'd like that very much."

Chapter Eleven

MAX

I BARELY MAKE IT out of the garden and across the Callaghans' lawn before I change into my animal form, sunlight streaking across the moors and chasing me back to the seaside. I have much more stamina as a cat, something I'm grateful for as I'm loping in between the brush and wildflowers in order to return "home." With every footfall on the grass, a new thought comes to mind, drumming a persistent beat of realizations inside of me about Ellie.

She makes me feel whole.

I can't believe we kissed.

After midnight, I'll see her again.

I haven't had many intimate nights that ended like mine and Ellie's did. Usually, a kiss or two is just the beginning of the evening, my tongue down someone's throat in an alley behind a bar. Just as often, it would start with me leaving a satchel of coins on a countertop somewhere, buying my way into the bed of a woman who I could pay off to make me forget about my duties and remind me that, for a short period of time, I was just a man with a need.

It was always formulaic and predictable after that. The undressing, the motions, and the conclusion. Some of the women were kind enough to let me stay after the candle on their bedside table burnt out, but most of the time, I was finished and gone before the flame died. No need for connection because that's what I was trying to avoid. Connection meant duty and duty meant marriage and children and carrying on with the Blossom fairytales.

As I approach the abandoned church, I find myself thinking about how I want more with Ellie. I don't want her to marry another man. I can't bear the idea of her living a life that she doesn't love and leaving Loch Gàrraidh behind to go wherever her new husband wants to live. Because that means she will leave, and I won't have any more nights with her in the garden or any mornings on her blankets with the summer breeze coming through the windows. That realization strikes at my heart as I duck through the front gate, escaping down to the basement before anyone has a chance to comment on my arrival.

I cross the cool, hard floor and sprawl out in front of the shelf of apothecary jars to rest.

I lie there for a few minutes, feeling the time drag past. I try to block out the pale sunlight glowing through the small cellar window by rolling over to face the shelving unit, silently reading the labels on the various bottles until I begin to doze on and off.

Belladonna, scarlet beans, foxglove powder, dandelion water.

I'm admittedly well-educated in what these specialized things could be used for. If I'd completed my education at Blossom, I'd have an even better idea of potion-making and creating enchantments made with the contents of these vials. Despite my advanced abilities stemming from old books about creating concoctions and tonics with basic plants, though experimentation, I quickly deciphered how to apply my magic to enchant mushrooms and flowers. Once I had that skill perfected, I needed a new challenge: charming the locals of Loch Lomond with horticulture tips.

But then, I lost my magic when I was changed. It was ripped from my soul, leaving an emptiness that I thought couldn't ever be filled. But Ellie... she reminds me that there's more than the typical Blossom magic that can be torn away. There's magic we create in our lives—love and compassion and understanding—within ourselves and with the help of others, too.

Nightshade berries, aster flowers, rose stems, beetroot. If I combined two of them together, I could make a love potion. But I'd need some of that cherry wine in order to create the right texture...

As soon as I think about cherry wine, the taste of Ellie's kiss returns to linger on my tongue. I think about it and try to decipher all the underlying flavor notes until I finally fall asleep, metaphorically tumbling into a vast emptiness.

I find myself dreaming of seeing Ellie in the daytime, but not as a cat—as a man. I dream about eating sandwiches with her in our own garden and playing croquet on our own lawn and swimming naked in our own lake somewhere far away from Loch Gàrraidh where nobody would look for us or tell us we had to be something we don't want to be.

In the dream, though, evening does come. Ellie's allegedly gone to bed, and I'm up in our study, reading through letters from my family that unconvincingly beg us to return to Scotland. I'm sitting at a desk with a quill in my hand, poised over some parchment in an attempt to respond as politely as possible, when I realize there's no being polite when it comes to explaining why Ellie and I ran away.

I write "Dear Mother and Father" before I spot Ellie in the doorway. Her red waves cascade over her shoulders and down her back as she stands there, a gauzy purple dress showcasing every curve of her body that I've come to know intimately. She holds up a lantern, lighting the room, and raises a question that's become more frequent lately.

"Max, are you ever coming to bed?"

There's worry lacing her gaze because she knows I've been trying to write a response going on for a fortnight now. But seeing her standing in the middle of our manor on the black-and-white diamond floor reminds me that my duty is to her, not to Scotland. Not to a life that we left behind. Not to the fear that we were taught to believe was normal.

So I nod and rise from my chair, crumpling the paper and tossing it in a drawer.

Of course, because it's a dream, it ends there.

I don't know how long it takes for me to wake again, but when I do, the basement is almost completely dark except for a few enchanted lanterns. I'm still in my animal form, which is convenient because sleeping on a hard floor is relatively uncomfortable, and I yawn and stretch out my legs.

"Fuck, you scared me," I curse, taking half a step backward as I realize that Alastair is sitting on the small bed, licking his paw.

Alastair smirks as best as a cat can. "Imagine how I felt when I came down here to get away from the *Clodder* and you're here on my rug."

"Sorry, I just... I needed space."

"That means you told her then, I presume?" He sets his paw down on the rumpled blankets, looking toward the dwindling sun reflecting off the shelves of glass vials. The kaleidoscopic colors decorate everywhere the light touches, from the small table and chairs to the oversized sliding ladder along the ledge. The sky certainly knows how to paint a pretty picture.

"How'd you know?"

"You were out all night again."

I look away from Alastair because it feels like every time I gaze his way, he's able to read my mind. "I try not to stick around here that often. It makes me feel depressed."

"...Now."

"What?" I furrow my brow.

"It makes you feel depressed *now*. Being here never made you depressed before. Well, maybe a little. But we all are at the start of our curse. I thought you were coming around to the idea of being one of us."

I don't say anything because he isn't wrong and there's no point in denying it. Alastair will see right through the lie. Instead, I watch the multicolored light from outside the window shift against a collection of green bottles. I stare at it so long that I can feel the sun sting my eyes, and I'm forced to blink away the glare of the waning day. In my peripheral vision, I can see Alastair kneading the old, knitted bed covering with his large paws.

"So," he finally states with certainty. "Something happened then."

"Something happened."

His kneading doesn't stop, but it does slow slightly and he closes his eyes. I wonder for a second if he's going to fall asleep in the middle of our conversation, but then he continues. "Something that would break the enchantment?"

"I don't know, Alastair. I mean, we..."

I cut myself off because I'm not sure I should be telling him that I kissed Ellie. Or that Ellie kissed me back. Or that she asked me to kiss her and that we kissed each other until moments before I turned back into the cursed version of myself. It's probably not allowed. Maybe he will tell Blossom and then something horrible will happen to Ellie and

I'll feel like the worst person in all of Scotland because I was responsible for it.

"You can say it, Maximilian. Trust me, there's nothing these old ears haven't heard from the others before."

I know that Alastair's probably heard everything, but he hasn't heard everything from *me*. I've told him many things—about Loch Lomond, about the brothels, about what happened at Blossom—but my newfound experiences with a woman after being changed and cursed somehow seems different. Like it's something that I could ruin if I release the words from my heart and set them free into the universe.

My hesitation doesn't seem to bother Alastair. He simply waits patiently, leaving me with my thoughts. He is the type of individual who probably would allow me to mull everything over in my head forever amid a silence that thankfully isn't awkward or uncomfortable. But I know that there's no keeping the truth inside of me because I haven't stopped thinking about Ellie for a long, long time.

I clear my throat before speaking. "We kissed."

"...and she is still interested."

"That doesn't sound like a question."

"Because it's not," Alastair replies. "You don't look upset enough for it to have to be one."

"What do you mean?"

He finally settles, tucking his legs underneath him before blinking at me slowly. There's something about his presence that's always calming, and instead of feeling embarrassed at telling him about what happened with Ellie and me, I feel as if a small weight has been lifted off my chest. Someone knows. Someone knows that my curse might soon be broken.

"Maximilian, I can feel the possibilities for you in my bones," he begins. "It's as if my own curse might break, too, someday. Someday before I'm too old for it to matter anymore and I will die knowing that at least I loved once. This way, despite the fact that I'm falling apart and spend my days by the seaside away from the *Clodder*, I get to live vicariously through your victories. You remind me a lot of myself when I was younger. Back when my bones told me fewer things."

I can't help but chuckle. "You always say you feel things in your bones, and I have no idea what that means."

"You'll learn. Or maybe you won't. After years and years like this, you start to get a depth to your soul. I'm an old man, you know. I've felt many things in my day, and the body never forgets."

"You're not that old," I remind him, though the overcast blue-gray fog covering his eyes tells me that his vision might not be what it once was.

He laughs, the sound reverberating off the walls of the basement as he changes the subject. "You're going to go back to her tonight then?"

"Should I not?"

Alastair shakes his head. "You should. She likes you. Even if things don't end up the way you'd like them to, at least you can enjoy the moments you have with her."

"I don't want to use her affections—"

"You're not using them. You're feeling them. You're experiencing them. She's not one of the women you paid for time with back in Loch Lomond. They were intimate with you because you gave them coin to be. It was a business transaction. The Callaghan girl—Ellie—the way you feel about her isn't financial. It's emotional. There's nothing wrong with either, but since you've been here, you seem to have grown into the type of person who feels the second way rather than the first. Am I wrong?"

"You know you're not," I reply.

"Good. Then enjoy yourself. Falling in love is a beautiful thing."

We don't speak for a few moments as the familiar, nightly tingling rises in my spine. I've long since learned the careful art of being alone when I'm with someone, and with Alastair, this is often a comfortable position to be in. Nonetheless, I do find myself asking him a question that I haven't dared ask before. "Who did you love, Alastair? You never talk about her."

He waves a paw at me, dismissing my question. "She's not relevant right now. What's relevant is that tingling you feel—"

"In my bones, I know." I laugh, the tang of cherry-wine flavored nostalgia cascading over my tongue again. I don't know whether it's just a memory because it seems too strong to be only in my head. Is there a way to save tastes and remember them later? Is that a thing a cat can do? Of course, I'm not a typical cat, so maybe...

"Maximilian, it's a beautiful night to watch the stars as you turn into your human self." Alastair's voice disrupts my thoughts.

"Is that your way of telling me to leave you alone?"

He rests his head down on his paws. "Changing is so strange for me nowadays. I'd rather be by myself during the process, if you don't mind."

"I don't." I rise, the prickling in my neck growing stronger as I walk toward the staircase to leave the old cat be. "Thanks for the talk, by the way. It was... insightful, as always."

Alastair blinks at me slowly, showing me his appreciation in his facial expression, before I sneak up the stairs. The foyer of the church is empty, and I quickly crawl through one of the cracks in the door before heading through the gate and toward the seaside. Outdoors, everything is quiet except for the sound of the waves and the rustling grass, the other Bèists all gone to who-knows-where. Maybe my conversation with Alastair was overheard by someone and they opted to clear out the rest of the *Clodder* to give us privacy. It wouldn't be the first time.

I sit on the gray rocks of the shoreline, salty sea spray dotting my fur, waiting for the moment the tingling in my spine dissolves into numbness. I've been told that the sensation is what keeps me from screaming bloody fucking murder as my body is rearranged from my existence as a Bèist into my human form. Sometimes I think I'd prefer to feel something when it happens, because blankness—even temporarily—is a hell all on its own.

Before I was cursed, I would have said that I'd already experienced nothingness when I found myself standing in an empty field and staring toward the imposing building of Blossom Preparatory Academy. I was deadened and emotionless to the fact that I had arrived at my final opportunity to fit into society. That early autumn, there was no breeze brushing my skin or drizzle prickling the hairs on my arms, and the sound of new students arriving was limited to an indiscernible hum of hushed conversations and sturdy shoes crunching on crushed rock. It was a curious kind of hollowness—but nothing compared to the barrenness that comes with changing.

Tonight, though, I find myself deep inside my own head, trying to force my body to become human again. I want it to happen as quickly as possible so I can find my way to Ellie's bedroom, as requested. I need to see her, especially since her sister had previously mentioned that Ellie's betrothed would be at their house for the day.

What if she's decided it's easier to marry a man who she doesn't love?

Can a few magical nights in a garden change her future... and mine?

I don't have much time to think about either of those questions because the oblivion of changing falls over me. It's peculiar in so many ways because I can watch as I switch bodies. I can watch my paws turn into hands and fingers and feet and toes; see my dark fur dissolve into the shadows. I can watch the enchantment take over and clothe me in one of the few outfits that I had brought to Blossom.

I've barely gotten my feet back underneath me—two feet now, instead of four—before I start rushing away from the seaside and toward the Callaghan house. It's merely a dot in the distance, the rocky moors and brambles and wildflowers between us. I'm about a hundred paces from the church when I realize I haven't been breathing, and I force myself to pause and suck in a mouthful of late summer air. It smells like wild roses combined with the chill of an early frost and something else I can't quite place.

As I'm trying to identify the third scent, I reach up to brush a lock of hair from my face.

Something catches my eye as I move my hand.

My palm is lightly glowing green.

It can't be—magic? My magic's been gone ever since I was changed. It's what happens to everyone who becomes a Bèist.

"You don't have magic. Blossom took it when they cursed you." My words cut through the stillness of the moors, and I shake my head like I'm trying to get the thought out. *There's no way I have any magic now. They wouldn't just give it back to me without proof of the curse being broken, would they? They control so much of society with their seemingly infinite powers...*

When I look back down at my hand again for confirmation that I'm actually seeing what I think I'm seeing, there's nothing there. No glowing light, no tinge of green radiance on my skin. Must have been the way the silvery light of the crescent moon was reflecting on the bushes.

Despite the realization that I was mistaken, my heart is still pounding as if my magic had been suddenly and mysteriously gifted back to me. But that wouldn't make sense. Blossom would never do something like that out of the goodness of their hearts. There would have to be a reason and also undeniable proof that I had earned it back, and I don't think I can offer up either of those things in a way that the Academy would accept. And the cost would be too high for me to pay.

Stepping forward, I continue my walk across the moors amid the hope that Ellie hasn't changed her mind about what happened before sunrise. As I've learned in the past, not everything that transpires in the dark feels the same in the light—not every kiss means more than a split-second spark, and not every word is a promise. Sometimes they're just tiny faults in the universe that are meant to remind us of what's possible.

I make it to the edge of the garden as the nightbirds begin their calling, and I spot only a few lanterns and candles left lighting up the home. The most obvious glow is coming from Ellie's room overlooking the back lawn, but there's still a brightness in Sophia's bedroom as well, flickering shadows dancing in between the gap in the curtains.

I catch my breath beneath Ellie's window and stare out across the back lawn. Moonlight shimmers on the loch with unusual brightness, the lake's surface looking like glass from my distance. There's no helping but to remember the night Ellie saw me as a human for the first time, high as anything and testing my limits. I have a feeling that tonight might test my limits even more—but in new ways.

Moments later, there's the distinct sound of a windowpane sliding open, and Ellie's musical voice pours from the second floor of the house.

"I've been waiting for you."

Chapter Twelve

SOPHIA

The moon glow makes pale patterns on the floor of Huntley and Pippa's room, spilling light over the rug between their beds. The two of them have already grumbled about their washing-up and bedtime, and now we're at the part of the evening where their exhaustion has gotten the better of them. It's taken longer than usual to get them to sleep because of their excitement at having a houseguest, but once I know they aren't pretending to rest—their quiet snores giving them away—I sneak across the threshold and quietly shut the door.

Our afternoon and into the evening went by quickly, despite Iain and I holding up most of the conversation. It was difficult to avoid mentioning his question about Ellie with her present, though I'm certain her continued silence throughout the conversation spoke volumes. I have a feeling that by the time I pulled a bottle of wine from the cellar and plunked it on the table for the two of them to imbibe, he was wondering if I had lied to him about Ellie's feelings.

Of course, that she appropriated more than half the bottle revealed more than I ever could have with a single untruth.

I tried, I tell myself.

Lantern in hand, I amble down the hallway past Ellie's closed door and duck into my own bedroom with a sigh.

You can't always help someone who won't help themselves, Sophia.

I do my best to remind myself of Mother's words as I change for bed, releasing my hair from its ponytail and shedding my second-favorite dress. For a moment, I stand in front of the mirror and stare at myself in my ivory underthings, red curls erupting over my bare shoulders and a puddled mound of fabric at my feet. I'm not pretty like Ellie. I don't have that timeless, classic beauty. I'm thin in the wrong places and round in others, though the freckles dotting my nose are something I've always adored. My father said they were caused by the kisses of buttercup flowers. I know that's not true, but it's kind of a nice thought.

As I examine every inch of my body, including my bandaged hand that's still a little damp around the edges with dishwater, I find myself wondering if a man like Iain would see anything in me. He may have wrapped my hand and our touch may have lingered for a few seconds longer than necessary, but that doesn't mean he felt the same burning heat that I did. It doesn't mean that his heart skipped any beats at all.

Before I get too wrapped up in analyzing my peculiar reaction to Iain's presence, I might as well face the truth. He's a proper, polite, and attractive military man who is going to take my sister off to see the world, and I'm going to be left here in Scotland with a yard full of enchanted cats.

I sigh for the millionth time—approximately—and step out of the sea of fabric to fetch something to wear to bed. Just as I'm pulling on a light nightdress and a delicate summer robe, there's a faint knock at my bedroom door. It must be Ellie, though I can't imagine what she'd want at this time of night.

Maybe she just drank too much wine.

Tugging the robe around myself, I pad across the room. However, when I pull the door open, the person standing on the other side isn't Ellie. It's not even Huntley or Pippa.

It's Iain.

Instinctively, I nearly shut the door in his face so he doesn't see me in my night clothes. He shouldn't be seeing me like this, especially not after midnight, and I certainly shouldn't be seeing him like *that*. It's not appropriate. He's betrothed to Ellie.

Iain's hair is ruffled, as if his hand has run through it too many times in exasperation, while he sports a loose white shirt that's partially undone at the collar, exposing the very top of his chest. A thin chain with some kind of rectangular pendant hangs from his neck, and he's still wearing the same slacks he had on earlier, as though he hasn't truly gotten prepared to go to bed yet.

His presence piques my curiosity more than it tells me to send him away.

"Is everything okay?" I ask, keeping my voice low so I don't wake the children—or Ellie.

"I thought I should check on your hand before I turned in for the night."

The gesture is so kind that I internally scold myself for feeling attracted to him. He's a gentle man; a considerate one as well. Surely, I'll be matched with someone who treats me with equal compassion. I don't need to picture myself with Iain. I *shouldn't* picture myself with Iain.

"I thought you had already gone to bed." I shift my weight against the door.

Iain shakes his head. "Have you ever been physically tired but your brain won't stop thinking?"

"Often."

"That's what happened once I was alone."

I crease my eyebrows together. "Because you were... thinking about checking on my hand?"

Running a hand over his face, Iain clenches his jaw. There's a little ripple along his skin that shows up as quickly as it disappears. "Can I tell you something?"

"Of course."

He rakes his gaze over my wrapped hand before he speaks. "Everything about this terrifies me."

"You mean being betrothed?"

Iain nods. "I'm just following the rules. My whole life has been about following other people's rules. I want to do the right thing by Ellie, but it's hard because I don't feel... wanted."

I open my mouth to lie to him again, to tell him that Ellie will come around to his affections, but he shakes his head as if to tell me not to bother.

"My own mother said I can change her mind. Ellie's, that is. Did she tell you I'm being sent to England? That Mother wants to rush the wedding so Ellie and I have our formalities in place before I'm deployed? I think she's worried that nothing will be left of our family's future if I'm... no longer."

"Formalities? You mean your vows?"

"Amongst other things." Iain doesn't elaborate, but I can only imagine what he might mean. The primary purpose of marriage is to continue a family's lineage, and there are only so many ways to do that. Ways I don't want to think about when it comes to him and Ellie.

"Why are you telling me this?" I say softly, peering down the hall to make sure Ellie and the children aren't listening from the corridor.

"I don't know," he replies. "You seem good at keeping secrets, and I've had the entire ride from Edinburgh to think about how I'm being told that your sister's future depends on me. But it seems as if your sister is under the impression that her future depends on... someone else."

There's a moment where I wonder if Iain saw Ellie with Max, but then I realize he arrived too long after sunrise to have spotted Max at all.

"Being scared isn't a weakness," I note, trying to push away the strange feelings I've been having ever since I opened the front door. Is there such a thing as falling for someone the first moment you lay eyes on them? I quickly shake this thought off, doing my best not to allow myself to entertain it. It doesn't matter. These uncharacteristic feelings don't matter. "I think both you and Ellie are terrified. My mother and father were terrified, too, when they met."

Iain casts his gaze over me, a little chuckle rising in his throat. His timbre gives me gooseflesh across my arms and causes a shiver to rise in the back of my neck. "My mother scared my father. She was like Ellie in her younger days. Careless and wild. My father is quiet and does what he has to. Doesn't make waves. That's the impression I get of you. That you don't want to make waves either."

He can read me like a book, something that has me both fascinated and petrified.

"Iain, I thought you were here to check on my hand."

The way his name falls from my mouth surprises me, the whisper sounding uncharacteristic and coquettish. I should call him Colonel Gallagher from now on. Iain is too personal, too private, too... *intimate*.

"I am, but you haven't let me in yet. Or we can go downstairs if you prefer. I didn't mean to intrude on your evening by prattling about my anxiety."

I look over my shoulder at the lantern still gleaming brightly on my bedside table, two blue velvet chairs in the corner of the room unmarred by the cats of the loch. We could sit there, he could examine my hand, and then I could very politely ask him to leave. I'd have to do that before my mouth and my nervousness start to take over and I ask him something stupid, like why he makes me feel the way I do. Tending to my hand should only take a moment. I can hold myself together for that long.

"Oh—my apologies. Please, take a seat in whatever chair will have the best light."

Iain nods, gingerly entering my bedroom as if he knows he shouldn't be here but can't help himself. I'm about to close the door but then I think better of it, crossing the floor and picking up the lantern.

"Where would placing this help the most?"

"Maybe the window ledge?" he responds. "There's quite a lot of light from the moon tonight."

Iain settles into the chair on the left, leaning forward with his elbows on his knees as I place the light and then take the empty seat across from him. Carefully, I place my hand into the one he has outstretched toward me, and he begins to unravel the bandage. I can't feel his skin on mine yet, but my body knows there isn't much between us, and my mind dares me to lift my finger ever so slightly to brush his wrist.

I can't do that.

I could say it was a mistake if he questions it, though.

Sophia, you're being ridiculous. Keep your hands to—

His skin touches mine, and I metaphorically crash back to real life. The bandage is off, my wound exposed to the open air, and Iain is sitting across from me still, running a thumb over the center of my palm. Every single bit of magic that I possess is going to force its way out of my body if he doesn't stop touching me, and for a moment, I think I stop breathing.

"Does it hurt when I press around it?"

I shake my head and reply earnestly. "No, it doesn't hurt. I just... thought that it might."

Iain smiles and looks back down at my hand as he begins to rewrap the bandage. The thicker the wrap over my cut gets, the more I'm able to catch my breath. "The good news is that it'll heal just fine. The bad news is that you'll need to keep it covered for a few days just so it stays clean."

"I think I can handle that. Mostly. With Huntley and Pippa running around, it might be a challenge, but I'm sure I can convince Ellie to help with a few things."

Iain briefly pauses at the mention of Ellie's name. "You know, Sophia, I think I'm nervous about the marriage for another reason."

"What reason is that?"

He bites at his bottom lip before speaking, the pressure of his teeth turning it red. "It's a little embarrassing to admit, but... I've never been with a woman."

"Never?" I raise my eyebrows. He must be joking? How could a man who looks and acts like him never have had the company of someone else in his bed? Shouldn't they be fighting over him instead of whatever wars he's been training for?

"Not once. Nothing."

"Not even a proper kiss?"

Iain stares at me, and I have the answer without him needing to use his words. Once he seems to know I fully grasp the truth, he plucks three pins from the ledge and secures my bandage as I respond.

"There's nothing wrong with that, you know. I've never been with a man and it—" I cut myself off because I suddenly realize I've just revealed a very private matter, and it's also a very strange thing to admit to my sister's fiancé. "I meant to say, just because you haven't been with Ellie or any other woman before doesn't make you less worthy of affection."

"She has, though. Been with other men, I mean. What if I'm... inadequate in comparison?"

"I don't think marriage is supposed to be about making comparisons."

He exhales deeply, releasing his tender hold on my palm. "It's wonderful that you think that, Sophia. But does Ellie?

Would she not compare whatever she feels with me to someone like Padraig who allowed her to be uncontrollable?"

The name Ellie warned me to no longer say hits like an unexpected wave, throwing me backward onto the figurative rocks. I lean back in my chair, my unbandaged hand running over the back of my neck. "How do you know about Padraig?"

"I'm in the service with his brother."

Ah.

"I don't think she feels any particular affinity toward Padraig, Iain. You don't have to worry about him."

"She doesn't feel any affinity toward me, either."

Of course, right at that second, I think about everything Ellie's said about Max and how he makes her feel. About the way her face looked when she came through the kitchen door this morning with grass in her hair and a flush on her cheeks. About how, when caught under the moonlight swimming naked in the loch, the two of them already looked like lovers instead of strangers. Max and Ellie's magnetism is what Iain should be worried about.

The two of us sigh in unison, and Iain chuckles, seemingly at the timing. "If only I'd met you first."

"Meaning what? That I could have warned you about Ellie's behavior before you agreed to anything?"

A smirk plays at the corners of my lips, but Iain shakes his head and lets out what sounds like an exasperated groan.

"I'm going to hate myself for saying this, but you can't tell me you don't feel it."

"It?"

"What's happening between us. My mind is as muddled when I'm around you as your face is rosy pink when we touch. I feel things in my heart that I thought I would never feel. Nobody has interested me like you have in only a few short hours, and I know now what I've been training to fight for. It's not all about duty and fairytales and Blossom and trying to avoid a war with England over old rules and stories that they don't even believe in. It's about needing someone so badly that you're willing to write hideous, lovesick poems for them when the world feels like it's falling apart."

My voice cracks because even though I barely know this man, I know he's the one my soul's been waiting for. "We can't, Iain. We have to stay apart. You need to marry Ellie or she'll have no prospects."

"I know, and I don't want to be the one to ruin her future."

I nod, nibbling the inside of my cheek, feeling anxiety and frustration and magic coursing through my veins. "Even if I feel something, we can't do anything about it. Even if we both feel the same, I couldn't let myself..."

Iain shifts to the very edge of the velvet chair, resting a hand on my knee as he whispers, "I'm only going to say this once, but have you ever listened to your magic, Sophia? Really listened instead of trying to nervously push it away? That's what I spent half the evening doing in that room by myself. I couldn't sleep because I couldn't stop thinking about what would happen if I was to be with you instead. What does your magic say?"

There's unbroken silence between us then, and I close my eyes and allow myself to feel everything, from my thundering heart to the ember-like flashes on my skin where Iain's touched me. I heave in a deep breath, trying to steady my pulse and calm myself as I've been told to do. But I can't focus. I can't focus on what my magic is saying because I'm focusing too hard on my anxious thoughts and the what-ifs and the understanding that I've already broken Ellie's trust in me by feeling anything for her fiancé at all.

My fingertips grow hot, little crackling sounds hitting my ears. But I don't open my eyes because I don't know what I'll see. Maybe Iain will be gone. Maybe this entire day will have all been a dream. Maybe my life will have all been a dream.

There's a little voice inside of my head that says something else, though: *open your eyes, Sophia, because maybe this is what you've been holding off on using your magic for.*

I listen to my tiny subconsciousness. I open my eyes, expecting the worst, but instead, there's a sparkling gold fire in my palm. It's the most beautiful thing I've ever seen, shimmering against the moonlight, sizzling like a dish straight from the oven. The magic feels like a dull pulsation in my veins, flowing through me with ease. I'm mesmerized, the flames in my hand offering release from my anxious thoughts and sending them burning into the night. When I finally close my fingers over my palm, my own personal fire smothers itself into a tendril of smoke.

"Feel anything?" Iain asks a moment later once the smolder has gone out and I've looked back into his brown eyes.

I don't know what to say or how to describe the experience I just had. *Was it normal? Was I supposed to create a flame? Was that my magic speaking?* Being rendered speechless isn't usual for me, and neither is the fact that I have a sob catching in my throat that I'm forced to choke down. I'm unsure why it's coming up because creating fire was beautiful and unexpected and—

"Maybe I should just go," Iain murmurs.

I shake my head vigorously, wild red curls bobbing around my cheeks. Iain can't go now because I don't want him to leave ever again. He's already leaving in the morning, which is much too soon. And who knows if he'll be back again once everyone realizes what I've been thinking and what I'm going to ask him to do.

Ellie will forgive me. That's the power of falling in love with a fairytale—everyone gets a "happily ever after" eventually.

"Maybe you should just kiss me," I say, the request fading into the dark.

Iain doesn't look surprised. In fact, he looks like he's been waiting to hear those words his entire life.

I could have waited for him to do something romantic—to tip my chin toward him or to recite some pretty words he'd read in a book once. He doesn't do either of those things, though, and I don't think I want him to. Instead, we wordlessly shift closer to one another in our chairs until our knees are touching, my nightdress barely concealing the curve of my legs against Iain's slacks. He runs his hand up the side of my neck and I lean into his touch, and a second later, we're falling into one another's lips in an embrace that is equal parts gentle and filled with many years' worth of longing.

I've heard first kisses are almost always messy. I think it was Ellie who told me that. But kissing Iain for the first time feels like we've already practiced a thousand nights over. It's not a simple and functional kiss like the one I had with George next to the heather bush. Iain parts my lips with his tongue, and we sink farther and farther into one another, my anxiety and nervousness vanishing more and more with every second that passes. Every worry I had fades into obscurity, and all that's left is the way Iain's mouth feels against mine—giving and taking pressure and feeling and desire.

It's only after a long while that I realize I need to breathe, and I nibble at Iain's bottom lip until he lets out the tiniest groan and slowly pulls away. My fingers are swathed in his shirt, wrinkling my newly-wrapped bandage, while my right leg has slid between his spread thighs. Sometime between the start and the end of the embrace, he pushed my robe to the side and shoved the hem of my sleeping gown up past my knee.

This kiss is a thief of time and decency.

"Sophia, that—"

No.

No regrets and no words and no reminders that we'll have to pretend in the morning that this didn't happen at all.

I press a finger to Iain's red-tinged lips to silence him, heat boiling in my stomach in a way I'm certain only indicates lustful feelings. I don't know that I've had immodest feelings before like the ones I'm having right now—the ones where I want Iain's hands to slide even farther underneath my dress and take my breath completely away.

Iain blinks at me, patiently waiting.

"Don't say anything," I murmur, sliding my hand from his mouth down his neck to his exposed collarbone. "Let's just do it again. But maybe we should close the door this time."

Chapter Thirteen

ELLIE

I'VE BEEN WAITING FOREVER for Max. An entire, breathless lifetime where I've been searching for my own version of the Blossom fairytales. A version where my life isn't controlled by a society that wants to meddle in my need for love and acceptance and reckless abandon. Now, with Max standing underneath my window, I find myself catching my breath and filling my lungs with nighttime air that's scented with wildflowers and an unmistakable cologne.

"I've been waiting for you," I say once I've opened the window. The breeze is still warm, though I can sense the looming autumn season—and with it, my planned departure from Loch Gàrraidh.

Max's smile could light up a completely dark room. "I've been waiting for you too, you know."

"How so?"

"I'll show you when I get up there."

My heart skips a beat at the determination in his words. "What kind of person do you take me for, Max O'Carroll? Just some woman who gives herself away to any man who manages to climb up a tree into her bedroom?"

There's the sound of a stifled laugh as Max pulls himself up on one of the thick tree branches. His muscles strain against his shirt, shoulders pressing against the fabric, the glint of light from the lantern in my window showing the tenseness of his jaw as he balances himself on the wide limb. "I know what kind of woman you are, Ellie."

"And what kind of woman is that?"

"The kind of woman I'd let break my heart on purpose."

It's my turn to chuckle, and I watch as Max skillfully scales the massive tree up to my bedroom. It's kind of a wonder to watch. Though he's not the first person to ascend to my window this way, there's something distinct about his gracefulness and willpower. It makes me wish I knew what was going on in his head as he reaches the windowsill, resting his heavy hand on the ledge.

"That seemed to be much more difficult than your usual climb," I joke, extending my arm to assist him off the branch. "Usually, I don't have to help you through the window."

"*Usually* you're kicking me out, not letting me in." Max takes my hand and I tug him through the gap. He doesn't let my hand go, and I don't release his either.

He smiles, a mischievous look on his face as he examines me. I changed the very moment I got back to my room, that purple outfit I wore to see Colonel Gallagher not even remotely suitable for the kind of night I had planned in my head. I've replaced it with a simple black dress with a corseted back and a bit of a lace hem. Something I've never worn for a man before because it's always seemed too... intimate.

"Usually, I'm doing things I don't need a cat to see. Especially a cat that may or may not have been the subject of a curse, retaining his human mind."

"*Usually* you're also—"

Everything in my body is screaming for Max; screaming for his touch and his lips and his hands on my skin. I need him again. I need to feel the way I felt when we kissed in the garden and the whole world melted away because I don't want to remember today with Colonel Gallagher and Sophia and the long conversations in the front room. I certainly don't want to remember that our days and time and summer are coming to a quick close, even though we've only just found one another.

I can't wait—I can't stop thinking about him and the way his voice dances in my ears like the songs of the nightbirds.

"Would you stop talking and kiss me?"

"Is that all I'm good for?" he murmurs, pulling me close enough that I catch the familiar scent of greenery on his shirt. "Kissing and stories?"

I grin, wrapping one hand around the back of his neck and sinking my fingers into his hair. "Absolutely."

Max is just starting to smile as I pull him down to me, our lips meeting amid the lamplight and moonglow. My heart starts to pound the very second that he presses his tongue against my mouth, deepening the kiss straightaway and drawing a moan from somewhere in the back of my throat. I want to drink in his entire essence—the feel of his shirt, the taste of his kiss, the sensation of him and the nothingness that exists around us as we fall into oblivion. He tastes like sea salt and summer air, and as we pull deep breaths and low groans from one another's bodies, the flavor of him submerges me.

Max is an ocean of his own.

Eventually, my lungs scream for both breath and for more of Max, but breath wins—just barely—and we separate, gasping for air.

I loosen my grip on the back of Max's neck and draw my fingers down his chest.

Max, meanwhile, looks at me with his beautiful green eyes. "*Fuck*, Ellie."

"We can do that, if you want." The words slide out of my mouth so quickly I almost wish I could take them back. Wish I could say something with a little more elegance and politeness than implying that Max came here tonight just to take off my dress.

"Do what?"

I'm certain he knows what I'm referring to because his fingers are already wrapped in the ribbon that holds the back of my dress together. One tug and everything will float to the floor, leaving me bare and ready for him. I've been ready for him since we met, but tonight feels like the right kind of night to show Max the depth of what that means.

"I—" I want to tell him that I want him to ruin me. I want him to fuck me until I can't breathe any longer, until I can't remember my name, until the only things I can see are stars and the moonlight and him. But something is wrong. Something's wrong with the idea of Max fucking me, and I think it's that we're *just* going to have sex tonight and that's it. It's the idea that it'll be without consequences and he'll go back to the seaside and eventually we'll never see each other again.

"Ellie, I'm not fucking you tonight."

"You're... not?"

"You don't deserve to be fucked like you're just some available body." Max's gaze feels as if it's penetrating deep into my soul. "This bedroom isn't part of a brothel in Loch Lomond or anywhere else in Scotland, and I don't think you invited me here because you needed coin in exchange for the things that we want to do to one another. I think you want more than that. I sure as hell need more than that."

My insides grow warm, a metaphorical fire burning in my stomach. "What do you need?"

Max leans in slowly and kisses a line up my neck, ending at my ear lobe. He nips at the soft skin while his hand loosens the ribbon on the back of my dress just an inch, then another inch, until my dress is just barely staying up. I'm probably going to perish right here on the floor if he doesn't get me undressed and into bed with him in the next five seconds.

"I need you, Ellie. Nothing more." His voice rumbles in my ear, and the vibrations resonate down my spine. "But I'm not fucking you. We can have sex. We can be intimate. But I can't call it fucking because there are so many strings attached between us that I can't do you the disservice of saying it's anything else."

For the first time in potentially forever, I actually feel cared for by a man. Padraig—well, Padraig was another story. He doesn't care much for anyone except himself. The other men who were passing through town were happy to have a diversion. But Max... I feel ways for him I haven't felt about anyone else. Ways I don't know if I have words for other than maybe I'm falling in love with him.

"Okay," I whisper, my fingers finding the buttons of Max's shirt and gently unfastening the one at the top to begin to expose his chest.

He nips at my neck, pulling the ribbon the final inch. However, instead of letting my dress fall to the ground, he grasps it with his opposite hand to keep me covered. The whine that escapes me is unconscious, but it feels so good to let out the noise and have it echo against the walls.

"You're going to make my heart stop, Max."

He chuckles, licking his bottom lip as he pulls back from having his teeth on my skin. "Tell me something before I let this dress go."

"Anything."

"Do you want this?"

I don't even hesitate before I nod. "I've never wanted anything more than I've wanted to be with you."

With that, Max releases his grasp and allows the dress to fall to the floor in a small heap of black fabric and soft ribbon.

"Oh *hell*, Ellie."

I have nothing underneath the gown; no slip and no lingerie. I've planned it that way so I would be exposed to Max completely if this moment came—the unexpected expression on his face worth every second that I had to spend alone with my thoughts of him. I can sense the moonlight on my skin as I smirk at Max, his gaze licking me up and down and back up again.

"You couldn't have warned me?" His voice is a heavy whisper, like he doesn't want the world to overhear. One of his fingers traces the line of my breasts, slowly and meticulously.

I shake my head, a small shiver running up my spine as his hand dances along my skin. "I figured it would be better as a surprise. Fewer ribbons and underthings to unravel."

He nods, watching me with wonder as I unbutton the rest of his shirt and free him from it. Without the black shirt covering him, and in lantern light, I can see every bit of damage on Max's body—scars on his chest, a birthmark on his shoulder, a long-since healed scratch on his waist. I'm ravenous for him, and I skim my fingers across his muscles, down his sides, and toward his hip bones, tracing figures over every blemish along the way before I start to sink to my knees to remove his slacks.

"Get up, Ellie." It's not a command, more of a suggestion, so instead of doing as he says, I stop in my tracks.

Have I done something wrong? I can't remember the last time I worried about having done something wrong with a man. Every one I've been with so far has liked having his—

Max gently takes my hand and lifts me back to a standing position. "I don't need you on your knees for me. I should be the one bowing for you."

I crease my brow. "That's not necessary, really."

"Don't tell me no man's ever…" He waits for me to say something, but there's nothing for me to say.

I should feel awkward, standing here naked in front of Max while having this conversation. I would feel awkward with any other man because this would mean our evening isn't going as planned. But Max is so close that I can practically feel his heart beating under my hand, and he brushes my long, red hair away from my face before kissing me softly.

"Let me show you something," he murmurs into my lips.

It's at this moment I realize that sex has been my power over other men, not their power over me. It's been a way for me to feel in charge of my lack of influence in my own life. Same with Allure. Same with parties. Same with every affair with Padraig and every stolen bottle of wine. It's all been about trying to manipulate a future that doesn't allow for change or difference or inconsistency—a future that values fear and control and rigidity over everything else.

But with Max—I'd drown the whole world in my need for him and the affection he offers.

Max guides me to the edge of the bed, gesturing for me to sit as he unbuttons his slacks. They hang on his narrow hips, his hard length pressing against the fabric as he sinks down to his knees in front of me, placing one hand on each of my suddenly trembling legs.

"You can tell me to stop whenever you want," he assures me.

I have a feeling I'm never going to want him to stop, but I nod and suck in a breath. Max slowly spreads my legs, watching me carefully, his fingers dancing up my bare thighs. I watch him back, the green of his eyes almost glowing in the darkness as he stares up at me from the hard floor. I can't believe nobody's fallen in love with his eyes before now.

Before now?

Ellie, I ask myself. *Are you in love with Max?*

I don't have time to think about my question because Max dips his head toward the gap between my legs, dragging his tongue up the softest and wettest part of me. There's no identifying the sound that comes out of my mouth, but I do know that I see the stars I was hoping for. They only last for a second, and once they start to clear, I grasp Max's shoulder with my fingernails—*hard*—and he licks me one more time before cupping my heat in his hand.

"More," I rasp. "I don't know what kind of magic that is, but I want more of it…"

Max chuckles, kissing the inside of my leg instead of putting his mouth where I want it most. "This is how a man should always treat you, Ellie. Like you're something to be savored."

I'm breathless as I respond. "I don't want another man. I want you."

"Perfect. Because I don't ever want another man to put his fucking hands on you ever again."

I can't help but laugh, but the sound is cut short and accented with a moan as Max dips downward between my thighs again. This time, he slips a single finger inside as he tastes me, and I find myself falling back against the mattress and closing my eyes. My entire body tightens around Max's finger, little waves of pleasure washing over me as I grip the blankets and feel every movement of his tongue on my most sensitive areas.

Forever wouldn't be long enough to experience this decadence, and I revel in it for as long as I can before every one of my nerves feels like it's on fire.

I'm writhing on the bed when Max shifts the angle of his wrist, and my body quivers in response to his touch. I can't stop it—it's a sensation I've never felt before. A full-body tremble that has my fingers tingling with impending numbness and my leg muscles constricting and my heart thumping so hard I'm certain he can feel every pulsation.

"Max—" I think I say his name, but I can't be entirely sure until he responds.

"I know, darling."

It's the endearment that does it. I never thought I would have an orgasm to a man calling me "darling," but I find myself sinking hard into Max as I reach the absolute precipice of pleasure. Every one of my muscles releases at once, and I bite my lip as I try not to whine so loud that I wake up everyone in the house. But it's so difficult not to let out a noise when my body is screaming in ecstasy.

No spoonful of Allure could compare to the way I feel right at this moment, and I bask in it until my pulse slows and I catch my breath.

How did he do that? It had to be something magical, right? I know he's supposed to have lost his magic when he was turned by Blossom, but no man has ever done that to me before; I've never had a feeling like that either...

Max rocks back on his heels once I've recovered, and I sit up, lean forward, and rest my forehead against his.

Once we're breathing in time with one another, I curse under my breath. But it's the good kind of cursing, the kind that's usually followed by a drag off a clove cigarette or a pull from a glass of wine.

"Where'd you learn to do that?" I finally ask. I have to know if it was some kind of enchantment or if he's actually that good with his mouth.

"It's a secret I picked up in my travels."

"Truthfully?" I lean back a little, noticing the playful glint in his eyes.

"Of course not. There are just some things a man wants to do to a woman he feels affectionate toward."

I can't help but glance downward, noticing his slacks have begun to slip off his hips just enough to expose the chiseled muscle at the top of his length. "Well, come then. Show me the other things you'd like to do to me before the sun comes up."

"Oh, we have lots of time."

"We'll never have enough time with autumn coming."

My heart is in my throat the moment I respond. I shouldn't have said that, but it's the truth. We have limited time. Summer will end. I'll be sent to Blossom unless we run away together like we did in my daydream.

Max nods somberly before rising from his crouched position. He takes a few steps toward the lantern and turns the dial down to a low flame, then adeptly slides off the rest of his garments. His silhouette smolders in the moonlight as I adjust myself on the bed; he's all thick muscle and disheveled hair. A low whisper resonates in my bones as he gestures toward the bedside table with the green ribbon piled on top of it.

"Do you want to take something before we..."

I almost ask him how he knows where I keep my contraceptive, but I'm sure that as a cat, he's seen more than his fair share of things come in and out of the nightstand.

Sliding open the drawer, I pull out a condom and a small vial, quickly drinking the latter before handing the former to Max. As he sheathes himself, I try not to stare. While it wasn't polite to look or think about him like that in the loch when we were swimming during the party I was supposed to be hosting, I'm fairly certain that a look is now permissible.

So, I look.

It's just a quick peek, but as my luck would have it, Max catches me. The realization of what I'm doing seems to be the reason he chuckles. "Acceptable?"

My face flushes with heat, but I still manage to respond as I fall back against the pillows. "Very."

Faded light glows on Max's upper body as he makes his way onto the bed, and the mattress shifts as he carefully positions himself over me. Our fingers knot together on the blankets, layers of fabric bunched up under us, my hair splayed like red flames. I feel safe here, underneath Max and amid the sea of coverlets, like nothing in the world could possibly touch our embrace—not even the daylight.

"I never thought we'd be here," Max breathes, pressing his hips into mine. His cock is firm against my wetness, only needing a slight change in position for us to be fully intimate. "I never thought I'd be able to show you my human form."

"Aren't you glad you took a chance at the party?"

He squeezes my hand, and I shift my hips so he finally can enter me. The sensation of him inside my body causes the two of us to groan—Max a little louder than me.

"You have no idea, Ellie."

Slowly, Max rocks his hips against mine, moving a little bit deeper with every thrust. Our hands stay tangled together, his tongue tracing patterns up and down my neck as I feel myself stretch around him. His actions are practiced and skillful, but still tender and calm, like he doesn't want me to feel the way I always felt with Padraig and the other men I've fucked. Like I just existed for their convenience.

I'm not having sex with Max for convenience, and he's not here in my bedroom as a way to pass the time.

Ellie, I ask myself once again because now seems to be the time for my thoughts to fall back to the question. *Are you in love with Max?*

A little voice in the back of my head responds quietly: *yes, I am.*

Finally, I can tell that Max has filled me because he pauses with our bodies aligned and our gazes lock.

"God, you feel good," he sighs, grinning like a fool. "I could live in this feeling."

I can't help myself. I unravel my fingers from Max's grasp and grab the back of his neck before pulling him down to me. "Let's live in this, then. Run away with me."

"For tonight?"

"Forever."

I don't think Max thinks I'm serious. That's fine for now because the idea is out in the universe instead of being stuck inside some daydream in my head.

"Forever, then." He shifts his hips, slipping out of me and then back in again before our lips meet.

We kiss the entire time we're intimate; lips, tongue, and sometimes soft nips with our teeth. I can't call any part of what we do "fucking" because I find myself agreeing with Max that we aren't *fucking*. There are more feelings involved than that. I may have fucked Padraig—or did he fuck me?—but with Max, the slow and deliberate and passionately gentle sex has me by a chokehold. Somehow, it also wordlessly reminds me of what I used to think love was about.

I don't know how long we last into the night in each other's arms, but by the time the two of us are about to finish, the lantern's light has almost burnt out and half the candlewicks have descended into darkness. Flickering shadows dance against the walls and leave the outlines of flowers I picked from the garden a fortnight ago and forgot to water. I know Max and I have our sensual silhouettes plastered along the bedroom as well, the gentle movements of our hips swaying in the dark.

"I'm close, darling," Max murmurs, nipping at my bottom lip as his free hand rakes down my thigh. I can feel him stiffening inside me, his muscles taut and in need of letting go.

Something about the name—*or is it the way he says it?*—drives me wild in the best way. I don't know what to do to help him finish, one of my hands already snared in his hair while the other is pinned to the bed. With one quick movement, I gently take the soft spot underneath Max's ear in between my teeth and close my lips on it, sucking and licking at sensitive skin. He lets out a low and guttural growl, an unexpected sound that shakes my soul, and then he thrusts one final time, groaning and shuddering in release.

He stays inside of me for a few moments longer, the two of us breathing in unison, until he rolls over onto the other side of the mattress. I stretch out my legs, hips screaming for even a brief respite, my body feeling empty and hollow without Max's fullness inside it.

"Ellie," Max sighs as we lie there and look over at one another. "I think we should do that again some time. But next time, I don't want you to lie on your back and think of Scotland."

A laugh breaks free of my throat as I reach for a blanket. "Absolutely not. I'll be on top."

Chapter Fourteen

MAX

Once I've removed the used condom and wrapped myself in one of Ellie's blankets, she nestles against my side, head on my shoulder. Her red hair forms a curtain over her breasts, skin peeking through the strands and begging my hands to traverse every intimate inch of her again. However, I don't want to disturb her rest, so I try to distract myself by regulating my breathing and begging my heart to slow down so it doesn't explode out of my chest. It takes a few moments of deep breathing, sucking in the scent of wildflowers and summer air, but eventually, I find myself dozing in and out of a light sleep.

I start to dream, but when I realize I'm dreaming, my brain immediately wakes me up. I can't sleep—not when I risk being here until sunrise. I can't allow myself to shift in Ellie's bedroom.

Trying to keep myself awake, I run my fingertips along Ellie's bare arm. She lets out a little sigh and places her delicate hand on my chest. "That wasn't anything like I expected, you know."

"What did you expect?" I ask, looking down at her and shifting my weight slightly so I'm able to do so at a better angle. Plus, the movement will keep me from dozing off again.

"More of the same, I guess. Is it what you expected?"

I roll a few thoughts over in my head, trying to remember what I thought Ellie would be like tonight. Of course, I'd considered the potential that we'd end up in bed together, but it wasn't like I had seriously deliberated what might happen after we got to that point.

"I'm not sure, to be honest. I'm never certain of what to expect with you."

"Is that a good thing or a bad one?" she questions, absently tracing a line up the center of my stomach.

I roll over to face Ellie completely, propping myself up on my elbow. "I'm naked in bed with you. We just had what I would describe as very... *emotional* sex, and neither of us ran off afterward when we realized what we'd done or said or felt. I think that means it's a very good thing."

Her laugh spills over the otherwise silent room. "It was emotional, wasn't it? As opposed to just fucking, like you said. My other experiences were always kind of hollow in comparison, now that I look back on them. Hollow and transactional."

"That's how it always felt when I was back in Loch Lomond. Like it was a business deal."

"It was, in a way, though. Wasn't it?"

I nod, biting the inside of my cheek. It was probably impolite to bring up my history with other women just now. Especially where I've got one of Ellie's sheets wrapped around my bare ass and her slick thighs imprinted in my mind. "We don't have to talk about the past."

"What happened in Loch Lomond doesn't worry me, if that's what concerns you." She pushes a lock of hair over her shoulder, exposing her neck. "I suppose, in some ways, the things I did with Padraig and the other men who came to town were the same as you lighting a candle in a brothel and seeing if you could finish yourself off before it was blown out."

I fall flat on my back against the blankets and pillows again, staring up at the uneven ceiling. She's trying to justify the things I've done for pleasure, but I'm not sure who she's doing it for. "Not the same. Definitely not the same."

We rest there amid the quiet bedroom for some time, the darkness surrounding us more deeply as time goes on due to the fading candlelight and lantern glow. Despite the fact that I know the night will eventually dwindle into a typical foggy morning on the moors, I'm determined to wring every second out of this evening before I change back into my other form. I don't want to leave Ellie alone, the two of us forced to breathe different air—mine on the seaside and in the abandoned church while hers is here in Loch Gàrraidh with the flower gardens. But like Alastair said earlier, changing is a strange process. I don't want Ellie to see it. She doesn't need to be exposed to the truth of what it looks like.

"Max?" Ellie's questioning voice interrupts my thoughts. "You do know that love isn't a transaction, right? Sex might be, but love…"

She trails off at the end of her sentence, as if she's suddenly realized what she's said aloud, and my insides unexpectedly feel as if they're coiling into knots. *Did she just use the word "love" while we're lying here in bed together? She couldn't have. Someone like Ellie, someone betrothed to marry a military colonel and who will be leaving Loch Gàrraidh behind couldn't truly fall in love with me, could she?*

"I don't think love is a transaction," I reply. "I think it's a reaction. A state of being. Love is a reason for existing."

"Then you must understand how I feel."

"Torn?"

Ellie sighs. "That, too. But mostly, I feel like you're *my* reason for existing."

A smile quirks at the corner of my lips, and the bedroom becomes a tiny bit brighter with every moment that passes by. It's a peculiar development with only one possible cause: more light. If there's more light, it means there are more candles, there is more oil in the lantern, the moon has suddenly grown much closer, or…

Instinctively, I look down at my hands. My palm is glowing the same pale green that it was on my walk in the field to the Callaghan house. It's not a strong light—faint and nearly ready to die out—but it's there. I can see it.

My magic is coming back.

I scramble to sit upright, nearly falling off the edge of the mattress. "Ellie, do you love me?"

For an instant, I think I might have ruined everything because the luminescence in my hand dies a quick death. Maybe I misunderstood the point that Ellie was trying to get across. Perhaps I'm hearing what I want to hear instead of the words that are actually being said. But then Ellie whispers in the dimness of the bedroom, and the glimmering green on my skin returns with a vengeance.

"I do."

A single spark emanates from my fingertip. Just one, but it's enough to remind me that even though I'm cursed, a curse can always be broken. Blossom doesn't have a forever hold on me, and those who run the academy will have to find Ellie and me before they can curse her, too. They'll have to use their magic, their powers, their seemingly all-seeing eye to track us down. "Tell me again."

She blinks at me amid the emerald radiance before she repeats herself. "I'm falling in love with you, Max."

Two sparks this time, and Ellie sits up on the bed, immediately comprehending the magnitude of what's happening. We're slowly breaking through the enchantment.

"Max," she starts, heaving in a deep breath as she keeps a close watch on the glow in my hand. "I have no doubt in my mind that I'm falling for you. I don't care about the curse. I don't care if we can't live by the seaside and if we have to constantly run away from Blossom and the lochs. I want to show you the way you make me feel in one of the only ways I know how. I want you to know that we—this, us, *tonight*—aren't some kind of business arrangement. I want to be with you and I want to prove it."

"We didn't already prove it?"

She shakes her head. "We proved pieces. But not other parts. Specifically, not the part where you experience the things I desperately want to do to you. To show you the ways you make me wild. Fuck magic and Blossom and societal rules."

Ellie clasps my hand and extinguishes the light from my palm, descending us into the rosy glow of the remaining candles. Her gaze flickers to the nightstand that's piled with green ribbon, and she reaches for the length of it before winding the strip between her fingers.

"Are you trying to tell me something?" I ask, smirking. She wouldn't be the first woman who I've tied to a bed, but now she's the only one I want to remember doing it to.

"I am. Lie back."

I furrow my brow. "Do you mean me?"

"There's nobody else around. So yes, I mean you."

I do as she says, adjusting my position so my head is resting on one of her feather pillows. I have no idea what she's thinking, which isn't something completely unfamiliar to me by now, though I am incessantly curious about what she's going to do with that ribbon. As soon as I'm comfortably reclined, Ellie disentangles herself from the coverlet that was tight around her body and crawls atop me.

Thank fuck I'm still partially wrapped in my own blanket because otherwise she'd probably be able to notice the sudden twitch in my dick the moment she spreads her bare legs on either side of my hips.

With a playful glint in her eye—shit, she definitely felt it—Ellie slowly wraps the ribbon around one of my hands.

"This okay?"

I nod, watching as she loops the satin length a few times around my wrist, across my palm, and back again before crossing to my other hand to bind them together. She pauses as I suck in a sharp breath, her agile fingers on my skin making me want to say and do foolish things. But I say and do nothing. I let her continue to tie my hands with the green ribbon, leaving me to silently inquire about her plans. That is, until she slowly raises my arms above my head and loops the ribbon around a top rung of the otherwise solid headboard.

I can't help that I growl her name because being the one who is bound is entirely different than being the one who is doing the binding. "Ellie..."

My cock flinches again, but I'm so hard now there's no hiding the way she's making me feel.

"You want me to stop?" Ellie pauses, looking down at me, our hands and the length of satin bundled together against the wood.

"Never. Keep going."

She grins, quickly returning to her task of fastening a solid knot in the ribbon. "Don't tell me you've never had a woman tie you to her bed before?"

My heart's in my throat. "Actually, I haven't."

Everything inside of me wants to grab Ellie and pin her down and do unspeakable things to her, things that wouldn't be at all as gentle as the first time we did them. But I can't. My hands are tied, and she's done a damn good job of making sure I can't get them undone without a bit of finagling. And I suspect that the possibility of being able to finagle myself free was done on purpose to give me the option to get out of the bindings if I really, really need to.

I don't need to. I don't want to. I want to be bound to this bed and this moment and this night and to *her*.

"First time for everything." She leans back, admiring her handiwork. "Now you can't interrupt me."

"Interrupt you?"

Ellie smiles the most lascivious grin before separating me from the cocoon of blankets that I've created around myself. From somewhere in the dark, she plucks another condom, unwrapping the seal with her teeth before expertly slipping the thin cover over my cock.

Her fingers gliding over my most sensitive areas has me instantly straining against the ties. I'm certain she knows I'm more than aware that I can undo the ribbon any time I want, but something about not being able to touch her has me feeling a whole other level of feral.

"I need you," I growl, the tone in my voice almost unrecognizable. "Now."

Ellie tosses her hair, shifting her weight on me as she chuckles. I could buck my hips and have her riding me in half a second, but I'd rather play this game with her all through the rest of tonight. "Oh, that's not how this is going to work, Max. You're all tied up in me now. But you need to know something very important about women that I don't think you learned in Loch Lomond."

"Oh? What's that?"

"A woman can be fiery and sexual and in love while fucking you senseless."

Every time she curses, I get turned on a little bit more. "I thought you agreed that just fucking was hollow?"

"I'm about to prove to you that it doesn't have to be." There's lust and passion and a blazing inferno in her eyes as she watches me, waiting for me to give her permission to continue with whatever she's conceived in her head.

"Okay," I reply, smirking. "Change my mind and fuck me senseless."

Ellie nods before she reaches over my head to grip my hands. She winds her fingers between mine, squeezing gently. Then, barely an instant after I wonder if she's actually going to do anything, Ellie slides her wetness down my dick, clenching her thighs and immediately filling herself with every inch of me. She's just forceful enough that the sensation makes me groan, compelling me to pull hard against the green ribbon shackles.

"Goddamnit, Ellie."

Her gentle laugh sinks into my bones as she starts to rise and fall over me. Without the use of my hands, I can only apply pressure with my hips. We create a rhythm together, rough and tempestuous, our stifled moans ringing off the bedroom walls. I can feel the ribbon leaving marks on my wrists, biting into the skin as Ellie rides me. She feels better than anything I've ever experienced in this life, and I desperately want her mouth on mine, but I also badly need to absorb all the sounds she's making and not smother them with my own lips.

Ellie wasn't being dishonest when she said she wouldn't lie down and think of Scotland the second time. We move together with an obsession for one another, grinding our bodies together in the kind of fervor that usually becomes rather one-sided with the dwindling of a candle in a brothel. However, both Ellie and I are slick with sweat and need, and she sits up straighter, rocking back and forth on my length as she lets out a low moan and closes her eyes. One of her hands finds her breasts, and I watch on hungrily as she caresses herself while the other reaches behind her back to graze my inner thigh. A moment later, Ellie rakes her nails up my leg to the base of my cock, and my entire body trembles with the sensation.

I nearly curse again, but Ellie's core tightens around me, and judging by the way her body is quivering as she rides me, she's close. *I'm* close, but she's closer.

The whole world feels like it's melting into nothingness, and the only thing I can focus on is the way the rhythm of her body perfectly matches every twitch in my dick and every jolt in my heart. I'm not sure it's possible for me to get any harder, veins throbbing in between my legs, but when Ellie whines my name, I nearly shatter.

"Max..."

My mind is so muddled with sex and the scent of flowers that I don't think I remember any words in the English language, so I am forced to mutter a noise that hopefully resembles something Ellie might recognize. "Mhmmm?"

"You feel so fucking good."

I want to tell her she feels better than I could have ever imagined, and I want to let her know that she's right, that she's absolutely fucking me to the point of losing my words and my breath. However, I can't get any of those ideas out of my mouth because my carnal desires take over the moment she uses another profane word. I see red—but not the murderous kind of red. No, it's the shade of red that's mixed with the color of her hair and of cherry wine and of rose petals from the garden when we kissed for the first time.

Ellie's going to be the death of me.

Manipulating the end of the ribbon in between my fingers, I am quickly able to tug my hands free of the binding she's created. In one fell movement, the length of satin falls to the bed, unraveled from one hand and trailing from the other as my unconsciousness takes over my next objective:

be as close to her as possible, get her off, and then admit that I'm absolutely falling in love.

Green ribbon shadows us as one of my hands grabs Ellie's ass and the other finds her throat. I sit up and hold her hips to mine as I press my fingers into her neck before my teeth locate the spot on her skin under her ear where I know she likes being touched. In response, she wraps her legs around me, letting out a moan.

I tighten my muscles and push into Ellie once; twice. That's all I need before I am ruined by her, so close to my precipice that I'm not sure how I manage to choke out any words.

"Come for me," I rasp, my voice almost getting lost in her neck where I've buried my lips. At some point, I released my careful hold on her throat, sliding my hand to her breast, but I swear I can still feel the sensation every time she groans. Maybe it's something I'm feeling inside my body instead of across the palm of my hand.

Ellie shakes her head, red hair cascading over us. "I don't want it to be over."

"Darling, it's not over. It's just beginning."

"Are you sure?"

She's so fucking tight and warm and I don't think I can last another five seconds, so I just nod. But with that nod, Ellie lets go. She writhes around my cock, and I see stars as I come along with her, my heart banging out a symphony as I grasp for any part of her I can hold onto as she collapses against my chest. With my length inside of her, I can feel every twitch of her muscles each time they contract and release until we are left there, our skin damp and glistening, my mind blissful, and the satin ribbon coiled around us as if we've been magically threaded together.

She's still on top of me when I lie back against her mattress, her small frame crumpled against my body as she breathes heavily. My wrists throb with what I can only assume are future bruises from the pressure I put on my bindings, and every part of my soul feels at peace for the first time in a long while.

"Ellie?" I murmur into her hair, kissing the top of her head as the final shivers of my orgasm dissipate. The taste of her name on my lips is the sweetest wine I've ever had, and I can't wait to say it over and over again—both in and out of the bedroom.

"Yes?" Ellie's voice is a whisper.

I suck in a breath before I respond, hoping I'm not about to destroy the moments we've just spent together. "I'm in love with you. Absolutely and entirely."

There's a crackle of a candle burning out in the instant before Ellie replies. "This soon? And despite the things you've seen?"

She's not questioning me—she's questioning time itself. But in my heart, I know that she doesn't need to question time or space or the universe or anything else because it doesn't matter. When things are right, they just *are*. And we're right, tonight is right, and this darkened bedroom is right—all together, it makes the timing for our admission of love downright perfect.

Instead of answering right away, I gently lift her from me, take a moment to rise and rid myself of the condom, and note the pale imprint of pinks and yellows and blues along the edge of the moors. We have time. Not much, but some nonetheless. So, I return to the bed where Ellie's pulled a blanket up over herself and sink into the crumpled coverlets next to her. There are so many things I could say—so many admissions I could make—but I have a feeling that for Ellie, she's heard generic love stories so many times that I need to prove to her that my feelings are true. Even if the proof is just in being honest.

So, I decide to be honest and bare my emotions to her.

"I love everything I've seen of you, Ellie. Every inch of your skin, every depravity in your mind, every word that's slipped from your mouth when you haven't intended it to. I love all the ways you want to be more than this world, and the manner in which your heart speaks to mine without saying a word. I want to be consumed by you. I *am* consumed by you—body, mind, and soul."

She watches me, watches the words come from my mouth, and seems to absorb them all before she responds with a smile.

"Let's run away together."

I can't help myself when I nod at her beautiful idea. "Not today, though. We're almost out of time for tonight."

She peers over my shoulder and looks out the gap in the curtains. "Not today, then. But soon. We'll break your curse and we'll get out of these lochs . We'll leave Scotland. We can find somewhere else in the world to live where Blossom can't reach us. Where I can be reckless and you can be a man and we don't have to be told we're too careless or insolent or unsuitable for a proper partner."

"The right partner will love all the wild parts of you, Ellie."

Ellie grins. "You must be the right partner, then."

Insatiable, I roll over on top of her, pinning her to the bed. The green ribbon still trails my arm, but I don't bother to remove it. It can stay. Everything in this room can stay exactly as it is until I feel that familiar tingling in my spine. "We'll have to make a plan. Think about this. Figure out how we can get away from here together."

"We can keep having sex; that might help?" Her smile is cheeky and ravenous.

I bite the side of her neck, and she releases a tiny groan that makes me chuckle. "I have to go. Not because I want to. But think about this. Truly think about it and what you'll be leaving behind. Because once we run, we won't be coming back, other than through letters and anonymous gifts for the children. We won't be able to risk it."

"I know. You'd best go before sunrise. Who knows when Sophia and Colonel Gallagher will wake, and I'd better make myself presentable for his departure so I at least look like I'm not a complete heathen."

Dragging myself from the bed, I dress before kissing Ellie deeply and escaping back out the window from where I came.

Chapter Fifteen

SOPHIA

I unravel myself from Iain's touch and rise to close my bedroom door to give us privacy. However, as I'm about to flick the lock, I can hear what sounds like someone crashing through Ellie's window, along with a muffled conversation. It wouldn't surprise me if Ellie brought Max up into her room based on everything she said earlier in the day. If she's bold enough to have him here while Iain's supposed to be sleeping in the room below hers, then maybe I shouldn't be so worried about the fact that Iain and I just kissed. Now I'm here locking the two of us in my bedroom, wondering why I would have ever judged Ellie based on what might happen next between Iain and me

Nothing more than kissing, I tell myself. *There's no way to excuse any behavior other than a single kiss. In reality, Iain probably only kissed me so his future wife wouldn't have kissed lots of men and he had never kissed anyone. That has to be it. I'm just practice for him so he knows what it might be like with Ellie. What if he didn't even like kissing me? I probably wasn't the best choice since my only other experience was that time with George...*

The thoughts feel strange, but they are most likely the truth. Therefore, when I close and lock the bedroom door and Iain's standing directly behind me, I'm surprised. I didn't hear him rise from the chair and I didn't anticipate him being so close to me ever again.

"Iain, I—" I start to speak but I don't know what I'm trying to say. My mind is reeling over the presumption that he kissed me for no other reason than because he can… and maybe to know if he even *likes* kissing.

"I think we should do that again."

"Do what?" *There's no way he means he wants to kiss me again. Maybe we can pretend that nothing happened, or that he's the one who started it. I could pretend that I'm blameless for that prior intimate moment. After all, he's meant to marry Ellie.*

Iain blinks at me, and the look in his eye tells me that neither of us is above suspicion in the way we acted. It wasn't one-sided, it wasn't a kiss that one of us stole from the other. We both wanted it, and we both breathed it in and took it. I can't honestly think I'm not guilty. I'm guilty. He's guilty. The world is guilty of watching us express ourselves in the only way we've ever been told we aren't allowed to act.

"I just—I wanted to have one kiss that wasn't for duty or marriage or Blossom or society. A kiss because I wanted one from a woman who I've somehow just met but who is so easy to talk to and confess my fears to. A kiss that was for me to remember her by before I have to do the proper thing and keep up with my promises. Maybe that was a selfish desire."

"No, it wasn't," I whisper.

"It wasn't?"

I shake my head. I don't think Iain has the capacity to be selfish. He is so gentle, kind, and trusting of the world, which is everything I could want in a husband. Mother has to find someone for me like him.

But I don't want someone else with those qualities because they won't be Iain, and when my future husband kisses me—whoever he turns out to be—it won't be a kiss with the first man I ever felt sensual craving for. It won't be the kind of kiss where I'm worried about it being messy or strange or new. I think it'll just be a kiss. A kiss with a man who I might not love... just like Ellie doesn't love Iain.

"Sophia."

I gaze up into Iain's chestnut brown eyes, feeling every worry in my body melting away to allow pure magic to flow through my veins. His low voice encourages goosebumps to rise on my arms, and I can't help myself when I nod and fall into his chest, pressing my lips to his.

It happens gently—and then all at once.

In what I assume is fervor rather than obligation, Iain pushes my back into the bedroom door, pinning me between the wood and his body. I know I'm supposed to not want this—but I do. I want to be held here by Iain's muscles and his kiss for as long as he'll have me. I hope he'll have me forever, but at the moment, even tonight would be long enough. Or an hour. Another minute. The next five seconds. And then five seconds more.

We kiss there against the door until the two of us are out of breath, and then we kiss for an instant longer until we are forced to part and gasp for air. His broad chest heaves under my hand, and I feel myself panting, but my want for oxygen isn't larger than my want for Iain. There's something happening inside of me as we are joined there, together in my locked bedroom, doing something we shouldn't be doing. Doing something that nobody should be doing with someone else's betrothed.

I wasn't sure anything could be better than our first kiss, but this second kiss where I'm in between Iain's body and the wooden door surpasses my expectations by a mile. As we maintain our embrace, Iain takes hold of my unbandaged hand, tangling his fingers in between mine. I don't know what to do at all, so I let him guide my arm to find a home around his neck while he drags his palms down my bare skin before resting them lightly on my hips. Gently, he places my bottom lip between his teeth, nibbling and sucking at me.

My shoulders dig into the door as my heart pounds erratically. I could very well faint here in Iain's arms with the way he's kissing the breath out of me.

But I don't. I don't because he pulls away before I have a chance to forget that I need oxygen to stay alive. My hand slips down the front of his shirt, and I can feel his pulse hammering as he takes a step backward.

"I shouldn't—"

The words that come from my chapped lips sound like things I think Ellie would say more than anything that would typically come from my mouth. "Don't talk. Don't think. Just kiss me."

Iain smiles amid the bedroom light, the lantern blazing behind us and giving him a golden silhouette. "I was under the impression that I just came up here to check on your hand and was supposed to leave afterward."

As if to accentuate what he's saying, a couple of solid bangs come from down the hallway that suspiciously sound like a headboard knocking against a wall. Iain raises his eyebrow and cocks his head to the side as he looks at me, wordlessly questioning the noise. I know it's Ellie, and I know what she's doing... and probably who she's doing it with.

Better for Iain to know the truth now than to have him led on any longer.

"You're welcome to retreat back to the guest bedroom. However"—I pause to wait for the end of another series of thumps—"I'm not sure you're going to enjoy a night of listening to Ellie and her *company*."

I expect Iain to deflate at the news, but instead, he chuckles lightly as if he's known all along. "I suppose I shouldn't have expected anything less. She did seem awfully distracted this afternoon."

"I think she's trying to get everything out of her system so she can be loyal to you when the time comes." There's no way I can look at him while lying.

Iain raises his hand, tipping my chin so I'm staring deep into his eyes. "You don't have to lie to me, Sophia. She'll never be loyal to me, just as I clearly will never be loyal to her, despite my best intentions."

"I don't mean to lie…"

"You're trying to help her. It's a noble thing you've been attempting. But she clearly—"

Thud, thud, thud.

A smile breaks across Iain's face, and I can't help the grin that quirks up at the corners of my lips in response. Maybe, for once, Ellie's distraction isn't so bad, even if it is giving me a bit of secondhand embarrassment.

"I feel like this happens a little more often than you're letting on," Iain says.

I gesture back toward our chairs on the other side of the room. "We should sit somewhere else so we don't have to overhear… *that*."

Iain nods, crossing the bedroom floor as he responds. "At least she's enjoying herself. Good for her. Takes a certain kind of woman to know what she wants and to just… defy Blossom and everyone else."

"She's going to get turned into a Bèist, isn't she?" I sit back down in my chair and immediately start picking at the edge of my thumb where I've located a small hangnail.

"Maybe. Though they'll have to catch her first. From all my meetings with Ellie, she doesn't seem like the type to be easily caught."

We sit quietly for a little while, me staring down at my hands and Iain looking out the window. I don't know what he's thinking, and that bothers me, but I also know it wouldn't be polite to ask about a man's private thoughts. I read a book about it once, from Father's library. The learned ability to read minds wasn't all that useful for the people in the story and ultimately caused their demise. As I think about the demise of most people in fairytales—well, their demise or their eventual falling in love—the lantern reflects against the window, emitting just enough heat that I can feel the flame's warmth kissing my skin.

I wish it was Iain kissing me.

"You aren't as upset as I thought you'd be." I finally look up at him, and he's running a hand over his partially exposed neck.

"It's like I said, I had a suspicion. Maybe that's why I didn't try to stop myself from developing an attraction to you."

"It's strange though, right? For it to happen so quickly? The attraction, not the suspicion."

Iain shrugs. "I don't know. I've never felt this way before. Maybe it's temporary... but it feels like it isn't. Everything inside me is telling me this is how I'm supposed to be. It's not like we were told about the sensations that comes with attraction in our childhood fairytales, but maybe that's for a reason. Maybe as children, we aren't supposed to be thinking about placing more importance on our hearts than our heads."

"Maybe everything happens for a reason, then?" I suggest.

"I'd like to think so."

Iain reaches across the gap between us and draws me close. I allow myself to get swept up in his arms and his lips again, along with the light scent of leather and pine that seems to have taken hold of his clothes. My fingers can't help but dance along the buttons of his shirt that haven't yet been unfastened. Though I'm not practiced at the act of undressing a man, I do manage to undo two of them before Iain lets out a light chuckle into our kiss.

"I don't know if we should go any farther," he mumbles.

I gently pull away from his mouth, though the hold Iain has on my body is something I don't ever want to part from. "You're right. Maybe not until... another time."

A little voice in my head says I should tell Ellie before I start undressing her betrothed in the darkness of my bedroom. That Iain and I should both tell Ellie we feel something for one another and beg her not to go ahead with the wedding. But Mother would be so angry, and I'm sure Father would be too, if he was still alive. They worked so hard to find someone for Ellie to marry. To find someone Ellie might grow to love and who might grow to love her.

But things are different now. Nothing has ever happened with Iain and Ellie, and now something has happened between Iain and me.

"Another time." He nods, but we don't part ways. "However, that doesn't mean we can't continue to do what we've already done. I mean, the rules have already been broken. Can we break the same rule twice?"

I laugh. "You're incorrigible."

"And you're beautiful."

The compliment has me crashing back against Iain's mouth. I've never been one to be called beautiful. It's always Ellie. Ellie is the pretty one in the family, with her doe-eyes and enviable lips and curtain of wavy red hair that flows over her shoulders, never getting frizzy or unmanageable. I'm just Sophia, the second oldest Callaghan.

But not to Iain.

To Iain, I am much more than the "other" sister. And that realization makes my heart swell and my palms itchy with the need to touch his shirt lapel again. I wish I could tear the buttons from the holes they're nestled in, but he's right about needing to wait for another time. However, he's also right that we've let ourselves break society's rules, and what's one hundred more kisses to add to the pile of offenses?

We've already kissed. We can't take it back, and it's not like Ellie's going to care. She'll probably be thrilled that she has an excuse not to marry Iain. Mother wouldn't make her marry a man who feels affection for her sister, right?

Iain and I kiss and talk—kissing more than talking—as the night draws on and fades much too quickly into dawn.

The morning light flows in underneath my curtains, a lemon-yellow glow that reminds me the little ones will be rising soon. I suppose Iain should make his way down to the guest bedroom to rest before his long return to Edinburgh, and in return for the unforgettable night, I could head out to the stable to feed his horse. That wouldn't be suspicious. Ellie wouldn't suspect anything at all other than that I rose early in order to get a fire going in the kitchen, have the tea on, and make porridge for the children before Iain's departure.

The fact that he's leaving should puncture my good mood, but it doesn't because somewhere deep inside, I know he will be back. It might not be for me, not yet, but he will return with a horse, carriage, and driver, and maybe I'll be allowed to stow away in a piece of luggage so we can be together.

Sophia, calm your mind.

"I should leave," Iain notes before rising from his chair and peeking out the curtains. As he pushes them aside, daylight pours in, and I realize it might be later than I thought. "I didn't expect to keep you up all night. I didn't expect anything that happened, to be honest. But it's probably for the best that I at least appear to leave from the guest room in the morning. Good manners and all."

"Agreed." I stand, shuffling my dress back down around my knees and attempting to straighten the wrinkles in the fabric. "Modesty is important."

We cross the room and pause at the locked bedroom door like neither of us is sure how to end our encounter. Moments later, Iain bows and kisses the top of my head, sending a shiver down the back of my neck. I don't want to let him—or tonight—go. But I know I have to. At least for now.

"I'll see you in the kitchen in a short while. I'll listen for the sound of dishes breaking."

I playfully swat at him, the reference both good-natured and teasing, and he winks before unlocking the door and partially stepping across the threshold.

"And watch that hand of yours for signs of infection. I'd have to come back and treat your wounds," Iain whispers, his voice low enough that I can barely hear what he's saying.

I nod, gently shoving him away. "Go, before I won't let you."

He smiles at me, turning and walking away just as the click of Ellie's bedroom lock disturbs the tranquility of the otherwise silent hallway. My stomach immediately turns into a knotted mess, heart jumping into my throat. *Please don't come out, please just stay in your room...*

Iain freezes, and I'm petrified, my hand on the latch of my door. The world feels like it's moving at half its usual speed as I watch Ellie emerge from her own bedroom. There's a bright red flush on her cheeks and her lips, and she's wrapped up in a golden-beige robe that she must have pulled from the back of her armoire because I've never seen it before. Then again, I suppose I haven't seen my sister in a lot of things that she wears in the presence of male company...

Ellie notices me before she sees Iain, who is doing his best impression of a stag caught in unexpected candlelight.

"Morning," she purrs. "You're up early. Are the little—"

That's when she spots Iain standing there with his shirt half unbuttoned and wrinkles all over his clothes. He offers a tight smile, but our chapped lips and crimson faces give everything away. *She's going to kill me. What have I done? I'm going to be sent to Blossom for being—*

Then Ellie laughs.

"You can't be fucking serious."

Iain's stiff posture softens and he immediately starts to apologize profusely. This is probably for the best as I haven't figured out how to make words come from my mouth yet. In fact, I'm not even sure if I'm breathing.

"We—*I* can explain. It's not whatever you're thinking, and I'm sure that you and I, we... I'm sorry. I don't know how to explain it, truly."

My sister holds up one hand to quiet Iain's blathering, and then she turns toward me. "You have no idea how wildly convenient you've made this."

"You're not upset?" I squeak. I know how to handle her anger and frustration, but I don't know how to handle whatever this is. Indifference? Is one supposed to be indifferent in a situation like this one?

Ellie snorts. "Tell me what happened and then I'll tell you if I'm mad."

I look toward Iain, who has a look of absolute dread on his face. "I don't know if—"

"I don't mean right this second." She gestures toward the guest room, and then Iain. "You, go get your things and your horse. I suspect it's time for you to leave. We'll figure out how to explain it before you return to take me to Blossom."

"Sophia and I like each other, Ellie. And I know you have affections for someone else."

"And how do you know?"

Iain's face turns an even brighter red as his gaze flicks toward her bedroom door. I think he's hoping she'll get the message, but instead, she stands in the threshold with an amused look on her face. The stillness continues, waiting for someone to break through the quiet—us, or a child waking from a deep slumber.

"We... heard you with him," I say in a whisper, knowing that Iain isn't going to tell Ellie that the fight between her headboard and the bedroom wall made for quite an entrance.

She shakes her head. "It was nothing."

But I know it wasn't. It was Max. And I'm fairly certain that Max is everything to Ellie, even if he is cursed.

We stand there quietly for a few moments until Huntley and Pippa's bedroom door opens. Little Huntley smiles at all of us like we weren't in the middle of something, his innocence something that I hope never leaves him. Even if it does mean believing in fairytales sometimes.

"Hi," he says, one finger in his mouth as he stares between Ellie and Iain before his eyes finally land on me. "I'm hungry, Soapy."

The nickname melts my heart and my grasp on the door, and I kneel down to encourage Huntley to come to me. When he wobbles on his little legs down the hallway, I pick him up and hoist him onto my hip. "You want some porridge?"

Huntley nods, and I use the opportunity to escape.

Chapter Sixteen

ELLIE

Once Sophia bolts down the staircase with Huntley in her arms, I'm left alone in the corridor with Colonel Gallagher. We stare at each other for a few moments, neither of us seemingly able to think up something to say. I could tell him my mother is going to be extraordinarily pissed off that our betrothal is not going as planned, but there is no real need because he appears nervous enough already.

Of course, I don't love that he and Sophia overheard Max and me during our intimate evening. However, that realization would be much more awkward if I hadn't just caught the two of them sneaking around. I mean, honestly... Colonel Gallagher could have at least buttoned his shirt.

Instead of getting into details, I gesture toward the stairs. "Go. Before we wake Pippa."

Colonel Gallagher scampers down the steps like he's a child who's just been told off, and I watch him go with a little smile on my face. I meant it when I said he and Sophia have made this convenient for me. Max made it convenient first—by agreeing that we will disappear from the lochs together somehow. But this takes care of those I was most worried about leaving behind. Because if Sophia can spend a night locked up in her bedroom with Colonel Gallagher, she must really be willing to break some rules for his affections.

I leave Sophia and Colonel Gallagher alone for a while, taking my time getting dressed and brushing out my hair. There's no doubt in my mind that they're having a hushed conversation in between making breakfast for Huntley, together, like two lovesick creatures that can't do anything without the other. They're probably in the corner of the kitchen, discussing the intricacies of the way they feel as Sophia stokes the fire and adjusts the kettle to bring the water to boil. Colonel Gallagher and his brown eyes must be watching her with interest. The same kind of interest that I've seen in Max's eyes when he's feeling loving... and loved.

I can only imagine that this is what Sophia imagined her life to be like when she was to marry—a nice man who does his best, a small child, a home to take care of. It seems like the perfect, comfortable life for someone who isn't me. Someone who doesn't want to run away from the stories and the society that thinks anyone with values different from theirs is a reckless deviant who needs to be adjusted by an academy.

Sighing, I look at myself in my tortoiseshell hand mirror one more time before I opt to leave the bedroom, descending the steps to the first floor before landing in the kitchen. Huntley's sitting at the table, kneeled on a chair and shoving porridge in his mouth while Sophia and Colonel Gallagher watch over him.

"Anything to say for yourselves?" I ask.

Sophia glances toward Huntley, who is absolutely not giving us any attention at all. In fact, despite it only being a moment later, he's located a couple of additional spoons to amuse himself with, lining them up above his bowl like they're soldiers waiting for orders.

Colonel Gallagher starts to open his mouth as if to speak, but Sophia hushes him by touching his hand. I almost miss the gesture because it's so swift.

"Ellie, I don't know how to explain it. I just... *we* just seem to be inexplicably drawn to one another. It feels both sudden and steady all at the same time." Sophia keeps her voice low, but she smiles, and for the first time, I notice a sparkle in her eyes. It's a shine I've never seen on her before—usually she just looks at me with annoyance.

I wonder if I had that same sparkle when I was telling her about the way I feel for Max.

I glance toward Colonel Gallagher before casting a peek over at Huntley. He's still playing with his spoons and breakfast, humming the tune to a nursery rhyme to himself. Truly in his own world—a world where none of what the rest of us are talking about matters.

"You feel this too?" I ask, turning back to the discussion. Colonel Gallagher nods and I bite the inside of my cheek for a moment before responding. "Okay. We'll figure this out. We'll figure everything out. Because I don't think either of us plans on continuing with things the way they were before last night. At least, not with one another."

"Are you sure?" he whispers.

"Absolutely. But I need to think. And you need to go back to Edinburgh while I do that. And I need to talk to Sophia. Alone."

"Alone?" Sophia furrows her brow, a look of concern crossing over her face. I can only imagine her heart is beating a mile a minute as she tries to ascertain if I'm going to scold her or not.

However, the conversation is both more simple and more complicated than a reprimand. There are things I'm perfectly aware that Sophia doesn't know about moving into a relationship, and I don't think those things are proper breakfast conversation. Colonel Gallagher has told me before that he's never been with a woman, never kissed a woman, never touched a woman intimately, and I'm not about to be the person to explain to him—and Sophia—how to do that. They can figure the specific details out themselves, as they have clearly already started down that path.

"Alone," I repeat instead of clarifying that I'm going to teach her how to make a contraceptive potion and don't want Colonel Gallagher around when I do that. Huntley's young ears are still in the room, and though I may not be motherly, I do have a shred of common sense.

Huntley chooses this moment to look up from the spoons and his now-empty bowl. "Do I go now, Soapy?"

Sophia nods tenderly, stepping forward to the table and picking up the bowl. "Yes, you can go play if you like."

The little boy slides down from the big chair before he waddles off with a handful of spoons toward the hallway. I watch as he plunks himself down in the corridor between the front room and the kitchen, just out of earshot, and Sophia props the door open, presumably to keep an eye on him. There's a clatter of metal as he drops the utensils to the floor and then giggles with joy.

We stand around the kitchen in silence until the tea kettle whistles.

As Sophia removes it from the stove, Colonel Gallagher speaks. "I should pack my things and get my horse. I appreciate the hospitality and understanding."

"No tea?" Sophia asks, a sliver of desperation in her voice as she places the kettle down. I recognize what she's doing—she doesn't want him to leave just yet. She's experiencing the first fragments of love and desire for a man, and her mind and her heart are fighting for him to stay.

Colonel Gallagher shakes his head, running a finger along her hand delicately and discreetly. As he touches her, there's a little golden spark that escapes from Sophia's hand, which surprises me because she's usually so good at controlling her magic.

"It'll be fine. I'll stop for a rest halfway and grab something at a pub."

"Okay." She peers down at his hand, and I decide that's my cue to leave so they can have a moment alone.

"I'll go feed and ready your horse," I note. However, neither of them is truly listening to me. The entire kitchen could probably be on fire and they wouldn't be aware of it because they're so caught up in one another.

Stepping over Huntley and his spoon brigade, I slip on some shoes and head out the door and toward the stable. The sun has risen over the hills near Padraig's—ugh, *Padraig*—and is shining a beautiful cloudy yellow over top of the wildflowers. Little globes of dew run along the tops of the emerald blades of grass, the lawn damp with morning glory and mist. It wouldn't be as beautiful if I hadn't just spent the night with Max, though I already miss him terribly.

I shake my head like I'm trying to rattle out the thoughts of Max's mouth on mine, and his mouth everywhere else on my skin.

It'll be a nice day for Colonel Gallagher to ride back to Edinburgh.

I enter the stables, and the nicker of a big, bay mare greets me, her pretty head peeking over the edge of one of the wooden stall doors. We haven't had many horses of our own since Father passed away, which is rather unfortunate as I've always quite enjoyed their company. A few months after he died, Mother said we didn't need as many animals to care for as we wouldn't be riding and traveling as much, but I've always wondered if it's because they reminded her of him. Besides his library of books and the piano in the formal front room, the horses were his adored companions. Plus, they were a way for us to connect with one another in the wide-open spaces of the moors.

Now, Mother takes our two remaining horses and the carriage when she goes visiting, and coming to this side of the property always feels a little empty without Hazel and Charlie roaming in their field.

Tossing a few handfuls of hay onto the floor to amuse Colonel Gallagher's mare before I dig out two scoops of grain from a covered bucket on the dirt floor, I can't help but wonder what Max is doing right now. *How does a man cursed to be a cat spend his day until he can turn into his human form again?* I suppose a cat would normally sleep and run about while chasing down their meals, but for some reason, I can't imagine Max's cat form hunting mice or small birds. I picture him as more refined than that, like a man drinking wine and consuming appetizers at a casual party.

Lost in thought, I only realize how much time has passed once Colonel Gallagher enters the stables. The mare has just taken her final bites of her oats and I'm about to slip her bridle on when I notice the silhouette in the open doorway.

"You're good with her," he notes.

I notice his lips are red again, and I know that means he's been kissing Sophia. Hopefully, Huntley didn't see that because even though he might be little, he knows enough to tell Mother if he sees something he's not supposed to.

"Did you expect something different?" I don't mean for my tone to sound as flat as it does because that would normally indicate disappointment. I'm not disappointed, I'm just occupied, both with thoughts of Max and of what's going to happen next.

Colonel Gallagher shrugs, shifting his kit bag over his shoulder. He's trying to make small talk with me, which is kind but unnecessary at this point. "Do you ride?"

"I can, yes," I reply as I slip the crown piece gently over the mare's ears and then begin to buckle the latch at her throat. The term "ride" has a different meaning after tying Max to my bed last night and finding a rhythm over his hips, but I do my best not to flush as I think about that—or that Colonel Gallagher might have heard fragments of that event. If I was aware that he was going to overhear Max and me having sex, I might have tried to muffle my moans a little more. "It's been a long while."

He watches me fiddle with the bridle for a moment before I push open the stall door and hand him the horse's reins. We're careful not to touch one another, and there's something unwritten and unsaid in the way we speak—like we're keeping a secret from the world but it isn't to do with one another.

"I appreciate you not being upset." Colonel Gallagher fastens his luggage to the saddle before unrolling his stirrups. "I didn't want to upset you. That was never my intent. In all honesty, my intent was… well, not any of this."

I think about telling him that I wasn't being nearly as considerate about his feelings.

I don't.

But I *think* about it.

Instead, I say, "I know you'll take good care of Sophia once we figure out the specifics."

Colonel Gallagher nods, checking the saddle's girth before leading his mare out into the early morning sunshine. I follow behind, my dress dragging in the soft dirt, until we make it to a worn patch of grass near the fence lining the property. I hold his horse as he mounts, though I probably don't need to because the animal is so quiet that she simply stands and waits as he gathers up his reins and his feet find the stirrups.

"I do hope you find happiness, Ellie." Colonel Gallagher gives his mare a little pat as he speaks. "And I hope you find a way to break free from Blossom and everything else it is that you're fighting against."

I release my grasp on the reins near the horse's bit, nodding. "I'll see you when you come back to bring me there. Hopefully, we'll have come to some kind of arrangement by that point. I might not even be here. Maybe I'll run off to the seaside and live with the cats before then."

"I think that would make you very happy indeed."

An awkward pause follows, filled with the sounds of rustling tall grass and leaves and nothingness.

"Well, safe travels, then," I say.

"Take care."

Colonel Gallagher taps his boots against the bay mare's sides, and together, they trot off down the path leading up and over the hill past Padraig's and toward Edinburgh. However, I notice once he's just far enough away that he might think I don't notice, he looks over his shoulder toward our house. Probably in hopes of seeing Sophia.

When I enter the house after the horse and rider have disappeared over the crest of the moors, Sophia meets me at the door. I barely have time to remove my shoes before she is asking question after question. I don't have time to absorb any of them because she's talking so fast, and for a split second, I find myself curious as to when she turned from the serious rule-follower into the sister who can't get a man out of her head. Of course, I already know the answer—yesterday. Yesterday or this morning or late in the evening when she and Colonel Gallagher definitely kissed... at least.

"Where are the children?" I ask, interrupting Sophia's ramble.

"Upstairs with their—"

Cutting her off, I keep talking. "Good. Go to my room. I'll be there in a minute with some tea. There's something we need to talk about."

"Are you mad? You said you weren't mad..." Sophia trails off, picking at the edge of her thumb.

"Would you just go upstairs? I need a minute, and I think you do too."

She doesn't ask any more questions after that. Instead, Sophia takes off up the steps. A moment later, as I'm listening to make sure she does as I said, she crashes into my bedroom and the decrepit reading chair skids along the floor with a noisy slide. The sound satisfies me, and I pour the two cups of tea I promised. Carrying them up to the bedroom proves tricky as I'm starting to realize I'm exhausted from staying up all night with Max.

I manage to only spill a little onto the saucers as I walk into my bedroom and unceremoniously kick the door halfway closed.

Crossing the room, I set the tea on the nightstand before it strikes me that the room is messier than usual. My blankets are everywhere, the length of green ribbon is still on my mattress and partially tied to my headboard, and there are condom wrappers strewn along the bedside. It's more than completely obvious what happened here last night and early this morning, the breeze wafting through the open window Max escaped from not all that long ago.

"You said you weren't mad, Ellie. You're acting so strange that I can only assume that might not be true." Sophia looks disgusted at the state of my room, but I don't care. I fling a blanket over the disheveled bed and sit down.

"Shut up, I'm thinking."

She stops talking and leans back in the battered chair, her clothes wrinkled from what I can only assume were Iain's hands. I'm not even sure how to start this conversation that I'm certain as hell our mother never gave her. I had to figure out everything on my own with other men in my time before Padraig, and it was a difficulty and a surprise that Sophia doesn't need to face.

"Let me explain something to you," I start, fidgeting with my dress before I rest my elbows on my knees.

"You're mad at us, aren't you?"

"For fuck's sake, Sophia." I throw my hands up and lean back again. I thought this was going to be a simple—though awkward—conversation where I temporarily had to parent Sophia for once instead of her being the adult. "Would you stop asking me that? If nothing else, your incessant worrying about the way I feel is what's going to make me angry."

Sophia looks down at her feet and kicks a ripped wrapper away from her like it's poisonous. "Fine."

"But no, I'm not mad. To be clear."

She smiles a little but still doesn't look up.

"Like I was saying, let me explain something to you. You need to know a few things about... being intimate. Like how to brew a contraceptive potion."

All the color immediately drains from Sophia's face. "I don't—I don't even think that's something we're considering, Ellie. I shouldn't—I shouldn't even be talking about this with you. I'm not—"

I can't help the laugh that escapes me because Sophia's so inexperienced and raw in her emotions. She simply doesn't understand what awaits her—either that, or she does and she's trying to fool me. "You're not me; you're not reckless or a deviant or whatever word you want to use to describe people who do the things that I do. I know that. And I know you want children, but I promise you that you're going to want to do a lot of things with Colonel Gallagher once you realize how enjoyable those things are. Like kissing him and—"

"Ellie, I am going to jump out of that window right now if you say another word."

"But you two kissed?" I take a sip of tea and wait for a response as Sophia's face turns the color of a summer tomato.

"You kiss lots of people!"

I do my best not to laugh because the response is exactly the kind that I would have once given. "This is why you need to know how to brew a contraceptive potion to keep in your bedside. It's not like Mother is going to show you how to do this, so you can either learn from me or you can try to figure it out for yourself later."

Sophia deflates and nods, but her face doesn't get any less red. She hides behind her teacup, taking a long taste of the hot liquid that I'm sure scalds her tongue.

"Open the drawer," I start. "Inside the silver sachet are vials of contraceptives. You're going to take one unless you promise right this second that nothing else happened between you and Colonel Gallagher."

"I swear, Ellie. Nothing else happened. We talked and we kissed and that was it."

Nodding, I nudge open the drawer, and Sophia places her tea back on the table. She dips her hand in, removes the large pouch, and unties the strings, pulling out one of the small, sparkling vessels.

"You made this?"

"I did."

She holds the cork in and tips the vial back and forth in between her fingers, the shimmering liquid sloshing about inside the glass. "It's... quite pretty, actually."

"I added a little extra magic to it. It smells horrible but the flavor is tolerable. The mixture tastes like pears, by the way."

Sophia finally meets my gaze, and she offers me a little smile. "You don't like pears. Always said they were too grainy in your mouth."

"I said tolerable for a reason."

She shifts the concoction in the sunlight, little rays glowing through the apothecary vial and sparkling against the contents. The clear glass casts a spotty reflection against the floor, and for a moment, I almost forget that I'm sitting in my room having a conversation about intimacy with my younger sister.

"So how do I make this? I presume I need some special herb or flower or something from the garden? The most advanced potion I've made is strawberry-rhubarb tea. I'm not even sure I can identify all the flowers out there. That was more your thing with Father than it was mine."

"It's not that complicated, Sophia. Having the ability to make proper tea is perfect. The contraceptive is basically a magic tea, if you want to think about it like that. Everything else that we need, I keep in this room for a reason."

Sophia looks around, her gaze landing on the satin ribbon partially tied to the rung on my headboard. "I sure as hell hope that the other ingredients aren't things you used last night during your escapades with Max."

I roll my eyes. "I don't think that dried roses and enchanted loch water are exactly the type of thing that would make most people feel—"

"Please stop." The words are serious but she's giggling. "Spare me the details of the things that make you feel… that way."

"So what you're saying is that you don't want me to tell you—"

"Ellie!"

The two of us burst into laughter. It feels good to laugh with her again. It's been much too long since we connected like this. In fact, I can't really remember the last instance. It feels like it must have been years ago, before Huntley and

Pippa were born. Before everything got so complicated with Padraig and Blossom.

"Sophia?"

She smiles her brilliant smile and pushes a curl away from her still-flushed cheek. "Yes?"

"You know Colonel Gallagher will take care of you, right? He's a good man."

"I thought so. He's so gentle and kind. I think he'd be a good match, even if he wasn't the right match for you. Plus, maybe Max will be able to take you to the seaside. He seems like the seaside type."

"He does, doesn't he?"

The moment she says this, I begin to drown in thoughts of running away again. Thoughts of living in a little ocean-front cottage that we've taken over with whatever money we've procured. Thoughts of having a world to ourselves where we live among crashing waves and the invisibility of the breeze and the careful quiet of being together. These thoughts only last for a moment before Sophia's voice breaks through my contemplations.

"Ellie, are you okay?"

I find myself nodding a bit longer than necessary before I fully come back to real life. "Absolutely. Now, let me show you how to make that potion."

Chapter Seventeen

MAX

Daylight lasts too long in the summer, an unfair exchange for the short nights I get to devote to Ellie. She and I spend several wordless evenings together, and when I return from my time with her, I purposefully avoid the rest of the *Clodder*. They don't need to see me in a state of post-intimacy bliss, and I don't need to try to act normal in front of them. Therefore, I rest on the seashore—alone—during the day before traveling back to the Callaghan house once the sun starts to go down.

Because of my disconnected nature, it's a week before I come across Alastair once again. Despite the fact that he often frequents the breakwater where I've made myself comfortable during many long afternoons, I suspect I failed to spot him because he spends so much of his time in the abandoned basement apothecary. Additionally, based on our last interaction, it seems as if there's a lot going on in his head, and to be fair, there's a lot going on in mine, too. This particular morning, though, he manages to stop me.

I've already changed into my black cat form and am plodding along the edge of the seagrass as the high tide begins to wane.

"Ah, Maximilian."

I have a sense of déjà vu as I see Alastair sitting in between the long, dried brown blades of grass. The ocean's spray isn't as forceful this morning as it was over the past few days, waves lapping quietly at the rocky shoreline and barely touching the bottom of the breakwater. However, as I approach, I can see that Alastair's paws are damp, which means he's either taken himself for a long walk among the dewdrops or gone fishing for scraps along the coast.

"Good to see you," I say.

"It's been a while, hasn't it? Few days, at least."

I nod, taking a seat on the rock next to him before scratching an itch behind my ear.

"This disappearance from the *Clodder* must have something to do with the Callaghan girl, then?" Alastair asks pointedly. He's never been one to mince words, even if some of the things he says come out more poetic than others.

I rub at the ticklish spot for longer than necessary, using the diversion to try and think of what might be considered the correct response to his question. I suppose Alastair's going to be able to tell if I'm being honest, no matter what I say. He has that way about him—the feeling in his bones that he always mentions. The only feeling I have in my bones right now is that I want longer nights with Ellie and shorter days here at the church on the seaside without her.

A rogue wave comes precariously close to our feet, and I lick at my mouth to get a hint of the salty air. It's then that I realize I can still taste Ellie's most recent parting kiss. The flavor of the stolen cherry wine we shared in her bed has lingered so long now that I swear she's managed to enchant it.

I can feel Alastair's gaze drilling into the side of my head. "You don't have to say anything about the last few days. I can read it all over your face."

"There's nothing to read."

"Except about ten thousand unspoken words."

I can't help but let out a long exhale. "You're a master of unspoken words, Alastair. There are so many things you could have told me that you simply haven't."

"For example?" He's challenging my statement in a delicate way that only Alastair knows how to do. A way that reminds me he's heard everything, seen everything, experienced everything and still manages to exist here in the lochs and not completely give up… while keeping most things tucked away deep inside.

"About the woman you loved, for example."

His whiskers bristle, and I know it isn't because of the breeze. For a moment, I think that maybe I've stepped too far; pushed a little too much about something he hasn't dared to speak about to me before. But the ginger cat's outward demeanor doesn't change—at least not perceptibly. He sits stock-still, staring out across the ocean to whatever exists on the other side of the world. A brief look of loss and grief and pain flickers across his gaze, but it happens so fast that I almost completely miss it.

"She isn't important right now," he finally says, shifting his weight from one paw to the other.

"That's what you always claim."

"Because it's true."

I sigh for real this time. "Except for moments like now when I can tell that it's not."

"Maximilian, you're pushing your luck. There's nothing for me to say about her. Lydia was a Bèist, I loved her, and she loved me back," Alastair replies.

My pulse quickens as I realize he's spoon-feeding me pieces of information—perhaps intentionally, and perhaps not. "She has a name, then."

Alastair hesitates, and I don't say anything more because I want to offer him the opportunity to get out any thoughts of this Lydia that he's willing to offer me. It's a rare look into what's going on in his mind behind the façade of his emotional strength. This seems to be the ideal choice because a few instants later, he finally speaks over the sound of water rushing across the pebbles.

"Don't we all have names? Just some aren't allowed to be said with the belief that we are expendable because we wouldn't bend to the rules of society."

It is ludicrous, as it's always been. But then again, perhaps believing in fairytales long after your childhood is nonsensical as well.

"Why can you say hers, then? Is she still a cat?"

Alastair doesn't break his gaze from the spot where the sea and sky meet in the distance. He shakes his head. "No. She's not. Blossom caught up to us as her curse broke and naturally afflicted me instead. An eye for an eye, a Bèist for a Bèist, and so on."

"Is that why you said with Ellie and me… that they'd have to catch us first?"

The glaze that had started to form over his eyes is blinked away. "You'll always be on the run with her. Absconders of your prescribed futures."

"I'm fine with that," I reply.

Alastair blinks at me, his look serious. "But is Ellie? You don't want to end up in a scenario where you sacrifice yourself for nothing. Because there's always a chance that Blossom already has their eye on her and will find *you* no matter where you go. Will curse you both. Will find a way to separate you. Will take your life for your disobedience."

The moment Alastair says that Blossom might have their eye on us, I think of Padraig and his position at the school. I'm certain he has something to do with overseeing the rules and regulations, despite being a newer addition to the group of administrators and to the board at large. If he's part of a coordinated effort to monitor those who are cursed and those who are about to attend Blossom, it would make sense that he's been keeping a close watch—and then some—on Ellie.

If we can get away from him, and get away from Scotland, Ellie and I might be able to find freedom. We might be able to escape the boundaries of Blossom's rule on society, which most certainly doesn't extend beyond the country's borders. I'm almost completely positive of this because I've heard the gossip and rumors and news—England and Scotland are negotiating the very existence of Blossom and the lack of autonomy for those who show any independence from its laws.

"I'm not worried about curses. I'd burn the world down for Ellie, Alastair."

"But would you die for her?"

Death never crossed my mind, possibly because I'd been naïve in believing that we wouldn't get caught. But Alastair is right—if Blossom catches Ellie and me, they'll almost certainly turn her into a Bèist and then do worse to me.

But would I die for her?

I mull the question over in my head, allowing it to stir up as many thoughts as possible because it's an inquiry that requires deeper consideration. Despite walking through the scenarios in which I would die for Ellie, only one situation sticks in my mind, and it's not about death—it's about life.

Would I live for her?

As the query sits in my heart, I become wholly aware that the two are connected. And because they're connected, my body and soul scream a single resounding answer—*yes*. Yes, I would live for her. Yes, I would give up every breath in my body for her. Yes, I would die for her... but would I live? Absolutely.

"Without a doubt in my mind," I answer. But then it strikes me that there's so much more to say than that, and the words flow from my mouth like I'm writing a poem Ellie will never get to hear. "I'd crash a thousand Blossom Preparatory Academy meetings and profess my love for her just to die again and again in her affections. I would drown myself in this ocean if it meant she didn't have to take the hand of someone out of obligation rather than desire. I would bury myself alive in the gardens of Loch Gàrraidh if it meant I could be with her every day of my life."

"I don't know what that last one is supposed to mean, Maximilian," Alastair says with a smile. "But I think I get your point."

I smile as I look away from the old cat, gazing out across the grand expanse of waves and sea and clouds. We sit along the coastline for a long while, a gray coating of sea salt collecting on our fur and whiskers. I can't be certain, but I imagine that Alastair is thinking about this woman who left him. A piece of me wants to ask him more about Lydia, but I think he will say what he wants when he's ready.

The prolonged silence between us is comfortable but different from the kind of ease I feel when I'm simply existing with Ellie. Different from the way I felt when she and

I were in bed last night, noiselessly drinking the cherry wine she took from her family's cellar. The taste of it was identical to the drink we had at the party, and identical to the way I remember her lips tasting during our first kiss.

Maybe she stains her lips with the wine, and that's how they get to be the perfect red.

I think about this for longer than I've ever thought about a woman's mouth before.

As the sun begins to shift to its mid-noon position, I curl myself into a ball in a flattened nest of seagrass. The brackish air wafts up my nose and smells like seaweed and fish and something I can't quite put my finger—*paw?*—on.

I don't have time to identify the scent because Alastair speaks again, and that listening to what he has to say feels more important than sniffing the ocean. The ocean will always be here at the edge of Scotland. Alastair might not.

"Lydia was a beautiful woman when I met her." The words hang heavy in the briny breeze. "Whip-smart and wild, like your Ellie. That might be where she gets her recklessness from. Though I can't imagine Lydia would ever admit to living that kind of life before her curse was broken, so Ellie would be none the wiser."

Alastair shifts his weight again, like he's in an uncomfortable position on the rocks. It's either that or he's distressed about the direction the conversation is headed. I can't quite tell which might be more accurate. Alastair's body always seems to be aching, but now I can't help but wonder if his heart is the thing that hurts the most.

"I've been to the Callaghan house. A long time ago, but I don't think I ever told you that. Took a nighttime walk through the gardens and drank from the loch and wondered if I'd ever be brave enough to tell Lydia that I still feel for her. That I still have dreams about her."

It's around this moment that I recognize what Alastair is saying doesn't quite make sense. How would Ellie get her recklessness from a woman who failed out of Blossom years ago, back when Alastair was young? What would visiting the Callaghan house have to do with any of this? I can't see the relation between the things he's saying, and I'm immediately concerned that perhaps something more is happening than just an old man recalling hazy memories.

"Alastair, are you okay?" I sit up from the spot where I had only recently made myself comfortable, and he looks back at me and nods.

"You might as well be made aware, Maximilian. About Lydia and what happened between us. Especially if you and Ellie are growing increasingly serious, as I suspect you are based on the lies you're trying to tell me about the past several days."

"Not lies, just... personal details."

Alastair hums to himself, a grin quirking at the corners of his lips. "Like I said. Your expression gives you away, even if you aren't actually revealing anything with your words. Plus, I saw what happened with your hands in the field. Your magic is coming back. It wouldn't do that for just anyone."

"You saw?"

"I think most of the *Clodder* saw. They haven't been completely ignorant to the fact that you've all but disappeared."

I do my best to change the subject because I don't want to delve too deeply into that topic. Instead, my catlike curiosity is getting the best of me about Alastair's past. "Does Lydia have something to do with Ellie? Do they know each other somehow?"

"They do know each other." There's a long pause, one that makes me think Alastair is either waiting for me to understand the insinuation of his words or is attempting to find the right thing to say that will explain the connection. Maybe both.

The hesitation lasts too long for my patience.

"How, Alastair?"

He sucks in a deep breath of ocean air, filling his old lungs with the salty breeze as I do my best to wait for the answer. It only takes a second for him to gather his thoughts, but when he divulges the truth, it hits me like a rogue wave.

"Lydia is Ellie's mother," he says.

A powerful and invisible swell feels as if it is cascading over me. I'm frozen to the spot as I process the information, and I'm certain my heart is going to burst from between my ribs, cracking my bones and spraying them out into the sea. *There's no way this could be possible. From everything*

I've heard about the way she treats Ellie, there's just no way she could be Alastair's Lydia.

"Ellie's mother, the one who says Ellie is insolent and reckless and needs to be sent to Blossom, was a *Bèist*?" I'm surprised I even manage to get the words out because my mind is throbbing with a sudden influx of thoughts. *There must be some mistake.*

But when Alastair nods, I know he's telling the truth. There can only be so many Lydias in Scotland and in Loch Gàrraidh.

"She was the wildest of all of us in that class, Maximilian. Lydia dared the administration and the governance of Blossom to turn her. Wanted to be changed just to get the process over with. They took their time with it; I think they were under the impression they could tame her. It was like she was a conquest for them to prove their superiority. But they didn't know that Lydia didn't need taming. She needed understanding."

There's no mistake. It's Ellie's story all over again.

"And you understood her?" I question.

"Something like that. At least, I thought I did. I still find myself wondering if she manipulated my love to get back at Blossom's outdated rules for a proper society."

I don't know what to say in response. There aren't any words that feel right; no apology, no consolation. Just stillness and our shared existence and understanding. Or an attempt at grasping the way that Alastair's been feeling all this time—years longer than I've been here at the church and the seaside. Years that he's been hurting both physically and emotionally by his own aging body and sharp nostalgia.

I just can't believe that Lydia is Ellie's mother, and that there's so much of a connection between the lochs and the seaside. I've been with Ellie's mother in the kitchen before, with her serving up breakfast and leaving a little bowl of goat milk for me on the floor. At dinner, she often drops small pieces of cooked meat on purpose for tasting. Sometimes she even offers me a scratch on the head as she wandered through the house in her own thoughts. She never seemed like the rebellious type, but more like an overwhelmed mother who was dealing with four children who depended on her for a proper future. A future that may not have turned out the way she expected once her curse was lifted.

"What do you think would happen if you showed yourself to her?" I finally ask. It's a question he would ask me if I was in the same situation so it seems like a good place to start.

"I don't know. It's too late to be considering such matters. And this isn't about me anyway; this conversation was supposed to be about you and Ellie and whatever your plans are going to be."

I let out a breath, looking up at the fluffy clouds dotting the sky. There's a tinge of gray to them, a telling sign of rain to come. "Fair enough. But there's no definite plan yet. Just pieces of a plan that we're trying to put together."

"I'd make a decision before your magic completely returns. By that point, it might be too late to try to get away."

"You think it can really happen that quickly?"

Alastair nods. "I have a feeling that Blossom already knows that your magic has started showing itself again. I can't say for certain—it could just be my own superstition that they have eyes and ears everywhere in Scotland."

"But do you feel that superstition in your bones?" I smile at the joke, my whiskers twitching in amusement as I look at the ginger cat on the breakwater. Despite my joking undertone, my belief that Padraig's association with Blossom's "all-seeing eye" is only growing stronger. "Your bones haven't been wrong yet."

"They've been wrong before, Maximilian. Just they're old and rickety now so they have to say things a little louder."

"You make it sound like you're a million years old."

"I make it sound like that so you're reminded I won't be here forever, and you shouldn't be either. If you can run, I'd encourage you to do that. It's not the easiest path to take for the rest of your life, and maybe you won't want to run forever. But the lochs are no place for real love. The only type of love supported here is based on obligation, duty, burden, and sacrifice."

With that, Alastair rises from his seated position and stretches out, his front legs first, and then the back ones, before yawning. "I'll leave you to your plans. But maybe don't run off without saying goodbye. I wouldn't want to spend the rest of my life here staring out to sea and wondering if you made it free from Loch Gàrraidh."

I can't tell if he's referring to me or if he's thinking of Lydia.

"Understood. I'll be sure to come back before going anywhere else. Even if it's just briefly."

Alastair smiles, though it's a difficult expression for a cat to hold. "You're a good cat, Max. But I think you're an even better man. You're going to achieve great things, even if you do have to run away to accomplish them."

I think that's the closest Alastair's going to get to telling me that he'll miss me when I go, so I just nod as he walks away toward the church, storing his words in my soul.

Chapter Eighteen

SOPHIA

A FEW DAYS HAVE passed since Ellie's shown me how to make the contraceptive potion, and I've been doing my best to master it whenever the children are sleeping. I've managed to get the taste of pears to be much stronger than in my sister's mixture, which does a little to mask the terrible smell. I figure if I can trick my nose into thinking the liquid is made of fruit, maybe my tastebuds will cooperate as well. It's strange, though, relating with Ellie over something like this. Up until recently, I was convinced she was the deviant—the only one disinterested in living within the rules of society. But now, here I am, stealing her betrothed and making potions so I have the opportunity to be intimate without yet starting a family of my own.

The thought of it all makes me smile as I sit on the rock wall outside the kitchen. There's something nice about bonding with Ellie, even if the way we are connecting is more than a bit unexpected.

Because Mother is coming home this evening, I've let the children stay up late to play on the upper lawn and await her arrival. The night is just rolling in, the sunlight fading into an uncommon dusky blue mixed with rose pink that predicts a clear, starry night and a beautiful morning tomorrow. I'm both present and not—thoughts of Iain, his words, and his kiss taking over my mind as I absently watch the little ones.

Huntley and Pippa have been amusing themselves for the past long while playing in the grass. They've already cycled through picking weeds from the gardens and flinging the stems into the air, now tiring themselves out by running in circles and giggling. If nothing else, they'll sleep well once they get over the excitement of Mother being home from her trip to see Aunt Matilda.

Huntley stops and Pippa crashes into him, falling to the lawn with a laugh as he points up to the sky. "Look, Soapy, moon!"

I peer up into the approaching darkness. Above our heads is the shimmering shape of the moon, a bit pale since it's not quite nighttime. "You're right, that's the moon."

"Not time for moon!" Huntley cackles and falls to the grass with Pippa like he's just told me the best joke in all of Scotland. Moments later, the two of them are rolling around in the remnants of the garden weeds, fluff and leaves sticking to their clothes.

As I adjust my position on the wall, Ellie steps out through the open kitchen door with a cup of tea in her hand. The perfect amount of steam rises from the rim, a splash spilled on the saucer in true Ellie fashion.

"For you," she notes, sitting the floral-patterned teacup on the ledge.

"Thanks." I nod toward Huntley and Pippa, who have resumed running in circles. "You think Mother will be upset that I let them stay awake until she arrives? I couldn't bring myself to put them to bed. They're just too excited."

Ellie shakes her head. "Let them be wild while they still have the chance."

Smiling, I lift the tea to my lips and take a small sip of the hot liquid. It's strong, just the way I like it, and I feel it warm up my insides as it goes down.

"Listen, Sophia, I have something I've been thinking about the last few days."

"Something about Max?" There's a little *clink* as I replace the cup on the saucer before looking up at Ellie, who hoists herself up on the edge of the rock wall. I swear by the rough way she does it that she's going to tear the pretty blue dress she's wearing.

"I'm capable of thinking about things other than Max," she says with a chuckle. "This is about you and Colonel Gallagher."

"You can call him Iain, you know," I reply.

"Feels too strange. Like we're still betrothed or something. I can't imagine calling any military man by his first name."

She has a point, I suppose. It would be strange calling a uniformed man by his first name if one didn't have a relationship with him, and despite the fact that Ellie is still technically betrothed to Iain, I don't think she would consider her few meetings with him under our mother's supervision as "having a relationship."

"What have you been thinking about then if your mind and body and bed haven't only been occupied with Max?" I grin in her direction, and she gives me a playful nudge with her shoulder.

Ellie looks out over the gardens for a moment, into the distance where Loch Gàrraidh glimmers with the reflection of the dying day. "I think you should go with him when he comes to pick me up for Blossom. You can go with him to see England when he's sent there. You can do so many things once you're away from here, and there are no guarantees that Mother would ever find someone any nicer and kinder than Colonel Gallagher. I know it's fast. I know you're more the patient type, but I can't help but worry…"

As she trails off in thought, I furrow my brow. "What's worrying you?"

"Everything and nothing. But mainly that I'm going to run away with Max and I hate that you'll be left behind."

There's anxiety in Ellie's voice, which is something I don't recall hearing in her tone ever before, and yet I recognize it for what it is. Usually, she's so confident—and stubborn—about anything she's planning that it's not worth arguing with her about the fact that it might not be the best idea. However, I feel like I could tell her not to go and she wouldn't. But then she would have gone somewhere either way… to Blossom, instead of to the seaside, which is where I'm sure he'll take her since it's where Ellie's always wanted to be.

"I'm not surprised you're planning on leaving with him."

"You're not?"

I shake my head. "You don't love Iain. You love Max, and he loves you. Deeply and most ardently, from what I've overheard."

Ellie rolls her eyes, clearly aware of the evening events that I'm referencing. "We've been here at the house for our entire lives, Sophia. I can hardly bear the idea of being away from the lochs without you to keep an eye on me."

"You only needed my eye on you because you were engaging with men like Padraig. You'll be fine on your own with Max."

"And you'll be fine with *Iain*." Ellie smiles, putting emphasis on his proper name. "That is, if you want to go with him."

Do I want to go with him?

The question sits in my heart, but the feeling is light and full of joy. Of course I want to go away with Iain. I've wanted to go away with Iain since the moment he wrapped my hand in the kitchen. He's kind and good-natured and was willing to give Ellie a soft place to land despite it not being what he wanted for the rest of his life. He's loyal to our society, loves children, and is not too proud. A proper man that Mother and Father already approved of. Not for me, mind you, but approved of nonetheless.

But there's even more than that. There's more than him just being kind and good-natured and selfless. I find him ridiculously handsome, and I don't want to keep my hands away from him, which amuses me since I recall telling Ellie and Max to keep their hands off one another the night of the party. Perhaps I didn't realize how difficult something like that could be when one finds another they're so attracted to. And even more than the physical, there's the emotional. The way he makes me feel and the way that I feel about him. Like we're meant to be together and we fit together perfectly.

So yes, I absolutely want to go away with Iain. I want to support him in England as he's doing his training for work, learning the ropes of negotiating agreements between countries and other complicated matters. I could tend to wherever we live during that period—a small apartment in the city, maybe—and read books and cook dinner and have a proper relationship. More than anything, I want to get out of the lochs with him and start our own home where I can picture a future that makes me feel… happy. Secure. Successful.

Therefore, I nod.

"I've always wanted to see the world outside of Scotland," I reply. The sun is sinking below the edge of the horizon now, the moon becoming more prominent as Huntley points at it again. I don't know what he's showing Pippa, but the two of them are quiet as they watch the sky change colors. "I want to experience places in real life instead of through Father's books. And Iain is a wonderful man, from what I've seen. I'd rather take the chance to be happy now than later be forced into marrying someone I despise or who is cruel."

"And that's okay. It's okay to want to risk it. Taking advantage of possibilities isn't the worst thing in the world, despite what we've been taught to believe."

"Plus," I say with a small grin, "he's the first man who's ever made me feel interested in brewing a contraceptive potion."

Ellie laughs, and the sound echoes through the night.

A little time passes before there's the sound of a carriage approaching—horses' hooves clip-clopping on the packed dirt road that leads to the front of the house and then the stables. I can only assume this means that Mother will be home any moment. I slide down from the wall and call the children so I can attempt to brush the dust and grass off their clothes prior to her arrival.

"Guess who's almost home?"

Both the children whip around at my words before running to clutch my dress and bounce up and down. I'm glad I didn't pick up the hot tea before I said anything.

"Mama!" Pippa squeals, and Huntley's eyes light up.

"Yes, you're right," I reply, kneeling on the grass and running a hand over Huntley's back to remove the shredded weeds. "You see that dark spot near the neighbors' house? That's Mama coming home with Hazel and Charlie. We have to go inside now and get ready for her."

The two children toddle into the kitchen as fast as their tired little legs will carry them, leaving Ellie and me to follow close behind so they don't get into any trouble. When I look over my shoulder, Ellie's picked up my tea and is carrying it toward the house, allowing me to focus on Huntley and Pippa, who awkwardly climb the steps to get through the back door. Once they're inside, Ellie's caught up to us and sets the tea on the table, the kitchen aglow and warm with a small fire still in the stove. Huntley stifles a yawn as Pippa rubs at her eyes, the two of them calming down from their play outside.

"Are you sure you both can stay awake until Mama gets here?" I ask, guiding the children through the room and toward the door that leads to the hall. "I can put you both up in bed and you can see her in the morning if you want."

Huntley and Pippa shake their heads, though Pippa looks at Huntley first, presumably to see what he chooses.

"No, it's time for Mama!" Huntley's little voice is loud, and I pretend to be taken aback by his volume.

"Okay, okay. Let's go out front then and wave as she comes down the road. Do you think we can wave the whole time?"

Huntley and Pippa nod and push against the door to the hallway, their little hands leaving fingerprints on the dark wood. I lean over top of them and give the door a little nudge, and the two of them collide in giggles before they totter toward the front of the house. Holding the door open with my shoulder, I look back at Ellie.

"You coming?" I ask.

"Should I?"

"I'm not going to say anything to her about what happened with Iain, if that's what you're worried about. I think that's something we can keep to ourselves for now. I can only imagine she'd blame..." My words trail off because I'm certain Ellie knows she would be blamed for something happening to the betrothal, despite the fact that it wasn't something she could have prevented. Not truly.

My sister nods. "She's going to ask, though. She's going to ask how the visit with Colonel Gallagher went and if I was a proper lady during it."

"And I'll tell her that you were. I've been covering for you for a long time, Ellie. I'm not worried about you doing the same for me."

Ellie smiles, and the two of us walk toward the formal front room where Huntley and Pippa have located two spoons. They must have been left over from several days ago when Iain was still here and we were rather preoccupied in the kitchen.

"Where'd you find spoons?" I ask Huntley as he raps the back of one against the front door. I thought I managed to clean up all the utensils that had been scattered along the first floor of the house, but I clearly missed those.

Tap, tap, tap.

I don't get a response from Huntley because he's too busy with his makeshift instrument, but Pippa points toward the couch as she starts to drum on the entryway as well.

Tap, tap, tap.

"Are we going to take our spoons to wave to Mama?" Ellie asks the children, but they ignore her. I think they're used to her barely existing in their world, so it's almost like she isn't a part of tonight. As she realizes they aren't going to respond, Ellie deflates, like she's feeling a bit sad that there's no connection between her and the little ones. I know the emotion won't last because I'm certain Ellie knows her departure from the lochs will be easier if she has fewer connections to break.

I open the door just as the carriage is coming into clear view. The two little ones step out onto the grass, sticking close to me as the large horses trot up to the front of the house. Pippa has her hand on my skirt, clutching her spoon with dedication, while Huntley waves his up in the air. Thankfully, both Hazel and Charlie are calm horses, and they aren't perturbed by Huntley's squeals and giggles as they are brought to a halt.

Mother opens the carriage door and steps out, gathering up her soft-sided luggage before smiling at all of us. She doesn't appear to be visibly upset that the children are still awake—something I'm grateful for.

"Ah, hello!" she greets us, and Huntley runs over to her, spoon in hand. She drops her bag on the lawn and scoops him up in her arms, swinging him back and forth as she gives him a kiss on the top of his head. "Did you miss Mama?"

He nearly whacks her with the utensil as she sways with him, and Mother laughs before she looks over at us. The time away from the house seems to have done her some good, and judging by her happy demeanor, I can only assume things went well while she was away. Hopefully, the cancer has been completely removed and the issue is now resolved.

"How are my girls?" Mother continues to shift her weight back and forth with Huntley as the hired cab driver takes the horses and carriage to the stable. "How was the meeting with Colonel Gallagher?"

If Ellie could shove me without being noticed, she would have done it already. She'd only do it to say "I told you so," but I don't need the physical reminder because her words are already echoing in my ears.

"It went well," I spit out before Ellie has a chance to say anything or for Mother to grow suspicious about Ellie and I swapping glances back and forth. "Everything is in order and *Colonel Gallagher* seems like a very kind man."

I nearly choke over using his title because it feels strange to call the man who I kissed so passionately anything other than Iain.

But it's not Ellie who says something next, or even Mother. It's Huntley.

"I liked the man!"

Mother chuckles as she places him back down on the ground, where he nearly wallops her accidentally with the spoon again. "You liked Colonel Gallagher, did you? Did you know he's a soldier?"

"Like my spoons! He and Soapy did *psst-psst-psst* in the kitchen."

It takes a second for Huntley's words to register, but when they do, I am drowning in a sense of dread. I know that he's not truly trying to tell Mother that Iain and I were whispering together in the kitchen because he is too little to understand exactly what that might infer, but I still feel an immediate need to address his childlike allegation.

Mother looks at Ellie, then she looks back at me, presumably for some kind of clarity. The look on Ellie's face implies that she'd like clarity too, but the expression is disingenuous. It reminds me of the stories she used to tell—and the appearance she would have—when she started using Allure and didn't want Mother to know she was high.

I wish I could put on a face like that right now, but I'm so transparent in my emotions that I'm sure everyone is looking at me for a clue. *What can I say that will make it seem as if Iain and I weren't up to something untoward? How many women whisper with men and it* isn't *something untoward?*

I blurt out the first thing I think of and hope it sticks.

"Shhh, Huntley! Remember, we said it was a surprise for the wedding? We can't let Ellie know the surprise."

Huntley claps his little hand over his mouth, eyes wide, despite that what I've just said is a lie. "Oh! Sorry, Soapy."

"That's okay. We can tell Mama later. But for now, let's bring her bag inside and then get ready for bed. We'll have lots of time to tell stories in the morning."

"Will you tell a story, Soapy?" Huntley asks as I absently pick up Mother's luggage before guiding the children into the house. Out of the corner of my eye, I spot a black cat coming across the grass, the pastel sunset glistening off the animal's coat. I know it's Max without Ellie even having to tell me. His green eyes practically shimmer, and though I notice them and their color clearly from the distance, they make me think of Iain's deep chestnut gaze instead.

Within moments, I'm lost in my own thoughts of kisses in my bedroom and Iain's knee pressing between my thighs and the fruity taste of the contraceptive potion that Ellie taught me to make. The memories are fresh and vibrant in my mind, so much so that I nearly trip while walking across the threshold, catching myself on the doorframe before I fall head over heels.

"Soapy?" Huntley's voice breaks through my reverie, and I place Mother's bag down in the corridor. "Story?"

Mother scoops curly-haired Pippa up in her arms before she looks down at the little boy who has sleepy eyes, ushering him and his soldier-spoon toward the kitchen door. "Let's give Sophia a break so she can get some rest. I'll put you two to bed and we can read a fairytale together. Say goodnight to your sisters."

Huntley gives Ellie and me a little wave with his utensil before he, Pippa, and Mother disappear into the kitchen.

We wait a few moments before speaking, listening for silence that lasts long enough to tell us they're all upstairs and out of earshot. Once it has passed, I'm the one who says something first.

"Max is waiting outside."

Ellie nods, her glance not quite meeting mine. "I saw him too. Hard to miss with those eyes."

"Maybe try and keep things down tonight if you plan on sticking around the house. I'm not sure I can explain away your intimate encounters for much longer. Especially after saying that things with Iain went well."

"You won't have to keep doing that. You'll just need to pack your things and be ready to stand up for yourself when Colonel Gallagher returns."

I exhale what feels like every ounce of oxygen in my lungs. "I know. That's the part I'm worried about. Everyone being upset with me."

"It'll all be resolved," Ellie replies. "One way or another."

She isn't wrong, but the realization doesn't make me any less scared. *What if Iain doesn't come back? What if he changes his mind? What if...*

My sister's voice cuts through my anxiety. "Sophia. Your magic is showing."

When I look down, little gold sparks are spitting from my fingers, the pinpricks of fire dancing in the moonlight.

Chapter Nineteen

ELLIE

After another few minutes, I finally sneak upstairs past Huntley and Pippa's bedroom, tiptoeing by the doorway where I can see my mother reading to the children from one of their copies of the infamous Blossom fairytale book.

It's strange to know that everything I rejected in those stories is likely true, though it's harder not to believe in the book's tales now that I know what Max is. Now that I understand the gravity of what the future will likely hold once we leave the lochs behind.

When I make it to the end of the hallway, Max is pacing around my bedroom, and I quickly close the door to offer us privacy. We've been enjoying these short summer nights together; bodies bare to one another as we kiss and touch and are intimate. Though I expect to turn around and find Max barely a step away from me with his fingers ready to unlace my dress, I am surprised that once I remove my hand from the latch, he hasn't stopped wandering from one side of the room to the other. His bright green eyes glimmer in the darkness, a single lantern glowing dimly against the far wall.

"Is everything alright?" I ask, keeping my voice low so Mother doesn't happen to overhear and assume I have a visitor that she wouldn't approve of. Max's frantic pacing is causing my heart to race—and not in the typical way I'd enjoy when we are alone. "You seem worried. Has something happened?"

He nods without hesitation. "I think you might want to sit down."

I'm fairly certain all the color drains from my cheeks at precisely that moment, my mind doing somersaults. *What if he's trying to tell me that he doesn't want to do this any longer? What if he doesn't want to run away? What if Blossom has gotten to him and made a deal? Does Blossom even make deals with those they've turned into a Bèist?*

"Is whatever you have to say that bad?"

Max finally stops stalking his way around the bedroom, pausing long enough for the lantern light to flicker off his raven-colored hair. "I don't know, Ellie. But I'm worried that it might be this time."

I cross the room and take a seat on my bed, trying to stay calm. "What's happened? Are you okay?"

He nods, wringing his hands. I've never seen him look so anxious and concerned. "I'm okay. I just... I learned something today from Alastair. You remember me telling you about him?"

I do recall a few stories about the wise old ginger cat, including some tales of his quirkiness and reclusive behavior, and not really wanting to engage with anyone other than Max. "Of course."

"He told me another story last night." Max heaves in a deep breath, keeping his voice low. However, the subsequent words fall out of his mouth so quickly that it takes me a moment to absorb what he's saying. "This time, he revealed something he's never spoken about before. He told me about his past and the woman who he became a cat for. Apparently, he wasn't the wild one at Blossom. It was her—the woman. He was so in love with her that he gave himself up to Blossom in exchange for her freedom, and she left him at the *Clodder*. Went off and married someone else and started a family."

Does he think that... somehow that could end up being us?

"Max, I trust that you would never—"

He gently cuts me off. "I don't think you're going to, believe me, but he says that the woman he sacrificed himself for was your mother."

There's a weighty pause between us, the ambient noise of the house coming through the walls accompanied, in my imagination, by the faint rumblings of Mother saying goodnight to Huntley and Pippa.

"What did you just say?" I whisper before running my hand along the side of my face to shift a stray lock of hair. *Did he just suggest that Mother was cursed before she met Father? That she was in love with someone else and allowed such a trade to occur on her behalf—an eye for an eye, a Bèist for a Bèist?*

"He knows her, Ellie. Alastair knows Lydia—your mother. They were... together, I guess. A while ago."

"Are you sure she's the same Lydia?" I don't know why I ask because everything in my body is screaming that it has to be. Max wouldn't lie to me, and everything about his posture and expression tells me this isn't something he's made up for the sake of a jest.

He nods. "Alastair confirmed it."

My mind is racing. Could this actually be true? Mother always told us that she had no connections to Blossom and neither did our father, but now I can't help but wonder. Now... I feel a prickling sensation in the back of my neck that seems to indicate that I should fight Max on this even being true. But Max wouldn't make up this story. Though, I did think that Mother wouldn't lie either. Now I'm not so sure. If she did, she'd be a hypocrite and a horrible parent for treating at least one of her children the way that she has. For telling me that I'm a deviant when she didn't live differently than how I do now. For treating Sophia like she's meant to care for Huntley and Pippa and have babies and her own home and do nothing else. And for Sophia fucking believing that.

"She wouldn't lie." I bite the inside of my cheek until I think I can taste the copper tang of blood. "There's no way that she would lie about something like that."

Max stares at me for a moment. "I'm sorry, Ellie. I think she might have."

At first, I don't know what reaction to have. My mother was cursed and she traded lives with a young man who loved her so she could have a human future and could escape from whatever the life of a cat entailed all those years ago? I can't imagine it's that much different now, based on the things Max has told me. A lonely and wistful existence with minimal connection to others and limitless wandering, waiting for... anything.

Max finally sits down in the shabby chair, placing his elbows on his knees and brushing his hands through his hair. I wish I could tell him that I'm not upset by this news, that it's not going to affect me, and that I'm not furious at my mother for her lies. But I am. I am so livid that it feels as if I'm about to be sick to my stomach, the acid inside of me starting to boil and rise in my throat. The taste in my mouth quickly grows bitter, and I rise from the bed to stand next to the open window in hopes of curbing my nauseousness and anger.

I don't know how long I stare out into the darkness, but it can't be all that long because when I finally realize that I need to confront my mother, Max is still sitting stock-still in the chair. But there's more than just that. There's something more important than telling my mother that I know about her. I need to get out of here. Max and I need to get out of here as soon as possible before I feel my life being tainted any more by the lies.

"Max?" I say, and he looks up at me through his dark eyelashes. There's a certain uneasiness lacing his gaze, like I'm a spooked horse and he's trying to be cautious so as to not further upset me.

"Mhmmm?"

The words keep echoing in my head: *we need to get out of here*.

"There's a bag under the bed. Pack up my things; whatever you think I might need. I'll be back in a few minutes, and I want to be able to leave immediately."

"Ellie…"

"Don't. Don't tell me that I'm going to change my mind or that I'm making a rushed decision. We've been talking about this for a week. So don't pull away on me now."

I'm already out the door before Max has a chance to say anything more, my heart pounding and blood pulsing in my ears as I storm toward Mother's bedroom. I stomp down the staircase and crash into the kitchen, shoving open the door to the first-floor hallway before passing the formal front room. With every step I take, I feel my fury rising more and more. There's no appeasing the way that I feel, my fingernails digging into my balled-up fists so hard I'm sure they're leaving marks.

There's no taming me now. Perhaps I am insolent and reckless and all the things that Mother has told me that I am. But she was that way as well, and I no longer think she's trying to protect me. I think maybe she's trying to live vicariously through my experiences—to feel involved in the life that she gave up for *this*. Maybe she didn't even want this at all. Want all of us. Want Father and his library and all his quirks.

When I reach the end of the hallway, I don't bother knocking on the door because I don't care about Mother's privacy or being polite. I don't care about anything other than finding out the truth and having her admit to me that...

What do I want her to admit?

I don't know, because all I'm craving is confrontation and for her to admit the truth. I'm not wrong here. She's wrong. She's been wrong for projecting a fabricated image of herself, by not telling the truth to Sophia and me, by offering us fairytales and falsehoods.

The door slams against the wall as I burst into Mother's bedroom. She's digging through her bedside table with a bunch of letters in her hands as I make my entrance. Two pieces of paper slip between her fingers and flutter to the ground as she practically jumps a foot in the air.

"Ellie, you scared me! Is everything okay?"

I allow the question to hang heavy in the air, hoping that she's feeling a similar sense of discomfort. I know deep down in my heart that she isn't, but I can still wish for it. I can wish for her to feel my pain and my sense of betrayal despite the fact that she most certainly has no idea of what's going to come out of my mouth.

"No," I hiss. "Everything isn't fine. I know what happened to you at *Blossom*."

Another letter slips to the floor, the sheet of paper and the envelope both disappearing underneath the bed as my mother's mouth forms a small "O." For a moment, I think she's going to try to deny the truth and tell me I'm making up stories, but she doesn't.

"How did you find out?" she asks quietly. There's no tone of denial in her voice, and her shoulders slump downward with her long, exhaled breath.

That's a question I hadn't prepared an answer for, but I suppose it doesn't matter what I say. I could tell her the truth about Colonel Gallagher and Max and the garden party and how I used to fuck Padraig with the goal of learning how to make better Allure to try and forget about finding Father dead in his library. But none of it matters. Nothing matters now except that Max is upstairs in my bedroom packing me a bag and I'm down here trying to ascertain exactly why something was wrong with just telling me the truth.

"Does that really matter?"

Mother sighs a second time, setting the rest of the letters back in the bedside table's drawer, and then sits down on the edge of her mattress. "Of course it matters, Ellie. You probably heard some story during one of your adventures with that boy from up the hill who works for Blossom."

I swear I see a curtain of red flash across my vision. "Padraig? This has nothing to do with Padraig or my *adventures* or any other story, for that matter. If you must know, I met someone else at... a gathering. He's the one who told me about Alastair."

"Oh, don't say his name," Mother whispers. "You're not supposed to say his name."

"I think we both know that nothing's going to happen if I say his name. Hell, I could recite the name of every Bèist in all of Scotland, and we are more than well aware I was already going to turn into one of them anyway. But you... you stole Alastair's life. That's worse than any of the things I could ever have done. Worse than the drugs, worse than the parties, worse than it all. You made him—"

"Ellie, I didn't make him do anything. Please, shut the door so you don't wake up the whole house."

"I don't give a fuck if I wake up the entire loch. They deserve to know what kinds of lies you've been spewing to your own children. Did Father even know about this?"

My mother looks down at the floor, the skirt of her nightdress shuffling as she adjusts her weight on the bed. "Of course he knew. Nobody involved wanted to waste what was... given up for me. I came to love your father, just like I know that you'll come to love Colonel Gallagher. You'll be able to avoid a mess like mine if you marry him. You don't want to end up living life like this, knowing that someone forfeited their own freedom for you. I think the boy who is up in your bedroom is willing to do just that, and it makes me worried for you, Ellie. It makes me worried that I haven't been able to save you.

I'm not even surprised that she knows about Max being in my bedroom right now. In fact, I don't even care because who was she truly trying to save? It couldn't have been me. It was her own conscience. Her own soul. She's been trying to relive her life through fixing me—and I don't want to be fixed because having independence and individuality doesn't mean that I'm broken.

I hear a noisy squeak from the other end of the hallway, which tells me that Sophia must've come down earlier to see what the commotion was about, standing out in the corridor and listening in to the conversation. Let her listen. She's going to find out the truth either way.

"I've done my best to raise you all in the way I wish I'd have been raised, Ellie. I've been trying to honor the gift that was given to me in order to have a second chance—and give you all one as well." Mother's voice almost matches the intensity of mine, but there's an undertone there that's pleading with me to stop and let this realization go.

I'm not letting it go.

"Your best isn't good enough. Your best is hypocritical and selfish and you deserve every lie that I've ever told you."

Another squeak. Sophia's left.

"I'm sure you think I'm a bad mother, but society ruined me too. I don't know where Alastair is, and it kills me every single day." Mother says Alastair's name tentatively, and I wonder how long it's been since it last came out of her mouth. "I get to miss two people—your father, the man I loved and lost, *and* the man I never stopped loving. I already know I'm going to miss you, too, someday."

"You're going to miss me because you're driving me away."

"I'm going to miss you because being a woman here in the lochs is half about loss and half about moving on and doing your duty. I'm just trying to fix the things I did wrong when I was your age, and it pains me to know that somewhere out there, Alastair probably thinks I don't treasure his sacrifice. At least your father knew how grateful I was for the life I was given." It's almost as if my mother is looking through me, like her next words are in another person's voice, someone speaking to both of us. "If someone loves you enough to surrender their life for yours, you can't throw that away."

Her words encompass the two of us in a heavy silence that lasts at least five full seconds. At first, I don't know what to say because I'm still furious, but there's a little piece of me that almost feels bad for her.

I mentally squash that fragment of my soul as if it was a lingering pest.

"Do you, though? Do you even care? Have you tried going to find Alastair since Father's passing? Have you tried doing *anything*?"

"Ellie, it's not that easy. I don't even know if he's still alive."

"Of course he's alive. You'd have known that earlier if you would just fucking try and be honest with yourself. And with Sophia and Huntley and Pippa and *me*."

With those words, I step back through the threshold and pointedly slam the door. I don't care if it's the middle of the night and if everyone at Padraig's and beyond the moors can hear our argument. It won't matter if the neighbors come by in the morning to ask what happened because I'll already be long gone.

I sprint back upstairs, hurling myself into my bedroom. I'm surprised to see that Max isn't alone—he's carefully watching over Sophia, who is packing my travel bag. She's clearly almost finished, meticulously gathering everything from the top drawer of my bedside table and placing it into the top of the luggage, the bag already bulging with the things she must've figured I'd need. The two of them look up when I enter the room, their expressions accented by the sound of vials clinking against one another. Sophia quickly looks back down, nestling the glass in between folds of clothing so they don't break.

"That didn't go well, I presume?" Max asks, not even bothering to lower his voice to a whisper.

I shake my head. "Monumentally awful. We need to go."

Sophia fastens the clasp on my kitbag, hoisting it onto my dilapidated chair as she rises from her spot on the floor. "I heard what was going on downstairs. I tried to help Max get everything we felt was important to you. Hopefully nothing was forgotten."

"Thank you," I reply.

There are so many other things for me to say—I could tell Sophia how much I've appreciated her over the years. I could tell her I hope she's happy forever with Colonel Gallagher so she doesn't stop believing in things like love at first sight. I could tell her that everything is going to work out for the best. But none of the words come out. Instead, tears gather in my eyes, and I find myself feeling terrified at leaving her behind and maybe never seeing her again. Goodbyes are a little death, of sorts.

Instead, I say the only thing I can choke out. "I'll write to you."

Sophia stifles a sob, fiddling with the skirt of her dress. "I'll try to write too, but we both know my responses might not always find their way to wherever you go."

"It's the thought that counts."

"The thought, yes."

I nod in affirmation, a single tear slipping from the corner of my eye and streaking down toward my jaw. Sophia takes two steps forward and pulls me into a fierce hug, the kind of hug that can only signal the end of something pivotal. The end of our lives as children together, and the beginning of our lives as women—with different duties and goals and priorities.

I'll miss her dearly, but I know deep in my heart that she'll be fine.

Sophia murmurs into my hair, "I'll be thinking of you."

We hold our embrace for a few seconds longer, and I try my hardest to memorize the way I feel when her curls tickle my damp cheeks. It's the same way I felt as when I lifted her onto my lap the time she skinned her knee in the garden when she was seven. It's also the same way I felt when she let me cry on her shoulder after I found our father. After Huntley and Pippa were born. After the first man of many let me down. After I got too high on Allure from Padraig and thought I was dying.

Moments later, amid every one of my memories, Sophia steps away and swipes at her face with the back of her hand. "You should go. Before Mother comes upstairs and tries to convince you otherwise."

"You're right."

Max lifts my bag from the chair, heaving it over his shoulder. "Are you sure about this?"

I suck in a deep breath that smells of midnight air and dead flowers before gazing over at Max's beautiful green eyes. "I'm positive."

A little smile twitches at the corner of Max's lips, and he gestures toward me with one hand. I slip my fingers into his palm, and he guides me toward the window so we can leave the house that I've known for my entire life. It feels daunting to retreat from this bedroom for one last time, but I'm intoxicated by the unknown and Max's springtime cologne.

"Love you, Soph," I say as I crouch underneath the windowsill and slide one leg out into the night. I feel for the thick tree branches that climb up toward the side of the house. "Say goodbye to Huntley and Pippa for me. Make up a good story about where I've gone."

"I don't have to make up anything, Ellie. You're a princess and you're running away with your prince. That's how all the best fairytales end."

With those words and a small smile, I slip out the window and into the warm summer night, not knowing exactly what's supposed to come next. Just knowing that it will.

Chapter Twenty

MAX

Ellie descends the large tree with practiced ease, which tells me she's snuck out of her window many times. However, I'm nearly certain that tonight will be the last night for such things—from this bedroom, at least—because by morning, there will be no returning to Loch Gàrraidh. We will have separated ourselves from society here and been marked as the deviants everyone else seems to already know we are, be it as a Bèist or otherwise.

I yearn for Blossom's ignorance of our departure until we're far enough away, but I don't know how likely that is. Nonetheless, I can't help but wonder how much we'd be worth to them. We might be useful for the continuation of their stories and for the threat of punishment to others like us. We might be worth it to Padraig, who would likely receive some kind of reward for turning us in, as he will certainly find out soon enough about our departure. Though a little voice inside of me says that if Blossom seeks us out—through Padraig or another source—they may discover that Ellie and I have created a fairytale all our own that matters more to us than anything they've written in their book.

As I move from thick tree limb to thick tree limb with Ellie's bag hoisted over my shoulder, I allow myself to focus on what our legend would be called rather than the height I could fall from. *A Narrative of Roses. An Account from Loch Gàrraidh. A Tale of the Garden at Night.* One would think after climbing this tree enough times that I'd get used to the precarious nature of it, but going up as a cat is much different than coming down as a man. Cats don't tend to feel the same fear of tall places like some humans do… and like I am right now.

Once my feet hit solid ground, I hike the bag up on my shoulder from where it has fallen to the crook of my elbow. Ellie is already shaking like a leaf, her trembling hands giving her away despite the steady look on her face.

I offer her a smile that's meant to be calming.

"Where do you want to go?" I ask, gesturing awkwardly in an attempt to soothe her worries with a touch of humor. "We have exactly the whole world to explore now."

Ellie returns my smile with a grin of her own. She's clearly trying to hide her nerves… and maybe even the shock of finding out the truth about her mother and the family connection to Blossom Prep. It's a valiant effort on her part, but I can see through it. I'm not sure how to comfort a woman in this strange position—it's not exactly a situation I've found myself in before. Running away, yes—I've run away before. Many times. Running away with someone else? I guess I can add that to the list.

As I'm thinking about what to say, Ellie straightens, sucks in a breath, and brushes her hair from where a lock has fallen across her pretty face. "I don't care where we go because I just need to get away from this house and from Loch Gàrraidh."

I consider our options: *North, south, east, west. Inland, upland, to the sea...*

The sea.

I promised Alastair I wouldn't leave without a proper farewell.

"I think I have the perfect place. Plus, it'll give me a chance to say my own goodbyes."

She doesn't question the direction I start to head in, though she motions to take her bag from off my shoulder. I shake my head and smile. "I'll carry it. Don't worry."

"Are you sure?"

"I'm sure," I respond, heaving her bag up onto my shoulder. It's not that heavy, and besides, my heart is lighter now that we're together.

We find ourselves walking through the tall grass and amid the bushes and rocks, carefully watching our footing as the path disappears past the stables and horse pastures. Wildflowers crop up around our feet after some time, and the sliver of moon above our heads lights the way toward the shoreline that I know is far off in the distance. We'll reach it tonight.

Ellie saunters along at my side in silence for a distance before she delicately slips her hand in mine. I look down at our fingers, woven together like that first truly intimate night with the green satin ribbon, and the corners of my lips quirk up in yet another smile.

"Max?" she murmurs.

It's strange and wonderful to hear her say my name at night without being forced to whisper.

"Yes, darling?"

She squeezes my hand and I stop, turning. We're so far from her home—or, I suppose it would be best referred to as the Callaghan house, since she no longer lives there—that I can no longer tell if we are in or out of Loch Gàrraidh. There's an invisible border somewhere along these moors, undetectable underneath the canvas of sky that's the darkest shade of blue.

"Can we just… sit a moment?" Ellie asks.

"Of course."

I place the bag gently down on the earth to avoid breaking any of the vials that Sophia packed. Before I have a chance to sit, Ellie flops backward in the thick grass and the nighttime flowers with a chuckle. She's all flaming red hair and sparkling eyes and nervous energy, that fury I'm certain she felt when she was confronting her mother now something else. Maybe a little bit of anxiety, though I suspect it may be something more akin to finally having a taste of the freedom and control she's been seeking through other means. There's nothing that makes someone feel wild and reckless like rolling fields and the long distance from a home they can't return to.

Ellie props herself up on her elbow once her laughter fades, and she looks at me with wonder in her eyes. "I can't believe we're alone. Actually alone. For the first time in my entire life."

"We're not alone. You have me. You'll always have me."

"You know what I mean."

I do know what she means, but I need Ellie to know what I mean as well. That there's no alone when she's by my side. That I will live and die and breathe and exist for her as long as the two of us live. And maybe even more than that.

"There's still time to turn back, you know. If you've changed your mind. I won't be upset, and we can make it to the house before sunrise so your mother will never know that you ever left."

Ellie shakes her head, smiling brightly underneath the moonglow. "I can't go back *and* be with you, Max. We both know that. I'd rather run away with you for only a short while than spend the entirety of my life unhappy. Because my unhappiness would mean I'd be married to Colonel Gallagher, and that would break Sophia's heart."

"She didn't stop talking about him while we were packing, you know. Except for when she went to eavesdrop on you."

"I'm not at all surprised. Because I haven't stopped talking about you since we met at the garden party. Or when I ran directly into you while not paying attention to where I was going. I suppose that's a more accurate description of what happened."

My heart does a little flutter, skipping a beat. "Honestly?"

"Truly."

I collapse onto my back on the grass, staring up at the night sky. "I thought it had something to do with the allure of my eyes."

"It had something to do with Allure, alright," Ellie replies.

The two of us laugh without inhibition, and it's breathtaking to be able to express myself with her without having to worry about being overheard. There's no need to silence our chuckles or to quiet the contented way Ellie yelps when I roll over and grab her around the waist, pulling her on top of me. Her dress hikes up around her thighs as she sits up along my hip bones, most certainly able to feel the way my body is responding to this newfound freedom and her body perched on mine. One sleeve of her dress is slipping down over her shoulder, exposing her skin to a pale green glow that is most certainly coming from my palm.

I gaze up at Ellie with her halo of stars, and she looks down at me on my blanket of wildflowers. Together, we are lovestruck.

"Your magic…" Ellie breathes, running a fingertip along my wrist. The light touch causes gooseflesh to appear along my arm and a flurry of reactions in the rest of my body. I'm not at all careful when I wrap my fingers in Ellie's hair and pull her down into a deep kiss, sinking into her like she's everything I need to stay alive.

Maybe she is.

My heart pounds as we crash together there in the field, and I let out the kind of groan and growl I've been waiting all this time for. It's a sound that does not yield and does not have reservation, and Ellie responds with her own quiet whimper, biting my bottom lip as my hands slip under the hem of her dress. I want every inch of her here in this freedom, wherever we are between the lochs and the ocean. There's nobody around to see us. There's nobody around to know that we're breaking every one of society's rules. Hell, maybe there's no society here at all.

Ellie rocks her hips against my hand and my body, and I know that I need her. I could push up her skirt and have her right here amid the call of the nightbirds and the scent of lavender. But I want to be atop of her, watch her red hair drown in the sea of grasses and flowers, see her fingers grasp for the greenery as I have her reach the pinnacle of pleasure over and over again. And because I desperately want this very particular scenario, the need so great that it gathers like a knot in my chest, I can't help but tear myself away. I'm just about to turn her over when I open my eyes and notice the glow from my hand is stronger than it's ever been—a deep emerald that now encompasses nearly my entire arm.

And I'm warm. So incredibly warm, which tells me one thing. I'm changing. But why would I be changing now? It's the middle of the night. There's no sunlight to be found in all of Scotland right now; no reason for me to be turning back into a Bèist now unless…

Unless Blossom knows.

"Ellie—"

Heat continues to rise in my chest, hotter and deeper than anything I've experienced before. Within moments, it feels as if my entire body is going to incinerate—from far inside of my heart outward to my fingertips. I bite the inside of my cheek as the fire continues to grow, body tingling with invisible flames. Every beat of my heart coincides with a palpitation in my hand, the green light pulsating almost imperceptibly. My fingers find the long blades of grass and hold on to them as if they are the only thing keeping me from being propelled into the evening sky.

Ellie's face is aglow in the moonlight and the radiance of my magic and she crawls from her position on top of me. I wanted her to be the one gripping the grass in passion, but instead, I'm changing, tearing the multicolored flowers from the field in sudden agony. *Has Blossom found us? Are they going to curse me even more? Are they trying to murder me? Alastair asked if I would die for Ellie—is this the moment where I must make that ultimate choice?*

"Max?"

Ellie's voice sounds far away, even though I know she's right next to me. I can see her, but she's barely more than a silhouette. The ache under my skin is keeping me from being able to focus on anything except for the taste of seeping blood and the fact that I'm boiling; a kettle that's been kept over a stove for so much longer than necessary that eventually the pot itself is going to burn. I can't breathe, I can't move, I can't do anything but feel my mind race.

The curse isn't breaking. I'm changing. She's going to see me change into a Bèist. It's either that or Blossom is going to hurt me just enough that I have to watch as they kill her first. There's no way this is the curse breaking. A curse breaking should feel pleasant, shouldn't it?

"I'm right here, Max…" Ellie says something more, but her voice turns into distorted nonsense as the pain intensifies so much that I can't help but scream out a string of curse words that I shouldn't ever say in front of a woman. They flow from my mouth like a river as I start to shake, whorls of green smoke encompassing both Ellie and me. At least, I think that's what's happening. It might be a delusion. It might be something only I'm seeing through the pain.

This is not the pain of changing, this is the pain of my entire body—my essence and soul and spirit—being ripped apart and realigned to make an entirely different Max.

Then, suddenly, a wave of cold crashes over me like a pail of ice water has been emptied directly onto my chest. I gasp for breath, my body reflexively sitting up as I gulp for mouthfuls of late summer air. Stars dot my vision—large ones that sparkle—but they slowly dissolve into nothingness as I try to regain my bearings.

What the fuck was that?

I blink a few times to clear my eyes. Tendrils of pale smoke are snaking along the grass like Ellie and I have just put out a fire while the glow from my palm is slowly fading away. The night sky and the distant water still look the same as they did before—deep blue shades with tinges of ivory from the moon—and the only difference in the moors is that there are two bare patches where I pulled the grass and greenery from the earth in agony.

When I look to my left, Ellie is sitting next to me, her fingers wrapped in the loose fabric of my shirt sleeve. There's a look of relief on her face, which isn't what I expected to see. In fact, I'm not sure why I still have sleeves if I've changed into a Bèist. I'm also not sure why she isn't screaming at the tearing of skin, the ripping of muscle, and the complete adjustment of my entire body that's occurred in front of her eyes. It's not a pretty thing to behold on the best of days, the process only getting worse as we age due to the harsh effects on our bodies, both in the morning and at night.

But no, Ellie is kneeling in the grass next to me as if I've had some kind of momentary sickness instead of traumatizing her with my change. Before I have a chance to apologize and explain that I don't know what's happened, she slides her hand over my skin and it feels... unexpected. I look down at where she's touching me, and I'm surprised to see that I still have fingers.

No paws, no claws, no fur, no tail.

I didn't change. I'm still in my human form.

So then, what was that? I mull everything over in my head as quickly as possible. *A warning? A threat? A notice that Blossom is coming for us? Maybe we should keep moving.*

Not maybe... we must keep moving. Alastair will know what this was all about. We'll find Alastair and he'll tell us what to do next and where to go to hide. He must know the answer. He knows the answer to everything else. I can't lose Ellie already. We've barely made it out of Loch Gàrraidh. Have we even made it out of Loch Gàrraidh?

I release Ellie's hand and spring to my feet. "We need to keep going. We can't stop."

"Max." Ellie's voice is calm as she says my name, the word sounding like the most delicious music as it comes from her mouth. "Take a breath. I think I know what just happened."

How could she know what happened? She's never been a Bèist before. She's never changed before. She might be able to guess but...

I'm panicking. I never panic, and I hate the way it makes me feel. I'm not the kind of man who loses control of himself—not like this, anyway. Not with pain and worry because of Blossom's damned rules.

But I do need to breathe. I'm not breathing.

I suck in mouthfuls of air, and after a few moments, my pulse starts to slow and my mind clears just enough that I'm able to process a distinct, and much more logical, realization. That wasn't Blossom telling me they're coming for us. It couldn't be. They'd have no way to control my body and mind like that. They're an administration of sorcerers, of people, not the enchantment itself—

Oh, fuck.

They aren't the curse, but the curse has control *over* me. Until now. That entire ordeal was my affliction breaking—just like how it was described in the fairytales we studied in books and in our classes at Blossom. The school presented it as something that rarely happens; an exception to the rule that curses are meant to last forever. But if the affliction was to break, meeting whatever criteria that was put on the cursed individual, it would feel exactly like I just felt: like agony, pain, fire, and then a wave of cold to calm the senses and drop the Bèist from the enchanted body to their own.

"Ellie, that felt like—"

Her words come out at almost the same time as mine, but I let hers take over the conversation. "Did it feel like that story in the back of the book? The one with the prince and the princess who lived happily ever after for real?"

I nod, knowing exactly what story in the Blossom book she's referring to. "I think my curse broke. I think... I think my magic's back."

"Can you test it? See if you can—what sort of magic were you able to do beforehand?"

"Mostly parlor tricks. Elementary horticulture. Read a lot of books when I was younger about plants. But we might as well try it and see what happens, if anything at all."

I'm nervous again, but not panicked, as I kneel back down onto the grass next to one of the bare patches I created.

What if it doesn't work? What if my magic is wild and uncontrollable and I end up causing more damage instead of fixing something? I place my right palm over the dirt, and close my eyes. I don't know what to do. I used to always know what to do with my magic, but it feels like this is will prove or disprove the existence of it all, and I'm lost in the idea of creating the perfect enchantment.

I open my eyes again, and Ellie is there next to me, smiling. As I look at her, I recall the look in her pale eyes the split second before we kissed for the first time. She trusted me with whatever would happen the second she wasn't looking, she trusted that I would kiss her, and I trusted that she would kiss me back.

Now, I need to trust myself.

Come on, Max. It's worth a shot.

I think about flowers. About lavender, specifically. About the light purple hue capturing the moonlight and the tiny flowers waving back and forth amid a summer's evening breeze. I think about greenery unfurling from the ground and being heated by the warmth of my hand, rained on by the misty skies of Scotland, and taking root in the soil of the moors.

As I'm thinking about all these things, my hand gets warm, but I'm too apprehensive to open my eyes in case there's nothing happening and it's all in my head. I just keep pushing my magic through my veins, feeling the sensation of wanting a plant to grow as it washes over me. I try to direct it downward, focusing. A moment later, something grazes the underside of my hand and Ellie gasps.

When I open my eyes, there's a collection of tiny lavender stalks growing from the space that was previously barren... and my hand is glowing that true bright green again, the color of my eyes.

I almost can't believe what I'm seeing. My curse is broken and my magic is back. I've become the exception to the rule in the Blossom fairytales. I'm no longer an afflicted one—a Bèist. Someone society couldn't tame. I'm Max, and she's Ellie, and we are together here under the same moon and next to the brand-new flowers that I created with my magic.

I barely have time to react because Ellie's body crashes into mine and her hands find the collar of my shirt, pulling me into a kiss that says more than any words ever could.

Chapter Twenty-One

SOPHIA

I don't sleep well, my heart heavy with Ellie's unexpected departure. Despite knowing she and Max are going to be infinitely happier now, it is difficult to accept that I'm probably never going to see my sister again. It's a strange feeling, the awareness of her world now existing without me—and Mother, and Huntley, and Pippa—in it. Ellie's going to be living her own life with Max, on the run from Blossom Prep, and I'll be here in Loch Gàrraidh for the next little while, waiting for Iain to return and take me away.

After tossing and turning for what feels like a thousand nights, and after using the rest of my ingredients to practice making additional vials of contraceptive, I finally spot the sun starting to rise through the gap in the curtains. I throw myself out of bed, the blankets feeling both too restricting and too warm, and traipse downstairs to get breakfast ready for the little ones. It doesn't take long for me to prepare the water for my tea and their porridge; my morning habits are so repetitive that I barely need to be awake to do them. However, I *am* awake this morning, and I can't help but continue to think about Ellie. I wonder where Max has taken her, if he brought her to the seaside like she always wanted. I wonder how long it will take until

Blossom starts looking for them, or if Blossom is going to just let them go and consider them lost causes.

That doesn't seem likely. I can't imagine Padraig giving up that easily, let alone an entire administration.

Then, for some reason, as I'm stirring the physical pot on the stove instead of the pot of thoughts in my head, memories of Iain come flooding back. Memories of us standing here in this kitchen as I made tea for us and porridge for Huntley while Huntley played with his spoons and we whispered in the corner of the room about everything that had happened between us. Everything from the kissing to the way it felt when he had his knee between my thighs and his hands on my dress. I must get distracted because my cheeks begin to feel warm and, as Iain and I are just about to kiss again in my daydream, I burn my knuckle on the pot of porridge.

I almost curse, the pain sizzling along my hand. The hand that Iain bandaged the last time he was here. The hand that he touched. The hand that I grabbed his collar with and used to pull him into—

Sophia, just stir the pot. Stir the pot. Stir the pot.

Stirring the pot is not enough of a diversion; however, I don't have to worry about it for long because Mother pushes open the door from the hallway and strides into the kitchen.

"Have you seen Ellie this morning?"

I should have expected there wouldn't be that much of a good morning greeting based on all of last night's yelling. Mother is probably still frustrated about Ellie, though she's about to be a lot angrier when she realizes my sister isn't even here.

"No," I reply, trying my best not to sound tentative. It isn't a lie. Not exactly. I haven't seen Ellie since I woke up… but I did see her leave after midnight. Which was technically this morning.

I'm overthinking this.

Sophia, just stir the pot. Stir the pot. Stir the pot.

Mother doesn't bother saying anything more before she ascends the stairs, lifting the bottom of her blue dress so she doesn't step on the hem. As she disappears past Huntley and Pippa's bedroom down the corridor to Ellie's corner of the second floor, I grit my teeth. There's going to be a moment when she notices that Ellie's room is half empty and Ellie herself is nowhere to be found. That moment is likely going to be very upsetting for her, and I'm going to have to know what to say when she—

"Sophia! Where is your sister?" Mother's voice echoes down the hallway and staircase into the kitchen. I thought that maybe she would be panicked or upset or annoyed, but instead, she mostly just sounds sad. Like she knows that an inevitable moment has come and gone before she could do anything about it.

I don't say anything right away because I haven't yet prepared an answer. In fact, I still don't know what to say when Mother appears at the top of the flight of steps and asks the same question again. Just in case I didn't hear her shrieking from moments before.

"Where is Ellie?"

I shrug, tending to the porridge that is almost definitely overdone now. However, my feet are frozen to the floor of the kitchen in front of the stove, like somehow keeping the kettle between me and my mother will help protect us from the truth.

Sophia, just stir the pot. Stir the pot. Stir the pot.

Mother stomps down the stairs. "She's with that boy who was in her room last night, isn't she?"

"I don't know."

"I think you do know. You can tell me. I just want to know if she's safe with him."

I want to tell my mother that Ellie might have been more honest with her if Mother had been more honest with Ellie, but I'm not brave enough to say something like that. In fact, I don't feel brave enough to do much of anything except stand here and stare at my mother.

"Sophia, don't make this any harder than it has to be."

There's a pit of frustration in my stomach that exists on Ellie's behalf. "I'm not. I don't know where she is."

My response isn't really a lie. I really don't know where she is. Max could have taken her anywhere.

Mother sighs, lowering her voice to a whisper as the sound of the children waking up and chattering to one another begins to float down the stairs. "Please, Sophia, you need to leave this instant and take one of the horses and go find her. We're going to talk. All of us. I'll make sure you both know what happened at Blossom. I'm sure once she hears the whole story, she's not going to be doing any more of this running around. She will marry Colonel Gallagher as planned, and she will not see that other boy anymore."

"She loves him, you know."

"I know. But it doesn't matter as long as we live here."

I throw the wooden spoon into the pot of porridge. "Then why don't we leave?"

Mother shakes her head in a gesture that seemingly indicates that I don't understand. I hate the implication that I'm not adult enough to grasp certain concepts or ideas or understand the way the world works. If I'm old enough to care for two small children while she's gone to check on Aunt Matilda, I'm certainly old enough to understand why we don't leave Scotland behind for good.

"Sophia, just go."

Without saying anything more, I flee from the kitchen as fast as possible. At least if I ready a horse and go for a ride, then I can get away from the house for a while so I can calm down and give myself time to think.

By the entryway, I find a pair of my old boots and shove them on my feet before I trudge out to the stables. Maybe if I'm gone long enough, Mother will think that I tried to find Ellie. But I don't want to find her. I'm not going to look for her. I'll tack up Hazel and ride over the hills past Padraig's and listen to the wind and smell the summer flowers as they start to die off during the change in seasons.

Hazel is in her stall munching on an oversized pile of hay as I stomp through the doorway. She lets out a friendly nicker in my general direction, and Charlie lifts his head from the opposite stall to blink his liquid brown eyes at me. A strand of hay hangs from the horse's mouth, and it looks like he's smoking a clove cigarette like some of the older neighbor boys used to in the garden. The recollection makes me smile because it reminds me of Ellie. Despite her being gone now, I still have every memory of us growing up together.

It only takes me a short while to ready Hazel for a ride, and I toss a handful of grain to Charlie to keep him occupied as I leave the stable with the other horse. We emerge slowly into the morning dew, Hazel's coat shining in the sunlight while her ears flick back and forth at the sounds being carried along the breeze. I give her a little pat before picking up her reins and placing my foot in the stirrup to mount, settling in the sidesaddle as she takes a few steps forward.

I haven't ridden in a long time. Father used to take Ellie and me into the fields on our ponies when we were younger, but since he passed, the new horses have mostly been pasture ornaments and used for transportation into town when it's been necessary. Mother occasionally visits Aunt Matilda or her extended family, but Ellie and I both dropped riding more and more the older we got. It hasn't had the same appeal since Father's death, and Mother wasn't ever much of a horsewoman.

I've missed riding, though. But with Mother gone occasionally to help care for Aunt Matilda, and nobody else to tend to Huntley and Pippa—and sometimes Ellie—I haven't really had much time for leisure activities.

But today? I have time for leisure. I have all the time in the world—or at least until Hazel gets tired and my legs get sore and the sun goes down. Then I can go home with whatever excuses I've thought up during my long ride, and break the news to my mother that Ellie is nowhere to be found in Loch Gàrraidh. She's not going to believe me, no matter how long I'm out of the house. But at least being out of the house right now is better than being in it.

Hazel and I follow the winding roads around the lochs for the better part of two hours, lazily trotting around the countryside in the emerald green fields. The horse's hooves thud in the dewy grass as we seem to perpetually be heading in the direction of a line of sad-looking trees, spindly and skinny against the landscape. Wispy clouds stretch like long bands of cotton across the blue sky overhead, and I watch the wildflowers and scenery float past us as I fall into a sense of peace that I haven't felt in a long time.

There's something about riding a horse that makes one feel as if they've grown wings and learned to fly, I think.

When we make it to the line of trees that follows the crest of the hilltop, rather than hold Hazel back, I allow her a bit of extra rein and click my tongue to ask her to canter. She immediately leaps into the faster gait, and soon we are dashing across the summit toward the perfect spot where I know we will have a panoramic view of the entire countryside. It takes a minute or two to get there, but once we reach the top of the incline, Hazel is puffing and I'm trying to catch my breath from having the wind in my face.

I halt the horse and give her the reins; she drops her head and starts to nibble the grass. As Hazel relaxes, I sit up a little taller in the saddle and look out toward the lochs from my ideal vantage point. Once I shade my eyes, the early afternoon sun high up in the sky and causing me to squint, I can see far off into the distance. My house, Padraig's home, and Loch Gàrraidh glisten behind the gardens. The roads are beige, wiggling lines that connect everything together, from the buildings to the fields and paddocks and estates. Even farther off is the seaside. I think I can see it from here, sparkling a little in the sunbeams, but it might just be a mirage.

"That's where Ellie is, you know," I say to Hazel, who most definitely isn't listening to me. She takes half a step forward to grasp another mouthful of grass, ears flicking back at the sound of my voice. I can always pretend that she understands me so that it feels as if someone is listening. "Do you see it over there? The ocean. I should take you to the ocean sometime. I bet you'd like to splash in the water."

Hazel snorts and chews. I give her a little scratch on the withers and keep talking.

"I wonder if you have a sister out there somewhere. Maybe in Edinburgh or Loch Tadgh. Maybe a brother too? Maybe you had to leave them behind, or they left you behind. I bet that was a difficult thing for you, wasn't it, Hazel?" My fingers find her mane, and I start to absently braid the bits closest to the saddle, separating the locks into three strands. "I know I was never really sure what to do about Ellie before. But I feel like we were just starting to get to understand one another."

I flip the pieces of Hazel's mane over and over and over one another until there's a long braid down the side of her neck. When I let the end go, it only comes halfway undone.

As I watch the braid uncurl bit by bit, I wonder if maybe I'm not as completely undone as I felt last night. Maybe I'm only halfway undone without Ellie in my life. Because soon I'll have Iain. I'll be able to start my own family. I'll travel and see the world away from the vista at the top of this hill and the spaces the sunlight shines down upon here. As I watched my sister climb through her window after midnight with the love of her life, I might have been a metaphorical braid that came undone, but there's nothing to say that I can't be something beautiful and whole ever again.

"Thanks, Hazel," I say to the horse. She snorts into the grass before lifting her head and craning her neck around to look at me. "Are you ready to go home? It's another few hours back to the house at the slowest walk imaginable."

I pick up the reins and turn the mare around on the hilltop, and we begin to descend back to the moors and fields. We don't canter this time, or even trot, because the sun has peaked and the temperature is relatively warm. I let

Hazel amble along down the grassy knoll at her own pace, enjoying my ride and the quiet for as long as I possibly can.

An hour must pass before we are level with Padraig's property. He's out on the lawn, waving me down as I ride nearby. He probably thinks that I'm Ellie, coming over for an afternoon affair or something disgusting of the sort, the thought of which makes me stifle my own gag reflex. However, I don't want to be rude—well, I do... but I won't be—so I guide Hazel down the lane and bring her to a halt next to a garden of perennials.

"Afternoon," Padraig says to me, disappointment lacing his tone. I was right. He definitely thought I was Ellie.

"Same to you," I reply. I'm not sure what else to say to Padraig, so I sit there atop Hazel and look down at his dusty shoes. For an awkward ten seconds, he also looks down at his shoes, the silence extending for so long that I'm not sure why I even bothered stopping. It certainly wasn't to admire this man's footwear.

"What has you out for a ride today? Your mother must be home from her journey, I presume?"

"She is. Aunt Matilda is doing well, thanks for asking."

Padraig nods, glancing toward the front door of his house before he lowers his voice and smirks at me. "How's your sister doing? I thought I'd see her a little more after the party, but she's been keeping to herself lately. Hasn't even come over at night to—"

"Fuck off, Padraig. She's fine. In fact, she's better than fine. She..."

For a moment, I'm at a loss for words. *Am I supposed to tell Padraig that she's gone away? Am I* not *supposed to say anything at all because Padraig will certainly notify Blossom and the board?*

Thankfully, I don't have to say anything more because Padraig's wife comes out of the house with a toddler in tow and a baby on her hip. There's a dishrag in one of her hands and an apron wrapped around her plump waist.

"Pad—oh, hello! My apologies, I wasn't aware there was someone here."

I offer her a bright smile because she doesn't deserve my sarcasm and hate like her husband does. "I was just leaving. Passing by. Saying hello to the neighbors."

"Can I get you anything? Water for the horse?" She's too nice for a man like Padraig.

"We'll be fine until we arrive back home, but thank you. That's very kind. Was nice to see you... all."

Before either Padraig or his wife have a chance to say anything else, I turn Hazel and urge her into a trot. We don't move quickly for long, just to the end of the lane so I don't have to risk being stalled by another question. The moment we're out of earshot and their direct line of vision, I bring the mare back down to a walk and lead her onto the grass instead of along the dusty road.

We take the longest route imaginable back to the house, meandering along the fields, and Hazel lets out a long sigh once I slide off her back and bring her into the cool stable. Once I slip off her saddle and bridle, I bring her a scoop of grain and a bucket of water. She takes a long drink before diving into the pail of food, and I take my time brushing her and cleaning her hooves. I know I'm delaying going back in the house, so much so that I sweep the stables and brush Charlie before I finally notice my stomach is rumbling and I need something to eat and drink myself.

With a sigh, I close the barn door and walk to the house, my legs tired from a long day of riding and doing absolutely nothing that I was supposed to do. As I amble along toward the front door, I am reminded of the weakness I felt in my knees when Iain kissed me up against the bedroom door, and my face flushes just as I put my hand on the latch to enter the house.

Mother's already in the formal front room waiting for me.

"I can see by the fact that you're alone that you mustn't have found your sister."

I shake my head, unlacing my boots before placing them neatly near the wall. "I didn't find her, no."

"Sophia, please just tell me where she's gone."

I can't help the sigh that escapes me, and I'm certain this has already given me away before I even admit to anything. But I have admitted to it. Just not in the way that I think Mother wants me to. "I have an idea. And I think you have an idea as well. But you know as well as I do that she's not coming home. You'd have to drag her kicking and screaming back to Loch Gàrraidh. And I don't want to know what would happen after that."

"She really isn't coming back, is she?"

"I shake my head. "Never."

With that, I clomp down the corridor, through the kitchen, up the stairs, and toward my bedroom. However, as I'm about to open the door, I recall that I've used up all my supplies to make potions, and my only source of amusement for the remainder of the evening is going to be practicing getting the taste of pears just right for my contraceptive. I suspect there may be some flowers or herbs or tea left in Ellie's bedroom, so I creep across the hallway to see if I can find anything of use in her bedside table.

Ellie's bedroom smells like lavender and emptiness, and the aroma catches in my throat like a winter chill. I force myself to swallow it down as I pad across the floor and open the top drawer of the nightstand. Inside are some empty vials, which I snatch and put into my pockets, and also a sprig of something I don't recognize. It looks like a dried rose, but with a bundle of baby's breath attached to it. It's so flat and brittle that it's hard to identify. Underneath is a folded-up piece of paper with my name on it. It looks like it's been in the drawer for a long while.

Seeing my name is strange, but I know the writing is Ellie's. It doesn't look as practiced as the handwriting she'd used to write letters in the past year in Father's study, but I'm certain it's Ellie's nonetheless.

I pick up the paper and flip it over to where it's folded and sealed with a dollop of wax. *I can open it, right? I mean, it has my name on it...*

The old stamp crackles open as I slide my finger underneath it and unfold the note. Written on the aged parchment is a brief letter from my sister.

Sophia –

I've put something for you inside of Father's Blossom fairytale book. What better way to give society a big "fuck off" than to carve out the inside of their soul and use it for secrets?

All my love –

Ellie

I read the letter three times before I realize what's happening, and as soon as I comprehend the message, I rush down the hall toward where Father used to write his own letters and read from his thick books. A love of books was something he shared with Ellie more than anyone else in the house, so it's no wonder the room has stayed intact. It was the last space that Ellie ever found him, the last place she wanted anyone to enter or touch or alter, and the last place anyone else would have probably have ever looked for anything out of fear of infuriating or upsetting her. We've all left the space alone now that he's gone, and I wonder for a moment if part of the reason why Mother doesn't want to leave is because then she'd have to dismantle and risk ruining everything that's belonged to Father—from the library to the piano.

The door creaks as I open it, and there's the same smell of lavender in the room, but it's mixed with old, uncorked red wine and something else I can't put my finger on. The curtains are open, and the lowering sunlight cascades through the windows and creates shadows on the wall and Father's desk. The hardcover Blossom fairytale book sits atop the surface as if he placed it there only the day before, the floral cover so distinguishable that I know what book it is even from halfway across the study. I've read from Huntley and Pippa's copies enough that I sometimes think I see the gilded patterns in my sleep.

My hands tremble as I release the door's latch. I walk across the floor delicately and carefully, worried it might make a squeak or a sound that Mother will overhear. However, I'm fortunate that by the time I make it over to the desk and turn the book around, the only mark I've made is leaving my fingerprints in the thin layer of dust on the cover.

What could Ellie have possibly hidden inside of this book?

I stare down at the flower-patterned hardback for a moment before swiping at the dust. Father would have hated knowing that his stories aren't being read. Well, maybe not the Blossom stories, but he would detest that Ellie wasn't able to continue using his library after his death. But I think it was just too traumatic. Too personal. Too... everything. Because of it, I wonder how long that letter's been in her nightstand. How long something has been hidden in this room. How long she's been trying to deal with the loss of our father without saying a word about him.

I flip open the cover to the Blossom fairytales after a moment, my heart pounding hard and my hands feeling as if they're growing clammy just from being in my father's space. It's like somewhere deep in my chest I think his ghost is watching me—if I believed in something like ghosts. I suppose if I believe in fairytales then ghosts aren't that far off.

The book itself looks and feels like a normal text, maybe a little heavier than expected, and so I turn a page, and another page, and yet another, waiting for something to happen. However, there doesn't seem to be anything inside near the front of the hardcover, so I crack the worn copy in the middle, and that's when I notice something strange. The middle of the book has been carved out with a knife—just as Ellie alluded to in her note.

What better way to give society a big "fuck off" than to carve out the inside of their soul and use it for secrets?

Inside the whittled rectangle, which spans the thickness of at least a hundred pages, is Ellie's tortoiseshell hand mirror. Tears form in the corners of my eyes as I pluck it from between the book's ruined pages, looking down at myself in the reflection. My red curls have started to escape and run wild, freckles barely kissing my cheeks as I stand in the lowering sunlight. I always thought that Ellie was the pretty one who everyone fell for, but at this moment, looking into her mirror, I feel every inch as beautiful as she always told me I am.

As I brush a tear from my cheek, I notice there are a few specks of pink powder around the edges of the mirror's frame—old Allure that Ellie wasn't able to entirely clean from the casing. I almost prefer it that way. Not because I want to try to scrape the drug free and use it myself, but because there's something about the combination of Allure and the pattern on the back of the mirror that will always remind me of the afternoons Ellie and I spent in her bedroom wondering what our futures would hold. The mornings when I would try to wake her after a party. The late evenings where I'd try to keep her from getting completely inebriated. The times when she would bring me into her room and let me try on her dresses and show me how to fix the hems on my own.

I don't remember the days. Not individually. But I do remember the moments.

Placing the hand mirror in the pocket of my dress, I look down at the carved book, trying to determine what I should do with it. I don't know if anyone will care no matter what choice I make. But then I think about the words from Ellie's letter: *what better way to give society a big "fuck off" than to carve out the inside of their soul and use it for secrets?*

At that very second, I know what to do. I pull out Father's chair and open a drawer to begin to craft a letter to Huntley and Pippa. I'll place it inside, and someday, I hope they'll find it, knowing they too were loved with the same sort of ferocity.

Chapter Twenty-Two

ELLIE

We make it to the seaside at the crack of dawn, the sun just starting to come up and change the colors of the sky. There's a faint pink haze that appears low to the ground, but the nightbirds are still singing and the evening flowers are just closing as we approach an abandoned church at the edge of the coastline. I'm yawning, and Max guides me toward the doorway, indicating that the other Bèists are changing into their animal form and often do so in isolation away from the church. When we enter the darkness of the building, light barely seeping through the cracks in the walls and windows, I have to feel my way down the curved staircase to the basement where Max says there's a proper place to sleep.

He lights a lantern, and the flame's shadow flickers against a wall of multicolored vials. We're in an underground apothecary of sorts, something I never would have known was here if I was passing through on my own to see the seaside. To one side of the room is a small bed, complete with blankets and pillows, and I barely have a chance to eyeball the rest of the space before I collapse on the mattress.

Max sets my bag down on the table at the other corner of the room. "It's strange to see the sun rising as a man. I haven't seen it this way in a long time."

"We can go outside and watch it, if you'd like." I stifle another yawn, running a hand along my cheek to brush a lock of hair away. I don't want Max to miss any moments now that he's gained his magic back. Now that his curse is broken.

"You're tired."

"I don't mind."

Max shakes his head before crossing the floor and picking up one of the folded blankets sitting at the end of the bed. "We'll have plenty of sunrises to watch together, Ellie. Might as well get some rest before everyone finds out we're here. And before we have to say goodbye again."

He's not wrong. I get the feeling he's going to have a difficult time saying farewell to Alastair in particular. It seems like the old cat has been a good friend and advisor to him during his time here. But I have things I want to say to Alastair as well. Things about my mother and how I think, if he's willing, that he should show himself to her and admit to me the things he told Max. About missing her. About his sacrifice. Let her know that he's still nearby and thinks of her. As much as it pains me to think about Mother having affections for someone other than my father, I know deep in my heart that love doesn't have to be limited to one person over an entire lifetime.

"Come to bed, then," I reply. "Let's enjoy this proper mattress and these blankets while we have them."

Max chuckles, beginning to unbutton his shirt as his green eyes glisten in the lantern glow. "Are you trying to tell me something?"

"I'm not trying to tell you anything other than that you're insatiable for thinking that I'm inferring anything about intimacy in this strange bed."

"I've slept many times in this 'strange bed,' I'll have you know." There's a smile quirking at the corners of Max's lips as he shrugs off his shirt and hangs it on the bedpost. He twirls his finger at me, indicating for me to turn around so he can have the distinct pleasure of unlacing my dress. I can do it myself, but he seems to greatly enjoy the task.

I stand and spin so I'm facing the bed, our shadows being cast onto the wall. Max lets out a sigh from behind me as he runs his hands up my bare arms before gently pushing my hair to the side and kissing my neck. The sensation of his lips on my skin sends shivers up my spine, and the pleasant, prickling feeling flows down my arms and into my fingertips. He is smiling against me, mouth still pressed on my body as his hands undo the ribbon that's fastening the back of my dress.

"Max?" I whisper as I feel the dress loosen. "Will anyone find us down here if we—"

He chuckles for a moment, the low sound interrupting my tired thoughts. "Not here, Ellie. The first time we are intimate since gaining our freedom is not going to be in a bed in a basement apothecary in an abandoned church. I have something better in mind. It'll be for another night."

I'm voracious for his touch but understanding of his point. We aren't quite alone here in the church, based off my knowledge of the *Clodder* and their general activities. "How long can we stay?"

Max kisses my shoulder as he lets the dress fall, exposing a layer of ivory underthings. "Not long enough. Maybe another night or two. Now get under the blankets before I change my mind."

I consider hesitating just for the sake of it, but I know I'm too exhausted to try. I listen to what Max says and crawl underneath the blankets on the small bed and curl myself against one side, making as much room as possible for him. Strangely, despite how tiny the bed looks, we both fit on it with room to spare for the plethora of pillows and extra blankets. Perhaps it's an enchantment of sorts. Not one I've ever heard of, but I'm certain there are plenty of ways that magic can be used outside of what I already know.

I nestle against Max's side, one hand on his chest, where I can feel his heart beating. "I almost can't believe we did this."

"Almost?"

"There was always a part of me that knew I was going to have to leave the lochs behind. I just never knew how or when or why. Whether it was as a Bèist or as a woman, I knew there was going to be something to drag me away from that place. My father used to tell me the same thing.

That I was a wildflower. That I couldn't be tamed and that it wasn't a bad thing."

"He was right. I hope you know that. Your wild parts are the ones that I love the most."

A smile breaks across my face, and I let out a quiet laugh. "I love many, many parts of you, Max. Some of them I probably shouldn't talk about out loud in a church."

"It's abandoned, if that helps." Max raises his eyebrow before grinning down at me. "Though I'm not sure that makes a difference."

The conversation and the light in the lantern soon start to fade away, my thoughts becoming muddled and hazy as the sun rises outside the small basement window. There in Max's arms—and in the bed that should be too small but definitely isn't—I feel myself slip away into sleep. As I begin to dream about the moors and the gardens and that Max is a man now instead of a cursed being, I swear I can overhear the sound of waves.

Max and I doze until nightfall, somewhere in between different stages of sleep throughout the course of the day. At one point, I think I hear him have a quiet conversation with someone, but I can't be certain if it's a dream or something that's really happening. It's impossible to make out the words, everything sounding like a whisper. However, once dusk hits, I find myself awake and watching the light change on the wall of potion bottles amid the sound of Max's shallow breathing. He's clearly much more exhausted than I am—I presume the curse breaking took more out of him than he led me to believe. I'm not anxious to rise and visit the seaside though because I'm currently more than happy listening to the sound of the water through the partially opened window, and I revel in the quiet slice of freedom that we're experiencing together

Even though Max says we can only stay for a few nights, I think I could live in this underground apothecary forever. At least, I could if it meant that we'd be out of Blossom's reaches.

Max wakes a short while later, yawning and stretching.

"What do you think of getting something to eat?" he asks. There's still a sleepiness to his gaze.

I look around the room, which seems just as empty as when we entered it early this morning. There doesn't appear to be anywhere for food to be stored, so I can't help but offer him a questioning look. "What kind of food are we talking about? Because I'm not sure I have the same kind of preferences as a cat…"

Max chuckles, running a hand over my cheek. "We don't always hunt for bugs and mice, you know. Alastair brought a little back. He ventured out to one of the cellars close by. Must have been feeling generous because he returned with one of their bottles of celebratory wine, some cured meats, and bread with cheese."

"Alastair was here?" I *knew* I heard an unfamiliar voice in the middle of my dreams.

"He was," Max confirms. "Didn't want to wake you, so he said he would come back later. Mentioned something about coming down again once we're both clothed and proper."

My face heats up as I remember that I'm lying under this blanket in my underthings. "Did Alastair see—"

"Don't fret. You were buried deep in the blankets when he came down. He barely even knew you were here, let alone under the covers in your lingerie. I'm certain if Alastair knew that was all you were wearing, I'd have had a few more jokes sent my way."

"Should we go find him then? Would he be back in his human form by now?"

"I think so. He should have changed. Knowing Alastair, he's probably waiting upstairs in one of the empty pews. Normally, I'd find him at the breakwater on a night like this, but I happened to mention to him that I wanted to take you there tonight."

"I don't want to interrupt…"

"You're not interrupting anything, darling." Max kisses my forehead before he rolls off the mattress, and I immediately spot that he's already partially hard. He doesn't draw attention to it, doesn't seem self-conscious of it, but he does catch my glance as it hovers between his hips. "Okay, you might be interrupting that. But we'll take care of it later."

"Will we now?" I sit up in the blankets, one strap of my bralette slipping over my shoulder as my knotted hair tumbles over my exposed arms.

"If you'd like."

I can't help but grin, my mind already thinking of the scenarios we could get into out here on the metaphorical edge of the world. I've thought about what it would be like to be intimate amid the ocean waves, surrounded by the tides and the cool water. I always thought that Padraig would end up being the one to take me to the seashore, or that I'd reluctantly visit with Colonel Gallagher and have my fantasy half-heartedly come true. But now? I'm fully awake and I'm rushing to get dressed and prepare to eat so Max and I can... take care of one another.

I pull on my dress from last night, wrinkled from sitting on the floor all night, and Max runs his hands over the fabric to smooth it before lacing up the back. I adjust my skirts as I cleverly watch him dress in the reflection of the apothecary bottles, shrugging the shirt over his muscled shoulders. He starts to poke the buttons through the holes with his adept fingers, something I enjoy watching him do because it reminds me of how carefully he touches me. I gently bump his hands out of the way so I can take care of the task while he runs his fingers through the ends of my hair.

It's almost like we've been doing this—dressing one another and sharing a quiet evening—for years instead of weeks.

"Are you ready to meet Alastair?" Max asks once we are dressed, twirling a lock of my hair around his hand and giving it a gentle tug. My head tingles with the indulgence of his touch, and it takes all my concentration to respond with words instead of tearing his clothes off.

"I—I don't know," I admit. "I'm nervous."

Max's fingertips are still wrapped in my hair, and he gently draws my head backward, exposing my neck to him. When I'm at whatever angle pleases him, he sinks his mouth to my skin, nipping and kissing and licking at me as he groans. I can't help but let out my own whimper, a little louder than usual since we're alone down here in the basement, which encourages a chuckle to rise from Max's own throat.

"You still nervous?" he murmurs into the crook of my neck before his tongue traces a delicate line down toward my breasts.

I don't know whether to nod or shake my head. I don't want Max to stop, if that's the real question. In fact, I can't quite remember what I was nervous about because he's kissing the top of my chest, one hand clutching my hair, the other dancing along my collarbone. If he keeps doing this, we're never going to get any food because I'll be his meal and he'll be my dessert.

"Max..."

He growls under his breath, the sound low and carnal as he releases his grasp on my hair. I tip my head forward to look down at where he's bowed to me.

"I know we shouldn't. Just a moment longer. After lying next to you all night in your lingerie, I'm just..."

"Hard?"

The two of us laugh in unison.

"Nobody has to know," Max replies.

I raise my eyebrow in amusement. "I suspect they'll be able to figure it out judging by the state of your trousers."

He looks down, and my eyes follow his gaze to where it lands near the button fly of his pants. "I have to say, I love your consideration for my cock, Ellie. I'd like to show every bit of you the same sort of consideration later at the breakwater when I slip underneath the hem of your dress and take your wet p—"

A cough comes from the top of the stairs, and I nearly jump out of my skin.

"Fuck, Alastair—we were just getting things started." Max's tone is one of amusement as he speaks to the man coming down the steps.

"I'm more than well aware, Maximilian. I thought I'd just warn you that the rest of the *Clodder* is aware of it, too."

My face burns with the fiery heat of embarrassment. I don't want to be the reason that Max gets into any trouble with the others. I can't imagine they'd particularly appreciate overhearing... whatever we were getting up to. At least at home it was just Sophia who accidentally overheard some of my affairs. Sophia, who understood the way I am. Was. Whichever.

As Alastair reaches the bottom of the staircase, I finally get a good look at the man who Mother loved once. He's a tall, broad individual with big shoulders, a thin waist, and heavy thighs, a gruff looking face with a red beard and hair that's peppered deeply with gray. While his expression appears to border on the line of grumpiness, his gaze is gentle. In one hand is a bottle of red wine while the other holds a covered basket that I can only presume contains a bit of food for us.

It's strange, standing here in front of this man who could have, in other circumstances, been my father.

"You must be Ellie." Alastair offers a toothy smile, and I immediately relax under his soft stare. "It's a pleasure to meet you instead of hearing censored stories second-hand. Maximilian does seem to like to keep his cards close to his chest when it comes to love."

"I've heard stories of you too, Alastair. Kind ones, of course."

The man crosses the room and places the wine and basket down on the small table near the window. "I've brought sustenance. I'm sure you both must be starving after the walk and... everything else that happened on the way here."

"Oh, we didn't... I mean, it wasn't like that—"

Max chuckles, and I'm not sure why. "Ellie, he means about my curse being lifted."

"Oh!" I mentally kick myself. "Well, that was somewhat of a surprise. I wasn't sure if I believed it was possible. I wasn't even sure I believed in the Blossom fairytales until I met Max and he taught me otherwise."

"Sometimes the truth about magic is a little hard to swallow," Alastair notes, leaning against one of the chairs. "I've had my fair share of disappointments and heartbreak because of it."

I nod. "Speaking of—I know we've just met, but Max said we aren't staying long, and I just wanted to say that... I think my mother misses you terribly. She's looked for you."

The room falls into a heavy silence, and I swear both Max and Alastair can hear my heart pounding judging by the looks on their faces. It's either that or they are picking up on my thoughts running wild. I'm trying to figure out if I should have said anything at all about what happened in the past. Maybe I should have just let it be, and Mother and Alastair could have been forever lost to one another; two ships passing in the night.

Ellie, sometimes you really do need to think before you speak. You're not in Loch Gàrraidh anymore with men like Padraig who don't give an absolute fuck about you. This is practically Max's family. Maybe try being a little more like Sophia...

Well, maybe Sophia before she fell for Colonel Gallagher and invited him into her bedroom for a night of... whatever they did.

My own memory would have made me laugh if I wasn't in such an awkward situation.

Alastair heaves in a deep breath and runs a hand over his beard before he speaks. "I looked for her once. Like I told

Max. I went to the garden and thought maybe I'd be brave enough to find her and show her what I'd turned into. But when I found her, she was with your father. And since then, it's never been the right time for me to return. We've always just missed one another."

I love the lilt in his voice as he speaks, everything sounding like it could be rearranged into poetry. I can see why my mother fell for him.

Mother's words come echoing back to me, where she said she didn't even know if Alastair was still alive until I mentioned him. Perhaps he wondered the same thing about her for a long while. Perhaps being an adult with adult relationships is a lot more complicated than I've been led to believe—worrying about death and marriage and children and history and whether or not anything is as it seemed all those years ago.

"Maybe you can find one another again. When you're ready, that is." Max's smooth voice cuts through the darkening room.

"Possibly, but I think that'll be a story for another time, lovebirds." Alastair clears his throat. "Now, I highly recommend if you want some time alone with the wine and the other provisions that you head over to the breakwater. I suspect the others are going to be gossiping in the atrium for most of the night, and you'll have the entire shoreline to yourselves in case you get up to... mischief."

"Appreciated," Max replies, giving me a little bump with his shoulder. I know what he's thinking—more of what we were just starting to get into, and then some.

Alastair either ignores Max and I sharing a glance or he doesn't see it at all. I suspect it's the former rather than the latter, considering the way he continues the conversation while crossing back toward the steps. "And don't take off without saying anything. You know how to find me. Ellie, you hold him to that."

I smile at Alastair. "Of course I will."

With that, he retreats up the staircase and leaves us amid the darkness of the basement. Max walks across the room and fetches the wine and the basket. "How do you feel about eating by the ocean, then?"

"I'd love that. Do you think we can sneak back outside without the others spotting us? I'm not sure how much longer I can be kept from sustenance. Or from you."

"Absolutely. We'll just be quiet and slip out into the night undetected. I'm certain Alastair has distracted the others away from where we'll leave. He knows we'll make a quick escape to head to the breakwater."

I take the wine from Max, noticing before we flee into the salty air that the bottle has conveniently already been opened. As we creep through the church's threshold and into the long grass, I swallow a mouthful. It tastes like berries and edible flowers and is such a dark red that I'm certain it's staining my lips as I drink.

A fourth of the bottle has found its way into my stomach—the alcohol seeping into my veins—by the time we climb the embankment that separates the land and the sea. There's barely a breeze at the top of the barricade, which feels strange as there was almost always a soft wind in the moors. I thought the ocean would be blustery, but tonight, it seems peaceful and calm with the waves lapping against the shoreline and the large rocks of the breakwater. At the bottom is a bit of flat land, perfect for the two of us to sit down with the food and drink and begin our consumption.

Strangely enough, now that we've made it to the seaside, I feel more mesmerized by the ocean than the food. The taste of salt is heavy on the air, along with Max's springlike scent. We end up passing the bottle of wine back and forth as we pick away at the bread, meat, and cheese, unceremoniously removing pieces with our fingers and popping them into our mouths as we watch the moon's reflection on the tips of the waves.

"Have you ever gone swimming in the ocean?" I ask Max after some time. I balance a small chunk of cheese between two of my fingers and sandwich it between a thin slice of meat and a piece of bread loaf.

"A few times, when I was younger. Have you?"

I shake my head as I gulp down my mouthful of food. "I've only ever swum in Loch Gàrraidh. Father taught me how to swim early because I was so curious about the water. Didn't want me to fall in and drown."

"We should go in. It's not deep on this side of the seawall where it meets the grass."

"Would you save me if I fell in?"

"I'd take your rescue under consideration." Max rises and offers his hand to me, which I immediately take. His palm feels warm and my fingers are held securely as he lifts me from my seated position. "Maybe you'll even be able to make a Whimsey like the first night we met."

I can't help but smile at the memory of the party, the one where I first saw Max outside my bedroom window having a conversation with Padraig. So much has changed since then. "That was meant to impress you, I hope you know. I worked really hard on my Whimsey magic when I was younger so I could influence men into doing what I wanted."

He lets out a laugh that is uninhibited. "You never needed magic to sway my affections. They were there all along."

"I suppose that means I don't need to create a Whimsey then?"

Max's green eyes sparkle in the moonlight, a swirl of emerald smoke coming from his hand as he struggles to hold his magic back. "The only thing you need to do is let me unlace your dress so you aren't weighed down with that outfit."

"How thoughtful. I was expecting a comment that was more *inappropriate.*"

"I always have inappropriate intentions when it comes to you."

A grin cracks across my face. "Maybe you should create the Whimsey. You can use it to entice me into your indecent fantasies."

"Right now, my fantasy is having my incredibly hard dick inside of you while we're just barely out of eyesight of the shoreline. I don't know if we need any magic for that unless you have a vial of contraceptive hidden in your dress."

Wordlessly, I reach into my skirt pocket and remove a single, shimmering vial that I shoved in there sometime before we ran away. In one fell swoop, I remove the cork and drink the contents, the taste of pears flowing over my tongue and down the back of my throat. The mixture is barely in my stomach before I unravel myself from my dress and the ribbons holding it together, the fabric pooling at my feet as it falls to the ground. I'm left in only my ivory underthings as I slip into the ocean, Max only moments behind me.

The water is cold but not freezing, and the two of us stand together under the starlight with tiny waves lapping around our waists. Max presses his chest against my back and holds me there, arms crossed over my breasts and my fingers entwined with his.

"Do you think we'll be cured of our depravity now?" I ask with a laugh. "Or shall we send you back to Loch Lomond to some woman in your past who fell in love with your eyes?"

Max kisses my shoulder. "Darling, you're my depravity. And I'm not going anywhere else in Scotland or beyond without you by my side."

Chapter Twenty-Three

MAX

The stars at midnight with Ellie seem to look so different from the way they appeared when I was alone on the breakwater. The sky somehow seems more vibrant, the deep blue of the atmosphere interspersed with inky, everlasting clouds that occasionally cover small slivers of the moon. The water's texture has changed as well. I feel as if I can see each individual ripple. Maybe it's just a matter of looking for them now, watching the way they undulate around Ellie's waist where her body cuts through the ocean's surface. I had no reason to identify them before because everything in the world felt flat and empty.

Now, things are different. They're full of life and color and feelings that I thought I would never experience.

We stargaze for a short while, enjoying the freedom that comes with running away and the sensation of lightness that comes with having consumed half a bottle of wine.

"Do you ever think the shapes in the clouds might sometimes be the same as the shapes in the stars?" Ellie asks me, as if I'm going to know the answer to her question. Maybe I'm supposed let the words sink into the night and not answer it, but I find myself squeezing her close and resting my chin on top of her head.

"I love the way your mind works. Mine always seems to think about inappropriate things."

"I love those inappropriate things," she notes. I can feel her smiling from the way her body relaxes into my embrace. "But don't discount yourself. Your mind has beautiful and poetic thoughts as well. I think you've learned a thing or two about language from Alastair."

It's my turn to grin. "He does sound a bit like a riddle sometimes."

"Sometimes love is a riddle. Grief too. He has lots to be profound about."

I kiss the top of Ellie's head before she slips out of my arms and turns to face me. Fine strands of her hair tickle my chest as they catch in the barely-there breeze, and her gaze seems to penetrate my entire existence, filling me up with something deeper than physical desire. She sees me. She knows me on an emotional level, and those things—they mean more than sex or touch or self-satisfaction. We use those things to show our connection. They're our love language. Our own personal poetry.

Ellie runs a fingertip up my arm. "Do you think Alastair might try to find my mother some day?"

A part of me expected this question would eventually come.

"I hope so. I think deep down, Alastair is a romantic. I suspect he'll make some kind of grand gesture when he's ready."

"I hope he's ready sooner rather than later."

"You can't rush through a history like that. Most of the time, you can't rush through love at all. We just happen to be an exception to the rule."

Ellie nibbles at her lip, obviously considering my words, before disappearing underneath the water's surface. I watch a series of bubbles pop, and after a half a minute, she reappears a bit farther away from shore. She's clearly standing on her tip-toes judging by the way the waves lap around her shoulders, the moonlight dazzling off her ginger hair and naked skin. I let her be alone for a few moments, knowing she's probably just taking time to quell her worries about leaving her mother, the children, and Sophia behind.

Sometimes I wish I could read her mind so I could soothe her concerns. So I could tell her that everyone will be fine. I think she knows it, but it might help her to hear it as a reminder. I know I always liked Alastair's reminders...

Maybe I have learned a few things from the older man after all. Maybe I've learned a few things from being cursed as well.

How to run away.

How to be found again.

"Is it much farther until the water gets deep?" Ellie finally calls, dropping me back into our reality.

I look back at the coast before turning around again. "Not much farther, I don't think. So be careful."

Ellie nods and then beckons for me to join her. All around where she's floating is an ivory shimmer, telling me there's something magical happening. I don't hesitate before I swim out to meet her again, and I notice she's playing with a rainbow-scaled Whimsey fish, just like the first night we met. The same blue whorls come up from underneath the magic as they did in Loch Gàrraidh, only this time they're punctuated with an even darker shade of sapphire. The mirage is as beautiful as that initial evening with the Allure and the wine and the party, but the vision is nowhere as beautiful as Ellie.

She swirls her finger around in the water, and we watch the illusion swim around us in a sparkling loop. "It feels like forever ago that I was trying to show off for you. But somehow not long enough, in the sense that I wish I'd met you an eternity ago."

"We could have gotten up to some trouble. I think now we're just making up for lost time."

Ellie laughs before she takes her finger from just underneath the surface of the deep blue. The Whimsey disappears with a *pop* and a burst of sparks. Everything about the way she expresses her amusement makes me feel the kind of bliss I had only dreamed about before now. But there's something in her eyes other than just delight and diversion, and I think it's related to the thrumming in my heart that I've been pushing away until now.

I gesture toward her, and she floats across the gap between us until I'm close enough to rest my hand on her side.

"Max?" Ellie purrs out my name, the sensual tone of her voice going straight to the area between my hips. "Do you think that wherever we land in the end, we'll have a seaside like this one?"

"Once we know that Blossom isn't following us, we can land wherever you'd like."

"How will we know? That they aren't following us anymore, I mean."

I suck in a breath as her hands drift across the space between us and dance along my thighs. I can't see what she's doing underwater, but I can feel it, and she's dangerously close to muddling my mind into only thoughts of taking her here in the ocean. "That's a question I was hoping Alastair might be able to answer for us before we leave. Maybe there's a way we can stop running. Eventually."

The corners of her lips twitch upward. She knows what she's doing. She always knows what she's doing in moments like these, and it drives me absolutely wild. "Well, tonight we aren't running anywhere."

I nod. "Maybe tomorrow, but not tonight."

"Maybe tomorrow."

We stand there amid the ripples for a brief moment, Ellie's hand finally dragging across the front of my body and taking my length in her gentle grasp. I can't help but inhale sharply, tasting the salt in the air as I breathe. The feeling of her fingers touching my cock amid the cool sea water gives me a mixture of sensations that I haven't felt before: lust and love and heart-pounding need. Because I can, I close my eyes and tip my head back, thinking only of the way she works her hand, slowly, up and down underneath the water.

A thousand little vibrations go through every one of my nerves as she pleasures me until I'm almost certain there's no reasonable way that I'm going to be able to make it out of the water before I have to take her. But I need to make it so that I can show her what it means to not have to hold back. We need to make it to land before every single fragment of my body shatters and we are forced to wait until I recover.

"Ellie," I murmur, opening my eyes.

She looks up at me, and blinks once, twice. "Close?"

"Very. You have about thirty seconds to get back to shore."

"And what happens once I get there?"

There are so many things I could say, and none of them are appropriate. But we don't have to be appropriate any longer. There's nobody around, nothing watching us except stardust and moonglow and whatever has created this entire universe, and so I'm free to say what I want her to hear. To say it without having to whisper it in her ear or mutter it under my breath. Because of this realization, I reach under the water and slide my hand between her legs before I start to respond.

"Once you get there, I'm going to strip off your wet lingerie. Then I'm going to use my tongue to make you—"

Ellie smirks, releasing me and diving under the water before I have a chance to finish my sentence. When it finally strikes me what just happened, she's made it most of the way back to the bottom of the breakwater. I immediately start swimming back, dick throbbing and a smile on my face. The grin doesn't disappear once I make it back to the pebbled shore, nor does it disappear when I find Ellie's underthings already in a pile on the rocks and her lying in the grass waiting for me.

"Not wasting any time, are you?" I sink to the ground and cover her body with my mine, the grass swaying delicately around us. "Didn't even give me a chance to do the first thing on my list."

Ellie wraps a damp hand around my neck before pulling me close. "Maybe I wanted to get right to whatever's next."

"You might have to let me go if you want that particular *activity*."

"I'm never letting you go." She whispers the words like she thinks someone is going to overhear, but the grin on her face tells me she's not worried about keeping her voice down for long. I don't anticipate that she's going to find the habit of being quiet a hard one to break. "And I don't need that. I just need you and the stars and for us to be alone, together."

I gaze into her beautiful eyes. "And you said I was the one who had learned about poetry. I think maybe you've picked up some pretty words as well."

"Here I was thinking for so long that your own pretty words were just meant to be used with the women of Loch Lomond and in the brothels to get what you wanted. I've learned there's so much more to you. There's so much more to all of Scotland. To everything that lies beyond its borders."

"I never spoke to those women like I speak to you. My time with them wasn't for experiencing emotions."

Ellie runs her fingers through my hair, sending a tingling feeling throughout my scalp. "I know. The point was to experience an o—"

Before she has a chance to remind me of the lackluster orgasms I experienced at the bawdy houses, I collide with her lips and take the unspoken words from her mouth. We kiss and kiss and kiss there in the grass until my lips are chapped from the salty air and the pressure of our mouths crashing into one another, and then we continue to kiss some more. I hold myself there over top of her with one hand, the other cupping her breasts or sliding across the curve of her thigh or skimming her stomach until she reaches down for my cock and places it right at her entrance with a muted whine.

I pull away from the kiss just enough so I can speak. The wind has picked up ever so slightly, causing the long blades of grass to tickle at my bare legs and conceal our position by the breakwater. "Promise me something, Ellie."

"Anything."

"I don't want you to silence yourself and your desires with me tonight. I want to hear every moan. I want to hear you say my name as you come. I want tonight to be a symphony of the noises we couldn't make all the other times we were intimate."

She nods, seemingly impatient, and lifts her hips against mine until I sink into her as far as I can go.

"Fuck, Ellie." I groan. I seem to say the same thing nearly every time I enter her. "How do you always feel this good?"

Her body stretches and adjusts around my cock as I begin to move slowly in and out of her, my entire brain and body on fire.

She arches her back and digs her fingernails into my shoulder blades. "I... How—how do *you* always feel this fucking amazing?"

I know the question is rhetorical. I'm not supposed to answer, so I don't. Instead, I bow to Ellie and run my tongue along her neck before peppering her skin with a combination of kisses and gentle bites. My hips and hers start to move together, finding a rhythm that's slow and deep and steady, like the tempo of the waves as they wash ashore. Soon, we are lost in a world of our own—a world that consists of my throaty growls and Ellie's own lovely noises that make me feel as if I never truly knew a woman until I met her.

I don't want to remember any of those other women. I only want to remember the way she makes me feel and the way we fit together in delicate moments like these; moments where our existence is nothing short of flawless.

I twine my fingers in hers once I know I'm on the edge of finishing. The breeze is cool on my hot skin, and her hands are warm in mine as they are pressed into the fallen grass. She's letting out a whimper with every thrust, quietly begging for her own pleasure to topple into utter ecstasy.

"Ellie," I growl, plunging into her wetness once again, intoxicated by the moment. "You promised."

"Nobody will know?"

Her gaze is bursting with desire and passion. I don't think she'd care if the entire country heard us, but she manages to metaphorically bite her tongue until the very second I shake my head and respond.

"Nobody's listening, darling. Nobody except for me."

With that said, she lets out an exquisite, wild moan that ruins me. She's still in the middle of making the noise when my dick stiffens. I'm in another universe with her, clenching her hands as I violently come, while her entire body tenses in pleasure around me. I know there's a separate orgasm exploding inside of her core by the way she trembles, her gaze glassy and her bottom lip tucked firmly between her teeth.

I stay inside of Ellie until the last few quivers of our pleasure dissolve, and then I collapse next to her in the grass, naked and high on her affections. There's a fine sheen of wetness on my skin and hers, though I'm not sure if it's leftover from the salty water or the heat of the fading summer. It reflects the moonlight off Ellie's body, making her look as celestial and magical as the Whimsey she created earlier tonight.

Ellie stares up at the stars, a gentle smile on her face. She looks tired but happy, and I can't help but want to remind her that she's absolutely perfect. However, she speaks before I manage to get the words out, tilting her head to look at me.

"What happens now?" she asks. "Do we have to leave in the morning?"

I shrug, my thoughts scrambled from sex and satisfaction. "We can probably stay another night, if you'd like. I'll see what Alastair thinks when we get back."

"I'm not sure I'm ready to run away from here just yet. I'd like to see the ocean during the day. Maybe we can take that boat that's bobbing over by the cove and travel along the coast until we need dry land again."

"There's a boat over there?" I furrow my brow and sit up so I can peer over the grass a little better. "I don't remember ever seeing a boat."

Ellie smirks. "Maybe you just weren't looking for one. And maybe Alastair had something to do with it. I bet he found a way to bring it to us like he brought the food."

"I always knew there were worse places to be a cat."

"Maybe there are better places to be a man, though. Places outside of Scotland where they don't curse you for being a deviant. Places where we can pretend to be married and not raise eyebrows from those who think we'd otherwise be indecent for living and traveling together."

Marriage. The thought of it used to bother me, but with Ellie? It doesn't seem like the awful proposition that my parents brought to me years ago.

"You think about marriage like that?" I ask, reclining once again. "It sounded like you used to think having a wedding was the worst thing in the world."

"The worst thing in the world with anyone other than you."

My heart swells at the thought of being with Ellie forever, and I make a comment despite already knowing what her thoughts on the suggestion will be. "I mean... we are staying in a church tonight."

The sound of her laughter resonates over us and out toward the sea. "That's quite the hint, Max. I expected a little more romance and poetry when being proposed to."

"What would you have me say?"

The moon has lowered significantly since we started being intimate, the sun about to rise.

Ellie rolls over and fixes her eyes on me, feigning seriousness. "Something about how you've changed."

"You already know that to be true, in more ways than one. I was cursed to be a Bèist. Now I'm enchanted by you instead. Amusing how things like that turn out."

She nods as if she's contemplating what to say next. Despite the pause in the conversation, I'm able to spot a glint of amusement in her eyes. "Okay, then, maybe you'd say something about how you've never felt like how I make you feel."

I find myself chuckling, and I shift closer to her. I can play this game. "That's something we're both acutely aware of."

"Fine. Then something about how you didn't believe in love at first sight until—"

There's no chance for Ellie to finish whatever it is she was going to say because I throw myself toward her, grasping her around the waist and toppling her over my chest. I hoist her over my shoulder as I rise from the grass, the two of us bare to the world and the growing daylight as I stride toward the ocean waves.

"Max!" She's laughing, and it's the most wonderful sound in the world.

I carry her out to a spot next to the seawall that's just deep enough, splashing through the water with her bent over my arm until I'm up to my shoulders and trying my best to maintain an air of seriousness. I don't think it's working because she can probably feel my body quaking with my own deep chuckle.

"You have one more chance before I throw you in. What would you have me say if I was to propose?"

There's silence for a second, then Ellie retorts with the kind of response I've grown to love from her. "You'd probably tell me that I make your cock hard and that—"

With Ellie bent over my arm, I submerge us in the cool water.

It's quiet under the surface once the sound of the splash dissolves, and neither of us rises immediately. We are transfixed by something celestial and universal—something that doesn't require words to understand. Instead of escaping the depths, we both open our eyes and drift together there underwater, sharing a long gaze and a smile. Ellie's hand slips into mine only a moment before I desperately need to breathe, but neither of us floats back up to the top. Ellie pulls me into her and kisses me hard.

She is my oxygen and I am hers.

We rise after a moment, dripping in the sunrise and begging the sky for a breath that we haven't stolen from one another. The sound of us gasping punctuates the quiet slap of waves against the breakwater that holds us away from the rest of the world. Once I've cleared the water from my vision and brushed my hair out of my eyes, I lick my lips and taste both cherry wine and salt water, a tribute to Ellie from the first night we met amid a curse, and the first real morning I've experienced as a man in a year. She's captivated me: heart, mind, and soul.

I wouldn't dare have it any other way.

"Should we get dressed and go back to the church?" Ellie asks as I reach forward to brush a trickle of water from her cheek. "Might be a proper morning for saying goodbye if we get dried and dressed."

I peek over Ellie's shoulder at the pinks and blues and yellows that are spreading across the morning sky, feeling the gravity and magnitude of this moment as a man who will no longer change into a Bèist. Who will no longer be cursed to feel the pain of what society would have described as poor decisions and recklessness. Who will no longer be alone in this world with his thoughts and his nameless existence.

As I pull her close, savoring every second under this first—of many—sunrises, I murmur, "In a moment, darling. In a moment."

Chapter Twenty-Four

SOPHIA

The day after Ellie disappeared with Max, a letter from Iain arrived in the post box, which was truly impeccable timing as Mother had only just come to accept that my sister wasn't going to be returning home. Because I never tend to receive mail, I didn't even think to rummage through the stack of papers, and I left them on the kitchen table for Mother to sort through when she came in from the garden with Huntley and Pippa. However, because the pile was taller than usual, a few pieces of post slipped off the top and onto the floor. When I reached down to pick them up, I noticed my name handwritten on one of the wax-sealed letters.

It stared back at me in cursive script, and I huddled in the corner of the kitchen by the stove to open and read it in privacy.

Sophia –

I'm going to be arriving in a few days with the intention of collecting your sister. I think we'd all much rather that I collect you instead. How would you like to visit England with me for the autumn season? The weather is supposed to be lovely, and I'm certain we can enjoy it when I'm not busy attending to work matters.

Thinking of you always –

Iain

Of course, as I was smiling down at the page, my mother and the children came crashing through the back door in fits of laughter. Mother noticed the paper in my hand right away, and probably assumed I was looking at her mail when she asked what I was reading.

I glanced up at her. "Oh, just a note from a friend."

Mother furrowed her brow and started to walk toward me as Huntley left dirty footprints all over the kitchen floor. "One of the boys you and Ellie used to play with when you were younger? I wish she would have gotten notes from reputable men instead of deciding to run off in the middle of the night with someone who is probably no better than that man across the field."

Quickly, I crumpled up the paper so she wouldn't be able to read over my arm. I wished I didn't have to because I would have liked to keep the note with Iain's handwriting on it forever. "Yes," I lied. "It's from George. He's doing fine."

She looked as if she was going to question me on my involvement with George, but the moment she opened her mouth, Huntley and Pippa dug into the utensil drawer. The two of them had remained obsessed over their soldier-spoons ever since Iain left to go back to Edinburgh, frequently tearing up the kitchen to locate the silverware for play. Thankfully, the distraction gave me ample opportunity to throw the balled-up note into the stove, turning the written words to ash.

There was no way I could tell her about Iain and me at that moment. Now, though, days later, I'm standing in my bedroom smoothing the canary-yellow skirt of my very best dress. Staring at my reflection in the full-length mirror next to the window, I worry if I've made a mistake by omitting the truth. Iain is coming today, and I'm going to take my paisley luggage case and run off to England with him. I suppose it's not running off in the same way that Ellie and Max vanished. Mother will have a chance to say goodbye to me as I get into the carriage. She'll know where I've gone and with who.

The shock might be lesser, but it will still exist. It's something I'm willing to live with in order to find happiness. I don't want to end up being betrothed to someone I don't feel a connection to or don't love or who doesn't love me back. I don't want to just do my duty to Scotland and the lochs. I want to live my life with the same kind of passion as Ellie has found with Max while still believing in a measure of truth in the Blossom fairytales where everything works out eventually.

Looking down at the bag by my feet, I try to recall if I've packed everything that will be useful in England. My vials of practiced potion are squashed in between the fabric of my clothes, a few trinkets placed inside as well. I don't think there's much else I'll need that I won't have access to once we arrive. It's not like Ellie and Max where they ran away with nothing. Iain has steady employment and his own money, and I'm certain that his kindness and gentle demeanor will translate to providing me with simple objects or toiletries that I might have forgotten in my haste.

The sound of horses and a carriage soon comes through the partially open window, the early autumn breeze flowing through the bedroom. Summer is not quite a memory yet, though the cool evenings most certainly lead me to believe there will be snow in the not-too-distant future. As I think about this change in weather, I reach for the door to my armoire and pluck out my cape, tossing it over my shoulders. Then I hoist the luggage over my arm and look around my bedroom one last time.

Sophia, do you have Ellie's mirror? I think to myself.

Quickly, I reach inside my bag's pocket and feel for the tortoiseshell hand mirror. My fingers press against the reflective glass, leaving marks I'll have to clean off later. But I don't mind. I'd rather have the mirror with prints on it than accidentally leave it behind.

I breathe in deeply as I overhear the horses arrive in front of the house, their harnesses jingling as they halt and wait. Now's the time for me to channel my inner Ellie and be as brave as she was the night that she climbed out the window and left this house behind. I exhale and count backward from five before I open the door, walk down the corridor past Huntley and Pippa's room for the last time, and descend the staircase into the kitchen.

Mother's not there, which means she's probably already at the front of the house wondering why Iain's arrived. I'm certain she would have sent a letter telling him of Ellie's departure. Of course, Iain is already more than well aware of Ellie's affections toward another man, but Mother isn't completely privy to that information, despite the conversation we had the day Mother found out Ellie was gone.

I push open the door to the main floor hallway and stick my head out to try to get an idea of the happenings. As I suspected, Mother is standing in the entryway with the door open, Iain gracing the threshold with his tall and handsome figure. He looks up and gives me a wink and a half-smile.

"I don't understand what's going on," I hear her say. "I sent the message that Ellie wouldn't be here and that the betrothal would be... delayed."

"I don't think it's delayed, Mrs. Callaghan. I'd say it's canceled."

Mother shakes her head. "She'll come back. I'm sure of it. There are only so many places for her to go in this *situation*."

I adjust my bag on my arm, the straps cutting into my circulation, but it slips and bangs against the kitchen wall. The noise echoes across the entire house, and the whole world seems to stop turning for half a second, everything frozen in position. Slowly, Mother turns around on her heel and looks at me with confusion written all over her face. It takes a moment for her to seemingly absorb the scene in front of her, from my clothing to the luggage, to the way I've done my hair in a knot at the back of my neck with curls hanging around my face. "And where are you going in your best dress?"

There's absolutely more that she wants to say, but she isn't saying it. Something about my hair. Something about the rouge on my lips and cheeks that came from the pot I stole in the spring from Ellie's bedroom. Something about the coquettish smile on my face that doesn't seem to be fading.

Heaving in a long breath, I try to think of what Ellie would say. Of course, she'd probably have the perfect words. I don't have the perfect words; I rarely ever do. As usual, I'm just a bundle of nerves and anxiety, little gold sparks flitting from my fingers as I try harder and harder to keep them hidden.

"I'm going with Iain."

Nobody moves or speaks or probably even breathes until Mother responds. "Come out here, Sophia, and explain to me why, in all of Scotland, *you* would be going with him?"

Iain and I share a quick glance as I shuffle out into the atrium, not quite sure how to answer the question. There are way too many things I could say, and so many accusations I could make, but I'm hoping that realization is going to set in as Mother sees the bag slung over my arm.

"We—" More sparks fly from my fingertips as thoughts buzz like angry bumblebees in my head. *How much do I tell Mother? What does she truly need to know? Can I not just run out of here and climb into the carriage and refuse to say another word until Iain and I are past the town's border?*

Judging from the look on Mother's face, I won't be running anywhere if I don't explain to her in the next instant what's going on.

"We all came to an understanding while you were away with Aunt Matilda," I begin, hesitation lacing my voice. "You know that Ellie didn't want to marry Iain. She wanted to go away with Max and escape everything about the lochs, and she did. She's gone. I want to marry a man who is gentle and kind, and who I can see myself growing to love like you did with Father. Well…"

Iain beckons to me, and I suck in a breath before crossing the floor and placing myself by his side. I feel safe there, like I felt safe with him when his body covered me as we kissed against my bedroom door. Not that I think Mother would cause harm with anything other than a stare and some choice words, but there's a feeling I get standing with Iain, and it gives me the strength to continue speaking.

"You can't be serious." Mother rakes her hand over her face, across her jaw, and down her neck in exasperation. "Sophia, you still have another year before you're supposed to make any type of decision like this."

Fearlessness suddenly fills me, my anxiety melting away. I'm leaving. It doesn't matter what she says because I'm going away from here and I'm going to live my own life before I lose the thing I've been told to keep looking for. Before I lose the hope and kindness and sincerity from a man who clearly has a lot of those things to give.

"You mean before *you* make the decision for *me*."

She shakes her head. "I would consult with you."

"Like you consulted with Ellie?"

A pointed silence fills the entryway, as if I've just slapped my own mother in the face and we're waiting for the impact's aftershocks to disappear. I think my comment probably hurts as much as Ellie taking off with Max in the middle of the night because it's not something I would usually say.

Mother looks down at my paisley bag instead of at me or at Iain. "She wouldn't have ever listened."

"Is that what you were told when you were at Blossom? That you needed correction instead of compassion? You spent years lying to us about your own afflictions. And don't even try to continue to tell the stories because I heard your conversation with Ellie that night. I know there was another man. A man you might have hurt, but a man who loved you, too. You grew to love Father, but I think your heart's always been with the Bèist."

To my surprise, instead of bristling and fighting back, Mother simply nods. She looks as if she's still feeling defeated from losing Ellie, and maybe she doesn't have the strength to keep fighting for me. I'm used to that. Used to being an afterthought. But with Iain, I'm not an afterthought. I'm the entire thought, and it's not something I'm willing to give up easily—or at all.

"I wasn't trying to ruin your lives, Sophia," my mother finally says. "I was trying to give you all the best future possible. One where you weren't always being chased by

Blossom or the committee. A future where you fit into the fairytale stories that were recited to us and that founded our worldviews."

The sparks that were coming from my fingers have all but dissolved now, my thumping heart slowing to a pace that feels less like I'm panicking. "Then let me go with Iain. You know I'll come back if things don't work out. You know Iain is a kind man, or you wouldn't have asked his family to betroth him and Ellie. You know so many things about this world, Mother, and you know that you wanted to get away from it too before you realized Scotland couldn't let you go. Not entirely. It'll never let me go either unless I leave."

Iain slips his hand in mine, and we stand there at the front of the house for a while before he finally speaks. It's amazing that he's remained so patient through this heated conversation, allowing Mother and me to get out what could be our final words to one another for some time.

"We're going to England, Mrs. Callaghan. I have some training there for the season with the military. But I promise to bring Sophia back for the holidays with you and the little ones. I'm certain the gardens are beautiful at night with the snow."

I squeeze Iain's fingers as Mother's mouth twitches into the faintest smile. Winter has always been her favorite season, and it's like Iain knows exactly how to play to her heartstrings without being manipulative. The genuine nature of his statement is reflected in the chestnut color of his eyes, and Mother seems to see it too.

Finally, she lets out a breath.

"I'll hold you to that promise, Colonel Gallagher."

Relief washes over me like one of the seaside waves that Ellie used to always talk about. "Does that mean I can go?" I say.

"I'm not in control of your life, Sophia. I don't know if I ever was in control of you or Ellie. But you're right that I want you to be happy. If you think that this—being with Colonel Gallagher—is what will offer you a proper future, I can't be the one to stand in the way of it. Am I giving you permission? No. I'm giving you a blessing to move on because I know, in the end, your father would have believed in the things that you're saying."

"I know. But Father would have believed in you too. He wouldn't want you to be sad. He would want you to find that Bèist and create happiness, just like he created the garden at Loch Gàrraidh."

One of the horses outside stomps its hoof on the lane just as Iain carefully takes my bag, lifting it onto his shoulder. "Should we…?"

It's time to leave. I've said everything I can, and so I step out of the house into the pale sunlight, the sky punctuated with rain clouds that look as if they could burst at any second. Iain loads my luggage, and I step into the carriage with his assistance. I appreciate the lingering warmth of his hand as I take a seat and smooth my dress before looking out the open doorway at Mother.

"Say goodbye to Huntley and Pippa for me," I request. "Tell them I've gone to live out my own fairytale."

Mother nods, wiping away a tear as Iain climbs into the carriage. I give one final wave before Iain reaches for the door handle and pulls it shut. He gives a little tap to the roof of the carriage, and seconds later, the horses are turning around in the lane and we're making our way from what used to be my home toward something new.

"Are you ready to head to Edinburgh, at least temporarily?" Iain offers me the kindest smile I've ever seen, tenderly touching my hand that's resting on the soft seat.

"I've never seen Edinburgh. What's it like there?"

"Much busier than Loch Gàrraidh. I think you'll appreciate the change of scenery. I've arranged for a few surprises. Plus, there's a lovely room with a fireplace waiting for you. I thought you might like to continue having a space of your own."

"We'll have a space together, too, I presume?"

The horses pick up into a brisk trot, the carriage swaying gently back and forth with the change in pace.

"I wasn't sure how you'd feel about that," Iain replies, his face turning a soft shade of crimson. "Since we aren't married and all, I didn't want to make an assumption about our living spaces. In England, I'll be in the barracks for a portion of the trip, so you'll have our rented flat to yourself. I know this is rather... unconventional. However, Edinburgh is a bit more progressive than I think you're used to. Ellie would have taken advantage of it. I think you'll love the freedom it brings."

"Will people ask? About us, I mean. Our... relationship to one another?"

He shakes his head, taking my hand completely in his and running his thumb over my skin. "I don't think so. Besides, if you find me suitable once my training is over, then perhaps we can continue the fairytale in other ways."

A little gold spark spits from my fingertip as I think about all the things that could mean. "Ellie taught me how to—"

Iain breaks into immediate laughter. "I can only imagine what your sister taught you with that wild magic of hers, and I'm curious to find out in the future. But for now, I'd rather come to understand the things you've learned on your own. Like how you manage to take my breath away every time we kiss."

Now I'm the one who must be turning red, gesturing to the front of the carriage. "Iain! The driver will overhear."

"I can guarantee he's heard and seen worse than anything we decide to do back here."

The sound of rain begins at that moment, a gentle pattering against the windows. We listen to the sounds of the carriage as it passes by the countryside by until the change in weather steams up the glass and we can no longer see the direction we're headed. We are alone in a haze of one another and our own anxieties. Or at least I am, until Iain silently reaches across my seat and draws a little heart on the foggy glass next to my cheek.

The gesture makes me smile, and our fingers brush as I draw my own matching heart next to his.

Iain slowly dances his fingers across my arm before taking my hand, bringing it to his mouth and kissing the inside of my wrist. The feeling of his soft lips on my skin encourages sparks to flit from my fingers, but I don't feel the need to try to hold them back any longer. I let them flow from my hand in a waterfall of magic where they gather like cinders on the floor of the carriage. They create a fine sheen of gold for barely an instant before the entire carpet I've created with my magic fades into oblivion.

Moments later, I realize there are gilded glimmers coming from Iain's palm as well. The embers pirouette around one another as they momentarily float inside the carriage and collect at our feet, slowly melting together until it's no longer possible to tell which of them came from my hands or his.

"Sophia?" He says my name so perfectly. "I have a desperate need to kiss you. I've been waiting so long. I've been dreaming of it. I understand if you want to wait until we're alone or if you're scared and you want to—"

I press my finger to Iain's lips to quiet him.

"I think your kiss is the only thing in the world that I'll always want, no matter how I feel, whether I'm frightened or lost or happy or blissful. I think your kiss can make Scotland disappear and drop me into the fairytale world

I was taught to believe in. The best of them always have kisses. A kiss for good luck, a kiss for goodbye, a kiss that means the start of something, and a kiss that signifies..."

Iain gently takes my hand away from his mouth before sinking into my lips so I can't speak any longer. I melt into his touch and the light scent of leather and pine that seems to always take hold on his clothes. Nothing else matters other than us and the impatient need to drown in our own story. A story that hasn't been written yet, but that starts and ends with a curse and a kiss.

Acknowledgements

When I tell most people that The Night Garden started as a dream, they think that I'm joking. That is, until I show them the notes that I have on my phone from September 1, 2022 at 4:58 in the morning where I outlined the plot to what was originally supposed to be a somewhat dystopian Little Women crossed with a fairytale. While the story took a slightly different turn from what was written in my messages to myself, the key scenes from the dream all made their way into the final text of the book.

I'm so thrilled that you've picked up The Night Garden, and truly hope you love this little story that started one night while I was sleeping.

Of course, no book of mine is ever completed alone. I have to many people to thank for their support and kindness on the journey to producing the first book in this duet.

To my husband, Jesse, for always providing me with snack breaks and helping me walk through plot holes even when he doesn't know exactly what I'm trying to say. To Kennedy, Mandy, Zilla, Renée Shantel, and Stacie for being the best early / alpha readers I could have asked for. To Heather Ellis and Rachel Rosen for their expertise in making the book readable and beautiful, and Natascia Mora for her gorgeous illustration that graces the front matter and the hardcover. To Lara for being my bestie and for putting up with me and my multiple crying sessions per chapter.

Finally to you, the reader. Thank you for choosing to take a chance on my words. I hope you enjoy visiting Loch Gàrraidh.

About the Author

NICOLE NORTHWOOD writes fantasy and fairytale romance stories for adults that are atmospheric, intimate, and alluring. By daylight, she works as a project manager for an international medical company, while by starlight, she pens all the stories taking up space in her head.

Nicole and her husband share their home in Eastern Canada with a collection of multi-colored cats, a cupboard stuffed with tea, and a lifetime's worth of books.

Find her online at:

http://www.nicolenorthwoodbooks.com

Also By Nicole Northwood

Standalones:
Beneath the Starlit Sea
The Devil You Know
Coming Soon
Ballads for the Brokenhearted
Coming Soon

Fairytales of the Lochs:
The Night Garden (Book 1)
The Winter Flowers (Book 2)
Coming Soon

Printed in Great Britain
by Amazon